I0600570

COPYRIGHT

THE DARK SIDE OF DREAMS

A NOVEL

MARJORIE KAYE NOBLE

FOR ALFALFA

BEFORE

The Dark Side of Dreams continues the story of *Babylon Dreams*.

Babylon Dreams begins with murder. But is it really murder? In the 22nd century, many cheat death by escaping into an after-death virtual reality program. In 2123, Gunter Holden was CEO of Virtual Enterprises, Inc. (VEI), and oversaw the creation of his virtual Eden, Bali Hai. In 2183, Gunter exists in a folder, stored in Bali Hai. Tucked away in Gunter's memory files are the murders of his wife Laura and her lover, Jacob, Gunter's hated brother. When his victims escaped to Bali Hai, Gunter shot himself to follow them. The lovers soon fell into the Dreams. Virtual Gunter is alone.

In after-death VR worlds, youth, beauty, and fantasy are standard. An old program, Bali Hai's sun is often in the wrong place. Strange fish swim in its virtual seas. Gunter is anxious. Something is causing his file to fragment, forcing him to relive times best forgotten. Worse, he's losing his influence with the VEI Board. Rumors of unwelcome change make him desperate to stop the fragmenting and put his past in order, Gunter asks Tom, a new resident, for help. Tom agrees, but Tom has his own secrets. A merger shifts control of Bali Hai to a Christian sect. Gunter protests and Virtual Paris is erased. Then a mass deletion destroys the Christian sect. An animal cult led by a ruthless criminal now rules Gunter's world. Bali Hai falls into chaos. As Gunter confronts his past, he discovers unspeakable betrayals. Embracing the love that he had once rejected, Gunter's past is in order. On the night of a virtual carnival, Babylon Dreams waits.

". . . inventive and intriguing storytelling . . ."   Portland Book Review

"The futuristic world is so well developed that it seemed almost prophetic. . . .an impressively detailed, creative story . . ."   City Book Review

"A keen and absorbing what-if tale about VR and a digital afterlife."

". . . a Citizen Kane–type mosaic of the tormented antihero. The result is a challenging but compelling vision of a privatized, synthetic heaven slowly eaten away by ungodly capitalism, cupidity, and the sins of its founder."   KIRKUS REVIEWS

What Dreams May Come ...

"For in that sleep of death what dreams may come When we have
shuffled off this mortal coil, Must give us pause"

TABLE OF CONTENTS

PROLOGUE

SEINI Research Facility

Coral Triangle

April 7, 2290

Andi Sukawati

"They're gone. Why do you ask?"

"Curiosity, I suppose."

The American seems unafraid, untouchable. Is he?

"I'm curious; several hundred people settled here, on this island. Fishermen, farmers; many brought families. Where did they go? Mr. Sukawati, where did they go?"

What did he say? The surf crackles as it greets the rocky shore. *Who knows this man is here? He must report this.* "I'm sorry, sir, I can't help you."

Raising his voice, the visitor asks again. "Where did the people who lived here go?"

"How should I know?" Many things here are better not to know. *Sorry to be rude. What does the man want?* A gull swooped down, screaming as it landed on the angry eye of a temple sentry. He suppresses an urge to run. "May I ask why you are here? This island is closed to visitors."

The American sighs. "It's sad the temple's gone."

"I can't help you, sir. Other than my colleagues, no one was here when I arrived." To continue is madness. He does not want to die; he has a family too.

"Well, think about it. Did they migrate? Did they all transition to an after-death arrangement? I'm trying to understand. When was the temple sold?"

"I'm not sure."

"When the temple site became an after-death research center, was there any resistance?"

The only resistance stares back at them from the violent surf. The dvarapala, the temple guardians, are all that it is left. Most of the temple stones were pounded into gravel and now line the path that leads to the SEINI research center. It saddens him to think about it.

"Why should there be? People need work."

"Thank you." The American smiles. Obviously, he knows there are secrets here and hopes to learn more.

He returns the smile, nodding.

"You're welcome. I really must go."

CHICAGO, THE ELYSIUM

April 10, 2290

The Dream Answers Mira

She closes her eyes and thinks, "It's somewhere, waiting. Where is it?" Opening her eyes, she scans the room. Are the bedroom peepers working? The table scanner light is green, a definite 'no.' The laughing Buddha arrived yesterday, thank God. Henry will be back tomorrow, and he's against any type of mind recording, especially dreams. She'll have to keep it out of sight. Mira swings her legs to the edge of the smart sleep cushion.

"It's a true bargain and a miracle of comfort," she claimed, justifying the new cushion. Henry laughed and agreed.

Ah, success! The Buddha's tiny hand is beginning to glow. Removing the recorder from her ear, Mira turns the Buddha around and inserts the tear-shaped piece into the gold-plated base. Activating a holo projector, she rubs the statue's base.

The Buddha's eyes shine as Mira's dream begins to play. Holo images hover above the smiling Buddha and sharpen as the dream flickers. Then, her own hidden thoughts stream into her consciousness.

Lots of bright colors. Someone gives her chocolate coffee, but she's not sure she wants to try it.

"Try it and if you don't like it, it's alright. You must always be open-minded." It's Ravi's voice.

There's a distant sound of water falling. Ah, the colors tell her they're in a café, someplace in South America. The room has a bar. She was five during that trip and has few memories of it. She remembers how blue her father's eyes were and wishing her eyes were blue instead of brown.

There's a window and outside she sees a vine-covered trunk of a tree. A circle of red and blue stones surrounds the trunk. She whispers to Ravi, "Can I take a blue stone with me?" Her father shakes his head saying it wouldn't be polite.

Parts of images are in and out of focus. She becomes lucid, but only briefly.

Ask the question! What question? *Too late, someone new sits next to Ravi. She knows the voice from the memory files that Ravi has shared. Patel, it's Randall Patel, only he's young, not the old man who raised her father.*

"Ah, Mira," Patel says. You want to know where he is, don't you?" She's embarrassed, even Ravi doesn't know she's searching. The window has disappeared, and she sees a large, old-fashioned piece of paper with a message. The words "Bali Hai" are printed in large, bold letters.

"Not every search is an adventure. Some things want to be found." Patel pours the contents of his cup into hers and instead of coffee, the

letter "P" tumbles out, followed by hundreds of other "Ps," in reds and blues. Ravi often encouraged her to be skeptical when something looks like magic. Before she can ask Patel how he made letters fall from his cup, Patel floats away and the dream fades.

"Repeat," she commands. The dream repeats and there's her cup with its chocolate coffee and her father says to be polite. It is an hour before she's finished. What has she forgotten?

***

A closet

Old lamps and plain tables clutter what would have been their dining room. The living room's red couch, a gift from Henry's grandmother, is an island of comfort surrounded by walls of Henry's past. Wall hangings, colorful totems and keepsakes are remnants of the Yang family's history, from remote villages to San Francisco and their recent years in Ohio. She remembers Grandfather Yang's proud smile when he gave Henry these treasures, all preserved like insects in amber.

The kitchen walls, also belong to Henry and along with a few family digitals and holos, there are framed humorous sayings. Mira had protested, but he insisted. "The world needs jokes," he said. "So, unless you want to cook . . ." The jokes stayed.

Recently, the issue was her collection of antique books, piled against a dining room wall. "The books will stay," she insisted.

Henry was forced to admit, "Anything printed on paper is rare."

"Exactly, though books are more than paper," she countered.

"We could sell some and put the rest in the storage unit," he said. "It's difficult to relax with all this clutter."

"Not now. Ravi trusts me to keep them safe. When I talk to him, I'll ask if there are any books we can donate to an antiquity library."

Items carved in wood or chiseled stone sit or stand against one side of a narrow hall. Their physical presence acts as a respite from life's shifting realities. None are digitized, languishing in some folder. Henry doesn't understand; there's something poetic about these artifacts, a melancholy, like the beauty of a snowflake before it melts. All have been crafted by humans, touched, polished, and created from materials taken from the earth. Their textures and smells remind you that for now, you are a flesh and blood human, tethered to the earth.

There is no question regarding her great-grandmother's clock. The clock once belonged to Ravi's grandmother, and it greets Mira each morning. Next to the clock is an ancient desk, piled with vintage catalogues; the wisps of paper pressed into thin layers of clear protective film. Select pages have been preserved, and set apart, and hints of color remain in the ghosts of Christmas sales and the bright summer clothes of yesterday's children.

The papers, the antique books and 'your precious grandmother clock,' as Henry calls it, are safe for now, but Henry insists that she move the rugs, all, currently rolled and leaning on walls.

But where? Perhaps there's room in a hall closet. She searches the larger one, which holds artifacts from her childhood travels with her father, Ravi. Gifts from Henry's family, including several small, stacked tables and two old-fashioned blankets with vivid images of past Yang family members, are folded and sit on the top of the tables.

She clears enough room for six large rugs. Maybe Henry will agree to put the blankets in storage. Probably not. First, she'll see how much room there is in the smaller closet.

The door to the next closet opens with a creak. Incredible. How old *are* the hinges? The apartment building itself is over three hundred years old. Clearly too old. Donovan Hosseini, her new boss and current landlord, will never replace the hinges. He's too cheap. Like his security system, building maintenance is largely ignored.

"Light," she whispers. A soft light fills the closet. Ravi sent her boxes and bags for safekeeping including a set of blown glass vases from Venice. Perhaps Henry might give one or two of the vases to his grandmother. Ravi wouldn't mind. Is there anything else she could—

What is that? A piece of paper? Paper doesn't go here. . . Why isn't he more careful? Hopefully, it's not torn because it's very old, a reed blend used occasionally to advertise events. It was phased out almost two hundred years ago. And there is some old-fashioned printing on it! Henry must have put it away before she had a chance to study it. It's been a while, at least two years since they moved from their old apartment in Hyde Park to the Elysium, and she's been distracted. Doesn't matter; there's room for the rugs in here.

Putting on a pair of gloves, she teases the folded paper from its place against the closet wall. As she unfolds it, she wonders where it was displayed and who created it. There is a message in an old-fashioned print. As she reads it, she gasps.

VEI announces:

Bali Hai is waiting!

Are you ready for the perfect you in paradise?

It's never too early to plan for your after-death experience.

VEI announces:

UNEQUALED ENVIRONMENT OPTIONS

ACCESS TO THE BIO WORLD

MAJOR CITIES IN 10 COUNTRIES

NATURAL WONDERS

UNPARALLELED SENSORY DETAIL

PERSONAL SIMS AND ROLE-PLAYING GAMES

MEMORY LIBRARY

For information on Bali Hai, or other VEI destinations, such as

1950's USA, American Capitals, or Turn of the Century Eastern Seaboard.

Contact a VEI representative for programs and payment plans.

What else is in the closet? Ravi had stressed the importance of everything Patel had entrusted to him. She remembers the crate with things that had once belonged to R. Patel. She must have opened the crate, taken a quick look inside, and nothing more. Was the paper originally in the crate?

Her heart thumps and her hands are cold as she enters the closet again to examine the rest of what Patel placed in Ravi's care. Shining the edge of a glow rope into the crate, she sees remembrance cubes containing holos of the memory records of travels Patel and Ravi took together. There are two child-sized hats and a child's coat made of soft angora. Lots of room in the crate; she could move several rolled rugs and—there's a container. It's rectangular, a reddish brown, worn looking and very old. Is it made of leather? Horrifying, but fascinating, the case is a relic of the past when animals were butchered for profit. A traveling case of some sort and . . . oh God! **There it is!** The letter "P" from her dream!

As she presses her fingertip against the decorative "P" on the top of the case, it opens with a snap. Inside, in a square frame, a painting of a skiff floating on a moonlit sea is inside and printed on the bottom part of the metal frame are the words, *"To Patel, with love from Marcia. A piece of heaven."*

This is unexpected. Mira knew Patel had loved her grandmother, but incredibly, *she* had loved him! Surprising, but it makes sense because Patel went to great lengths to save Marcia's child. Of course, he loved her, but Mira never thought it was a love affair.

Did her grandfather know that he was not the only man loved by Marcia Evans? Her breathing is fast and shallow as reality recedes; she is lost, adrift from life. *Light is an intruder, unwelcome in this closet, a secret place, safe from the passage of time.* Is she dreaming? *Is that a wrinkle in the case lining?* She shudders, resisting paralysis. Gently, she tugs on the stitching until it breaks open, revealing a pearl-colored case, shaped like a cat's paw. She presses the middle and the claw relaxes, revealing a red crystal resting within a milky sphere. She rotates the sphere, and slowly, it spins to show its gold letters, GH-C glowing on the sphere's red surface. She falls heavily against the closet doorframe and its rusty hinges.

Mira knows she has found the missing mind-upload copy of Gunter Holden, her grandfather. She must keep it a secret.

Chicago, The New Aon Center

Byron Hernandez

Law Offices of Trammel and O'Connell

May 3, 2290

"If you are not a family member, why are you here? We represent the interests of families seeking contact with loved ones trapped in Shemathra's Realm. You are an employee of SEINI and a part of the AI DESIGN team. Your reasons for offering to help in my Shemathra's Realm investigation concerns me. Any evidence resulting from violating your employment contract with SEINI would be inadmissible."

He should have refused the meeting. Regardless, Mira Patel is here, at least her holo is, sitting in the chair programmed to receive confidential missives. What now? She tilts her head, as if deciding if she should continue or seek out other enemies of Donovan Hosseini and help them instead.

"I am a family member of a citizen of Shemathra's Realm, Mr. Hernandez. Before I tell you more, I need assurances this room is safe from hostile surveillance." Mira Patel folds her arms across her chest. She is a young woman with dark hair and eyes, attractive, but way too arrogant. Does she think she can intimidate him?

"Are you serious? We have cutting edge security. How safe is your location?" It's time to put an end to the meeting. "Ms. Patel, I appreciate your offer but—"

"It's Holden; my name is Mira Holden."

"Ah, okay. Let's agree on 'Mira' for now. Mira, you should be more careful when—"

"Hosseini's security system rarely functions because he refuses to pay for updates or maintenance. This is why I can safely tell you what I'm going to tell you."

"And what are you going to tell me? I'm out of time, Mira. I'll have you connect with my AI assistant, Millie, and she'll take the information. We'll get in touch."

"I'm the granddaughter of Gunter Holden."

"No, you're not. Are you aware Holden's bio death was almost two centuries ago?"

"One hundred and seventy-nine years to be exact."

"Mira, I wish I could give you more time, but—"

"I have a copy of Gunter Holden's mind upload."

Does she? There were rumors that Holden made a copy and hid it away.

"Okay, let's assume you do. Where did you find it?"

"First, you must believe that I'm telling the truth. I've sent my DNA in a separate file. Holden's DNA is on record at Cornell. My father was born several decades after Holden's death. I'll explain how that happened some other time."

"For now, let's say I believe you. A copy of Gunter Holden would be a valuable tool."

"I know. I intend to use it."

"I assume you possess an exterior aural interface."

"Of course."

"Here's a code for a direct B-QP link to this office. I'll be in touch."

"I know you will."

***

Byron Hernandez, "God, yes."

May 4, 2290

Byron Hernandez taps his foot as he waits. The tapping is a nervous habit his mother once described as extremely annoying. Millie has no opinion since she is his AI assistant.

"Your follow-up research on the Mira Patel meeting is ready."

He sighs, is it too much to hope that there really is a copy and she's telling the truth?

"Play report on Mira Patel." In response, a holo appears in the media frame. The holo is a sim version of his great uncle, Ivan who gifted his sim to Byron before Ivan's bio death at the age of cen- ninety-two. The AI sim version of Uncle Ivan speaks with his voice.

"Good morning, Byron. I understand you want to know about Mira Patel, an employee of SEINI. What is your first question?"

"Is Mira Patel the granddaughter of Gunter Holden?"

"Yes. Her DNA confirms she is a descendant of Gunter Holden."

"The same Gunter Holden who created VEI, Virtual Enterprises Inc?"

"Yes, that Gunter Holden."

"Gunter Holden's bio death was almost two centuries ago. She claims to be his granddaughter, not just his descendent. Can you explain?"

"Of course. You might recall that among Holden's Bali Hai memories you obtained, one concerned Holden's discovery that Marcia Evans, his first wife and business partner became pregnant with Holden's child. Records show that the embryo was removed and placed in pro- tected storage, where it remained. Seventy years later, Randall Patel, another Holden business partner, arranged for his cousin's daughter to be a surrogate and she gave birth to Ravi Patel, Holden's biological son. Ravi was fifty-two when his daughter, Mira was born in Tibet. Does that answer your question?"

"Yes, thanks Uncle Ivan."

"You bet." The holo disappears.

"Millie, I'll dictate a message, and you will send it to Mira Patel on her private receptor."

"Of course. Are you ready for your tea?"

"God yes."

CHICAGO, THE ELYSIUM

May 5, 2290

Mira Patel

A dim spring morning scatters its light on Mira's desk. "Work light." The morning retreats. She showers and then chooses a neu-cotton blouse and a pair of shapeless trousers. Brushing her hair, she studies the grooves etched in the frame of an oval wall mirror, an antique with a pewter frame. Once, it had been a serving tray in Indonesia until someone added a mirror. Last year, on her birthday, she discovered it wrapped in gold paper, a gift from Henry. Occasionally, Ravi refers to Henry Yang as Mira's "beloved," though her father does it with care. Mira rarely likes teasing.

"You like things with a past, I know." Henry said. "The frame is almost two hundred years old." He sat on a stool and watched as she studied the swirls and shallow grooves that formed an intricate pattern on the mirror's edge. Who made them? Who had polished them and for whom?

A faint glow on the inner edge of the frame signals a response from Hernandez. Reaching for a bottle of gardenia scent on a side shelf, she knocks the edge of the porcelain flower lid, upending it. Catching it just before it rolls and falls, she realizes how nervous she is. Everything depends on what she is about to hear. She pauses to regulate her breathing and calm herself. If Hernandez won't help, she'll find someone else.

Spraying the gardenia scent on her wrists, she rubs them together, then washes the tips of her fingers. The scent will confuse Hosseini's little spies, a collection of antiquated surveillance pests, usually nonfunctional.

"It pays to be careful," Henry had whispered when he gave her the bottle. He's right, especially now.

She studies her face in the oval mirror and imagines her grandfather peering out at her. Then, she touches her thumb to the glow where Hernandez's message waits. The glow becomes a transparent receiver, clinging to her thumb. She'll be careful to return it to the pewter frame when she's done. Moving to a comfortable chair, she presses her thumb to inside of her ear. What will he say? Seconds later, she hears the voice of Byron Hernandez.

Transmission date: May 5, 2290.

To: Mira Patel

Via T&O aural receptor

Mira Patel—Your information is of great interest. As I mentioned during our initial contact, we represent the interests of families seeking contact with loved ones trapped in Shemathra's Realm. Since you are an employee of SEINI and a part of the AI DESIGN team, the reasons behind your offer of help in my investigation concern me.

The after-death program, Shemathra's Realm, has closed all communications between Shemathra virtual residents and the bio world. Mass deletions are rumored. Bio families of Shemathra's virtual residents want to know what's going on. Are their virtual loved ones safe? Congressional hearings are being scheduled. Donovan Hosseini, who owns a controlling interest in SEINI, has employed an impressive legal team and Hosseini continues to be a virtual resident of Shemathra. Keeping in mind you are advised not to violate any terms of your employment agreement we are intrigued by your proposal.

Records confirm that you are the biological granddaughter of Gunter Holden. If Hosseini hired you with full knowledge of your background, I'm amazed. However, I urge you to be careful. He is dangerous. I would be grateful for whatever information you can send my way. If the file you mentioned is indeed a copy of Gunter Holden's virtual self, please consider uploading it to the Shemathra program. He might be able to go places and record events unavailable to your prying eyes.

I look forward to your next communication.

Regards,

Byron Hernandez, Lead Investigator

***

Henry

So, Hernandez is urging her to upload the copy. That's surprising. She thought he'd try to take it from her. She's reluctant and a little scared. Questions and answers fight for her attention. What will her grandfather be like? What will he think of her? Will he believe her? Will he cooperate? If he doesn't, what should she do? Regardless, she won't ask Henry for help after what he said. Maybe she will; she doesn't know.

She believes in herself. When she was twelve, she was home during a school holiday. Gita, her favorite Patel cousin, gave her a holo cube recording of the Patels celebrating Holi.

"Sorry you couldn't come," Gita said, "maybe next year." As she ate the bag of colored candies Gita had saved for her, Mira knew there would never be an invitation.

Later, as she entered her gap decade, she was pressured to consider an arranged marriage. If she agreed, her life would be settled, and she would be considered a Patel. Too late, she had recently discovered she was the granddaughter of the VR visionary Gunter Holden. At last, she was free.

She began her research into notorious Gunter Holden, a pioneer in the after-death industry. As she explored, she wondered how different life might be if she were no longer a bio and the right AI design could make a difference in the quality of her virtual existence. She would entertain romance, allow kisses, and fear no consequences. But in the bio world, young men are unpredictable. She had lost her virginity to a charming boy at Cornell on her birthday. Birthdays came and went, and so did lovers until she met Henry Yang.

She was leaving an AI seminar, when a girl with sleepy eyes gripped Mira's wrist, pulling her close. The girl whispered, "Are you really *the* Gunter Holden's granddaughter?" She bent her sleek blonde head as she stared at Mira's face as if taking note of its lines and proportions.

Mira turned her head away, saying, "Look, you're mistaken, I—"

The girl interrupted and pulled Mira closer. "They said you'd deny it." The aggressor was taller and stronger than Mira, her hands securely on the sides of Mira's face. "If you are, are you proud of it, or aren't you? Personally, I think you should be." The noisy hall grew quiet as people had begun to pay attention. Calmly, Mira began to tug on the girl's spidery fingers. The girl was irrational, and panicking would make it worse.

"Let her go, Sam." Someone intervened. A tall young man stood close, blocking the view of the crowd. "Don't be a problem, Samantha," he whispered. "If you're curious, do your homework."

Mira knew the history of her grandfather's loss and disgrace. VEI had collapsed during a hostile takeover, and Holden self-deleted, his place in history tainted by murder and scandal. Few were aware of all he had accomplished. Gunter Holden was a pioneer of the after-death industry. Her father, Ravi, was nothing like Gunter Holden, but Mira knew she was.

"Come on, Henry, aren't you a tiny bit curious?" Rolling her sleepy eyes, Samantha shrugged and turned away. Ignoring her rescuer, Mira made her escape. Henry was tall and too attractive; it was safer not to trust him.

The next day, Henry Yang insisted on sitting next to her. She thanked him again for helping her the day before, however, she said, she was fine now and didn't need his help. When she learned Henry was a rising star in the art of quantum security, she continued to ignore him. Like Gunter, Mira hated competition. He never discussed them, but she knew Henry had more offers than she did. Worse, he had completed research at Stanford's Virtual Studies in the virtual security division. Gunter Holden had gone to Stanford. If she were known as Mira Holden, she would have been accepted there for more than just a summer class.

Henry persisted, gradually breaking through her defenses. She resisted, saying she could take care of herself. Pausing his holo monitor showing daily AI options, he shrugged. "My Polish grandmother taught me to step up when I see someone being mistreated. She had no right to bother you."

"Your grandmother was Polish?" He must be mocking her.

He shrugged. "My grandmother *is* Polish, and like me, she is over six feet tall.

Mira shook her head, convinced he was lying.

"I see some skepticism." He turned off his monitor and faced her. "Grandpa's folks came from China As a young man, Ye ye was a tour guide. Okay, here's where the story becomes a great romance."

She shook her head but when she didn't leave, Henry knew she was ready to hear his story.

"She was a tall blonde exchange student," Henry's smooth voice reminded Mira of the storytellers from her travels with Ravi. "And a member of Ye ye's tour group. By the end of the tour, he announced he would marry her. This was news to Busia Alanna, but Ye ye was determined. He persuaded her to have dinner with him. Later, Busia swore she couldn't resist him."

"How romantic,' she said, aiming for sarcasm.

Henry laughed, "Yes, truly it was. It's your turn."

"What do you know about Gunter Holden," she asked him.

"Yeah, of course," Henry said, "something to do with the early after-death programs. Let's see, um . . . wait, I'll ask Alex, my AI. Better yet, why don't you tell me?"

"VEI," she sighed. When he didn't respond, there was no other choice but to finish telling him what he already knew. "He was the founder of Virtual Enterprises Inc. Gunter Holden was an asshole, but he was also a pioneer who expanded our realities. Bali Hai was his paradise, but VEI offered other worlds as well. His company was stolen from him. I'm his granddaughter. I intend to take VEI back. If we continue to see each other, it's important that you know." Was he telling the truth? True; her last name was officially Patel, not Holden.

He kissed her hand and nodded, "Okay, I'm warned."

Years later, she loves Henry too much to care. Every night, as he sleeps next to her, his arm rests on her waist and his warm breath on her neck soothes her as she dreams. Leaving him is unthinkable. Henry knows her secrets but refuses to share his secrets with her. What does he do when he goes away? His new employer is a phantom. No name, no location. What exactly does Henry do? A troubleshooter, he tells her. For whom? When he is gone for days, where does he go? It drives her mad.

When Mira accepted SEINI's offer, she basked in his outrage. "Why, Mira?" Henry demanded. "You'll be working for the most corrupt after-death group in the country. Seriously, Mira, you joined SEINI's AI development team? Why? You can go anywhere!"

"Not where YOU go." She countered. Soon after, they leased an apartment in Chicago's Elysium, a building personally owned by Donovan Hosseini. Renting a SEINI owned apartment was a condition of her employment. Henry had been furious until he realized how poorly maintained and managed the building was, especially its multiple surveillance systems. Better to be where Hosseini was over-confident and more prone to mistakes.

***

The First Day

As she had waited for the glide transpo, light fell in sharp ribbons on the narrow streets, melting a thin layer of snow. Air-scrubbers swarmed over and between buildings like wasps removing unwelcome intruders. Glimpsing a ribbon of blue sky, Mira remembered a World Media news story on urban flight. Was Chicago's population decreasing?

People are disappearing. Most of them were cen-thirty plus adults, leaving bewildered relatives behind. Where are these missing citizens? Some vanished from neighborhoods in New Orleans. Cultural time capsules of small towns in Wyoming had become deserted houses and empty diners. In the Ozarks, confused people in isolated communities searched for missing elders and found the heartbreak of decaying bodies in a deserted warehouse.

Is it because of Social Security's Virtual New Deal? A new branch of the after-death industry, the Virtual New Deal offers discounts on after-life destinations to citizens over the age of cen-fifty. People as old as the plentiful seniors of the Yang family are becoming scarce. Something is wrong.

The first time she crossed the New Chicago Mall panic made her stomach churn. The high rise, which formed a gleaming letter "H," could be seen, Hosseini often bragged, from space. Approaching the entrance, she was surprised. No holo promos with silken voices promising adventure and unending after-death happiness for lucky virtuals in "Celebrations USA" or "Medieval Splendors." There were no ads for Shemathra's Realm; its early media promotions had disappeared. Instead, the corridor leading to the Shemathra offices of the "H" building were a dull gray.

Ruling the herds of the "Goddess" Shemathra is Donovan Hosseini who entered the VR after-death Realm as Urcuchillay, the rainbow llama god consort. During her fellowship at Cornell's AI Institute Mira discovered what Shemathra's Realm really was and how it sprang from the ruins of Bali Hai, VEI's fabled paradise.

At the scanning gate, a heat barrier restricted unauthorized access. Her identity confirmed, Mira walked a long hallway, trembling as she entered a darkened room. Researching Donovan Hosseini, she learned he ruled by intimidation. A trap might be waiting. No way to refuse. Doors closed behind her. SEINI board members were present as holos forming a circle. In the dark boardroom, she was the only one physically present.

Hosseini appeared in a burst of pulsating color. Not a rainbow llama that day, Donovan Hosseini appeared as his human self in his prime at age seventy. Mira trembled when he began her torture.

"Hello to youz all," the monster growled, addressing the holographic board. "We're here to welcome the newest member of the SEINI team. Let's give it up for Mira Patel!" No one clapped. Pointing at her, he laughed, "So, just so ya know, this little genius may or may not have an interesting pedigree. Unfortunately, there's no way to verify, but rumor has it that the notorious Gunter Holden is perched on her family tree." Hosseini knew she was Gunter's granddaughter, but it was better to leave it in doubt—easier to label and diminish her at will. An audible gasp came from a woman with green striped hair.

"However," he smiled, "Mira's real grandpa may be just another dirtbag, Randall Patel! We all remember him; he was the brains behind VEI, a failed enterprise. VEI failed our Shemathra folks. What losers! The VEI guys, I mean."

He paused for applause, his head rotating as he stared grimly at the circle of holos. There was reluctant clapping. "No one here has a sense of humor all of a sudden?" Still, no roar of approval. Slowly, he rotated his head completely around, as if noting the face of each Board member.

"I get it, Patel was some kinda genius, okay. So maybe, better to be from a bastard with a good pedigree than the other one. Holden, I mean. All in all, I'll be watchin' you, Mira Patel." He says, waving his finger. "Don't misbehave, ya know what I mean? At SEINI, when you mess up, there are consequences. Do you understand?"

Barely able to breathe, she nodded.

His eyes spun round in their sockets until he became the rainbow llama. His llama coat shimmered into rolling clouds of color as he approached the trembling girl. Summoning a wad of llama spit, he hurled it in her direction. As she cringed, the virtual wad disappeared before reaching her. He whispered, "We're done here, you can go." The monster gone, holos of board members disappeared. Mira was alone.

***

The Copy

Days later, she avoided Henry's eyes as she told him she had found a mind-upload copy of Gunter Holden. "I learned there might be a copy when I was at Cornell," she said, her words unspooling in a soft reluctant whisper.

Henry tilted his head and listened to her explain how she had found the copy after years of searching. "I was stacking artifacts in the hall closet, and I remembered Patel had left personal effects with Ravi, who entrusted them to me." The daylight faded as her confession played. *I do not regret it.* "Henry, I found the copy!"

Lucas, Henry's cat, a regal Maine coon, purred as it kneaded the pillow next to her, usually a soothing sound, but not as she panicked, waiting for what Henry will say. Leaving the couch, Mira moved to an old wooden chair and cleared her throat. *Why is this so hard?* "I contacted Byron Hernandez. He's an investigator working for Tram—"

"I know who he is," Henry said quietly. "What did he say?"

"Let me show you!" Taking his hand, she led Henry to the closet where Patel's effects were stored. "Soft light," she said. "He said I should use it; no, he urged me to, in fact!" There was no need to apologize. Defiantly, she pulled the pearl-colored case of hard plasma, shaped like a sculpture of a cat's paw. The claw relaxed, and he saw the red crystal suspended within a cloudy sphere. She rotated the sphere to show him its gold letters, GH-C on the sphere's red surface, and held it up like a trophy won after a long battle. "This copy is Gunter Holden, my grandfather! Everything Gunter Holden was, his memories, all his plots and the dreams that stirred within him, on the day this digital copy was made, are within this crystal." She began to cry.

He took her hand, his voice an urgent whisper, "No one can know about this. Most likely, this copy was created when mind-uploading was new and foolish people made numerous copies of themselves. The IRS put a stop to it all when it levied a heavy tax on copies of mind-uploads. This copy is illegal and technically, the property of the U.S. government. Regardless, the copy must either be destroyed or stored someplace secure."

"NO!" She cupped the side of his face and whispered. "He's Gunter Holden and he owes me. A monster stole VEI and invaded Bali Hai because *he didn't protect it.* Holden's going to help me get it all back. My grandfather thought that rules were for others, not him. But I found his copy, and I will make new rules!" Returning the copy to the leather case where it had rested for almost two centuries, she went to bed. There was no more to say. As she tried to sleep, Mira wondered if she would dislike the copy as much as she feared.

***

Patel

Ravi is nothing like his father, Gunter Holden. When she was little, Ravi had told her stories about Randall Patel, his guardian, and the man who became like a father to young Ravi. It wasn't until boarding school that she learned who Patel really was. One of the founders of VEI, Virtual Enterprises, Inc., which dominated the after-death industry of the 22nd century, Patel, like her grandfather was a pioneer and a visionary.

Ravi rarely spoke of the sins committed by Gunter Holden, the infamous destroying of a rival company, resulting in the erasure of two million mind-uploads, and of course, the alleged murders. Although never proven, she was convinced that Gunter Holden had murdered his brother and his own wife, both mind-uploaded to Bali Hai. Then Holden shot himself and followed his victims into Bali Hai. Her grandfather hated to lose. She knows she is too much like him.

When Mira was six, someone told that she was lucky not to look like her Gunter Holden, her grandfather. "Your father has yellow hair like his dad," a Patel cousin explained. "Yours is brown, so it's different."

"I don't get it. Why is yellow hair bad? Ravi's a good person."

The boy sighed. "Patel paid my aunt to be your dad's mom, even though she wasn't."

"What do you mean she wasn't?"

"I mean, Ravi was a bean," he rolled his eyes. "They put the bean in her and then Ravi was born. And Patel paid Auntie. Everyone hoped Patel would leave us all his money."

"Was Patel really old?" Mira thought the whole story silly.

"Like, at least over cen-forty." The boy shrugged.

"That's not so old. Some people live to cen-eighty-five."

"It's still old. Do you want to hear what happened or what?"

"Okay, so tell me," she sighed.

"So, you're not really my cousin but it's okay. Everyone likes you."

"Why don't they like my dad?" Mira was indignant.

"For one thing, he's not really family." Seeing Mira's face cloud and the tears starting, he softened the blow. "At least they like Ravi more than Patel."

She frowned. "Why? My dad told me Patel was nice."

The boy shook his head. "Because Patel was rich, nobody says anything." Before she could ask him why no one liked Patel, the boy grabbed his glide scooter and was gone.

CHICAGO

Mira Past and Present

May 6, 2290

A bubble-note floats in the corner, away from peepers. The rose color signals it is nothing urgent. With a slight tremble, she says, "Message." The bubble disappears as she hears Henry's voice in her ear, telling her he will be back before noon and to think about dinner; should they go out? Bowing her head in relief, she whispers to the absent Henry, "Thank you for staying."

Ready to begin her current work assignments, she says, "California beach, project seating, level one audio." Her workspace walls disappear into rolling surf and a deserted beach. Her chair molds itself, providing support and tension relief. "Pause!" She hears the soft brush of an urban air scrubber hovering outside the window of her workstation. Her heart skips as a wind gust sweeps the scrubber away. Air scrubbers belong to the city, but Hosseini has influence. Enough to modify a scrubber and reprogram it as a peeper? Is that why it paused outside her window? She freezes, indecisive. Everything fades except her shaking hand. No, it would be cheaper and safer to update what's already installed. Hosseini would never agree.

For now, she thinks, augmented environment options are unwise. Too distracting. Rotating her shoulders, she sighs. The air scrubber is gone; her hand relaxes.

Rather than a neural link, on this system, her commands are spoken, a safer choice. "Monitor," she whispers. A series of bubble texts and holo messages stream in a media window, notices of meetings and company policies. There are fat bubble messages from Hosseini in his various forms.

As she prioritizes, Mira slides her fingertip on the edge of her necklace. Linked by thin gold chains is a replica of a San Francisco bridge. "Your grandfather gave this to your grandmother to honor their memories of a special bridge." Ravi told her. "Now this memory is yours too."

At boarding school, Mira often opened her bedroom window and held the gold chain linked to each side of the little bridge. As moonlight traveled on the golden bridge, she spun her future into dreams. If the moon was full, moonlight reflected on the golden bridge as it swayed. Like the bridge, her future, with its perils and rewards, hovered above the darkness.

When she was twelve, she often sat on the school roof while parents collected their daughters for weekends and holidays. A day before her thirteenth birthday, Mira met Leilani Three and decided not to kill herself. After another painful hour of watching her schoolmates disappear into glide-cars, she felt Three's cool hand on her shoulder.

She could still remember Three's voice with its tinny gurgle as the android whispered a warning. "Careful, you don't want to fall."

The sharp edge of the roof tiles had pressed under her child's knees as she swung her feet back and forth. Her black oxfords were loose. What if they came off and fell to the stones below? Good if they did; she hated those shoes. She imagined the screams below if her body slammed onto the hard stones, the blood spreading like a flower of rebuke. Her mother Rosalind had fallen; maybe Mira should too.

She imagined Rosalind still there, her body frozen, preserved in the icy glacier. As a young child, Mira had pretended that a climber saw her mother fall, reached out and caught her. *But maybe, Rosalind lost her memory and that's why she's still gone.*

"Thank you Three, I'll be careful," Mira nodded. Besides, if she fell from the gables onto the schoolyard stones below, her father would be alone.

"Let's take a walk," the android said. The next morning, a new pair of shoes with no laces and cushioned heels was delivered to her room. After that, Mira and Leilani Three walked on the mile path that encircled the school. Mira remembered Three's uneven gait as they followed another path to the lake. The android's gray face on its long neck lurched forward as they walked. Under Three's patient counsel, Mira's hopelessness gave way to ambition. Leilani Three was a joke to many students. They called her "the hen," imitating the android's strange amble. Three *was* like a hen. Ignoring the ridicule of her classmates, Mira became Three's chick.

As she matured into a slender young woman with dark brown hair and amber eyes, Mira needed clarity. If she wasn't a Patel, who was she? With Ravi's help, she searched for answers. Her mother

Rosalind's family was blank. As a newborn, Rosalind was dropped at a church door. DNA searches were forbidden and few records kept in Northern Ireland. Rosalind had spent her childhood adrift in a sea of rural doorsteps. But Ravi, her father, *oh there was so much history*! When he told her she was the granddaughter of Gunter Holden, a pioneer of the after-death industry, Mira began to research.

Familiar with fantasy VR programs, she had been surprised by how technological advances impacted the ruthless battles for control of the after-death market. Though his legacy was tainted by murder and the merciless destruction of another company, her grandfather was considered a visionary. Researching the rise and fall of after-death programs, she wondered where their virtual residents went when the companies, firms, and corporations they trusted failed. Mergers resulted in program changes for these unfortunate virtuals and too often, this impacted the quality of virtual life after death.

When she was eighteen, Mira took a summer class, *The History of After-Death, an Overview* where a casual remark during a lecture spoke of a lost mind-upload copy of Gunter Holden. After a sleepless night, she messaged Ravi, demanding to know if it was true. Alarmed, Ravi responded, assuring her that if there was a mind upload copy of his father, he was unaware. She promised herself and Ravi that if one existed, she would find it. But all VEI memory recordings and files were at Cornell.

Ravi sold several of his most prized artifacts and she applied to The Cornell Institute of Artificial Intelligence Design. In the VR Library at Cornell were the remaining records of VEI and Gunter Holden. Admitted to Cornell's Virtual Environment Department, she studied the specialized AIs that maintain after-death programs where mind uploading enabled people to continue existing after physical death. It was her AI designs that caught the attention of SEINI.

***

The world is the world

Hours later, Henry's back. She wants his support and advice in uploading her grandfather's copy to Shemathra's Realm. His arm around her, they sit on the red couch as their cat purrs softly.

"It's not only about VEI," she tells him, aware of the slight tremble in her voice. "Hosseini is bidding on Virtual New Deal contracts." Several older members of Henry's family had expressed interest in the Virtual New Deal. "My guess is that SEINI after-death programs will be at best, bleak, if not truly horrific."

Henry shakes his head. "There are other ways, people I know who can use Holden's copy, better than you. And they can protect him, better than you! I promise you; they *will* find a way to take Hosseini down."

"No, *I* found Gunter Holden," she insists. "*I* want to say what happens to him. We both know that whatever is hidden in Shemathra's Realm needs to stop. Help me find a way into Shemathra's Realm, and I will use Holden's copy to stop Hosseini."

She waits for his answer. Is he going to leave her, wish her luck, and tell her goodbye? When he reaches out, she collapses into his arms. Wrapping her in his mother's favorite blanket, Henry studies her face and strokes her hair. "Mira, I love you. If I could, I would forbid anything or anyone to hurt you. But the world is the world."

"I know," she nods and looks away. Outside the kitchen window they hear faint echoes of air cleaners, and the comings and goings of glide-trams. She drapes the edge of the woolen blanket around his shoulder.

"Whatever your plan," he chooses his words carefully, "however many precautions you use, most likely, you will fail. Hosseini is cunning. He knows you want to trip him up and he'll be watching." Henry shakes his head and shudders. "You'll never let this go, will you?"

Bowing her head, she whispers, "I can't." She refuses to fail because of fear.

He looks into her determined eyes and kisses her. "I'll help if you'll promise to be very careful.

THE ELYSIUM

Mira's new suit

May 15, 2290

Help arrives in a box. SEINI requires her physical presence at the H Building only two days a month, so Mira is home when help comes. Regardless, SEINI pays her to create hellish virtual environments and monsters to rule them. If any laws are violated, she will be blamed. For now, Henry has enhanced the security of her office Qu-COM while her grandfather's copy, legally a resident of Shemathra, will witness and record enough cruelty and broken laws to destroy Donovan Hosseini and restore VEI.

Hosseini has acquired government contracts tied to the Virtual New Deal. There are rumors that conditions have gotten worse in Shemathra. It's true. Shemathra has become a virtual hell. What if these programs go the same way? The SEINI "H" building teems with secrets. She is afraid.

On each of the room divider's lacquered panels, dreamy images recall ancient China. Panel tops fold into a sort of canopy for more protection against peepers. The helpful box is made of something smooth, its edges rounded, perhaps a challenge to grasp and move. But she easily lifts it, carrying it to her work area where a wooded path leads to a distant mountain, one of her favorite AR environments.

As Mira slides her hands across its creamy surface, the box opens. The garment inside looks bulky but weighs almost nothing. She thinks it looks like an old-fashioned pair of child's pajamas. Its soft rabbit feet remind her of the snowsuit she wore when Ravi took her to play in the Sierra Mountains snow. Because she was five, the memory is barely recalled, until today.

Incredibly, beneath the garment, tucked in the side of the box, there is an external drive, an antiquated device, not seen in over a century. Placing the ancient device on her desk, she is startled when it connects to her Qu-COM system and is recognized!

Like her suit, the new drive becomes invisible. Shifting colors, the drive merges with the contours of her workstation. Will SEINI security see it? Probably not, Henry is cautious.

What's next? "Vintage media," she commands, her voice shaking. The wooded path and the mountain are gone. Her surroundings are now the interior of a twentieth-century movie theater. Ornate curtains, draped and accented by baroque statues are on each side. Behind her are rows of seats and shadows of a faceless audience. In the balcony, blurred figures lean forward. On the stage, tasseled gold curtains stand ready to open.

As Mira sits in the center-row of this AR media environment, she isn't sure if she's ready. "Stop," the command barely whispered. The theater disappears. What will change when she wears the suit? Time to find out.

She begins by threading her arms and legs through the suit's opening and tugs on the open front until it closes with a snap. A gentle massage ripples over her body. There's a breeze, a pleasant sensation, as if recording a memory? *Oh, God, this thing is scanning me, translating me into code!* After embracing her arms, hands, legs and feet, the garment moves quickly from the back of her neck, until it covers her head and face causing her to panic until she discovers she can breathe. And her vision is more acute. In a corner shadow, she can trace the fine grooves in Ravi's flute collection. Enough.

"Release!" she thinks the command. Quickly leaving her, the suit slides back into its box.

***

Miranda Four

Days later, she uploads her digital self as an AI Miranda Four. Via a series of holos, Hosseini had taunted her, showing her holos of what went on in Shemathra's Realm. The non-disclosure employment contract she signed made her powerless. Anything she revealed, however credible would be inadmissible. And Hosseini made it clear that Mira would be seen as a disgruntled employee. She would be punished.

In Shemathra's Realm, she'll be seen as the AI Miranda Three, but she is Miranda Four, an AI free to release and direct the new Gunter

Holden. On her first day as Miranda Four, Mira enters the portal that connects to the Villa program, a remnant of Bali Hai. She is afraid. SEINI's penalties for misbehavior are barbaric.

Until it was forbidden, Shemathra members frequently manifested as human, especially during holo chats with bio friends and family, knowing they were free to return to their animal form. As the quality of human life diminished, the herd life offered guilt-free pleasures. Then Bali Hai became Shemathra's Realm, the ground shook and the Goddess announced a change.

"Our virtual humans require more memory to maintain their habitats, and taxes must reflect the expense. The choice must be made. Leave the impure human form, manifest in animal form and follow the herds. We welcome you!!"

The Wolf Goddess, her canines grinding back and forth, scanned the herds and terrified human virtuals. *"All are free to choose. Leave the peace of the One Will, only to embrace the sadness of human existence, but you do so at great peril. For these apostates, there is no going back."*

Most have renounced their humanity. Each year, before the Grand Stampede, followers of Shemathra are chosen to board a spaceship. They will travel to another universe where they will rule a new world. But when the ship leaves, a spray of white mist follows in its wake. Many of the faithful pray not to be "chosen."

Members who did leave the herds, often joined a human loved one. For others, it was the prospect of eternal, crushing boredom. These were Bali Hai virtuals who uploaded to enjoy the promise of pleasures and challenges. Unable to transfer to another VEI program, they rejected the herd life. Once the choice was made, it was irreversible. Anyone caught changing from their animal form and returning to their previous human, risked the slaughterhouse and erasure.

Herd life meant taxes waived, frequent entertainment events and privileges such as the stampedes through human habitats. Four legs were superior to the human two. Bio contacts were strictly regulated until Shemathra went dark, and all within her realm were lost to the outside. Human virtuals faced more punishments, fines, and the degradation of habitats. Ritual tortures and forced deletions began. Certain elite herds were closed to new members.

Hosseini takes pleasure in Mira knowing all of this. Spies roam everywhere, but especially where habits hold the dwindling population of human uploads. But Mira knows change is coming. Hosseini, confident and smug, is uninformed.

When Miranda Four uploads the copy, Gunter Holden begins to manifest on the transition post. Panicking, she puts him in sleep mode. Next time, she'll wake him up.

***

Childhood Memories

May 19, 2290

Before she becomes Miranda Four and wakes the copy, Mira reflects on what has changed since she contacted Hernandez. Skeptical of her claim of being Holden's granddaughter, he vetted her as a descendent of Gunter Holden and that her father Ravi was the adopted son of Randall Patel. Hernandez sent her the Gunter Holden memory files from Bali Hai.

She wrestled with the century-old Holden Bali Hai memories. Sad and infuriating, the truth flickers like an ancient twenty-first century film where the sin and bitterness end in a redemption of sorts. Defenseless against Hosseini's illegal takeover of VEI, and stripped of power, Gunter struggled to protect Bali Hai. Oh God, then there was another merger, and it was too late. Hosseini owned Bali Hai.

Her grandfather had changed as he learned the truth of who he really was and how as a child, he was brutally betrayed by the father he loved. Shaken by what she has witnessed, Mira wonders how to continue.

This Gunter is not the original mind-upload, whose Bali Hai memories Hernandez insisted she review. But this Gunter carries the same hungry childhood memories and fear of abandonment. He is not yet a murderer nor is he responsible for the mass erasures that ended Joy Forever. Still, this copy must answer for what the bio did, however unfair.

SHEMATHRA'S REALM

(The Return of Gunter Holden)

RECORD 1A.

Audio: Byron—these records are what occurred after uploading the virtual copy of Gunter Holden to Shemathra's Realm. In the interest of clarifying these encounters, I have included notes in the transcript of these events. Let me know if you have questions. Mira

Shemathra's Realm

The Copy

June 2, 2290

Transition Port 3

Gunter Holden (copy of original bio)

(Recorded encounter 1A)

Audio: Byron—the copy's initial confusion is evident. For the record, I am aware of the documented crimes of the original bio-Gunter. I have reviewed the memories you sent from the file of the original, uploaded when Holden was fifty-six. I plan to follow this virtual copy (made when Holden was forty-nine) by using a new version of SOC (stream of consciousness) software which, like the original Bali Hai memory records, allows us to hear his inner dialog.

Transition complete. Gunter Holden copy is now in Shemathra's Realm. COPY activated.

***

Gunter Holden wants to know.

Where did the dolphins go? They were—what's wrong with the ocean? It isn't moving. . . I don't see a sun, so where is the light coming from? It must be a program glitch.

"Miranda, what's going on? Hello?

MIRANDA!"

This can't be Bali Hai. Where am I? Think! What do I know? This can't be a VEI program. It's dismal, not even basic. And why am I here? Ugh, there's a spongy black substance under the sand. I get it; I'm the copy. Don't leave me here, MIRANDA!

"Miranda, where are you?"

Why doesn't she answer? Have I been forgotten? The bio me must know I'm here. Why am I still active? What if I'm dead? Is the bio me dead? This is not Bali Hai. Miranda must know I'm here. Is there a glitch in the transport software?

If I'm the copy, why am I here and not in a folder? Did someone upload me here as a sick joke? People can be petty, especially on the Board. I swear when I find out, they'll regret it.

What other explanation can there be? Is this an experimental program and I'm here to make notes? Ridiculous idea. Why would I agree? Why would anyone? Regardless, there will be MANY notes. Plus no one will EVER be permitted to upload my copy unless the bio ME gives them written AND holographic permission.

In the meantime, okay, notes . . . I observe no rock formations, nor a single blade of grass. Ah, there IS a limp palm tree. Wait—is that land over there? How do I reach it? There must be commands. What if I choose a command and it takes me someplace worse? Yep, there's land stretched to the right of the horizon. There must be virtuals! Human voices are coming from wherever the—

OH MY GOD, IS THAT A SCREAM?

Oh, God! There's no wind so it can't be . . . *I hear screams! There's nowhere to hide here*, nothing but the palm, like a prop in a bad play. This must be a joke.

Calm down and think! First, why should I be scared? *I AM GUNTER HOLDEN!* Second, I control *Virtual Enterprises, Inc.* I own it and ONLY I control it. That doesn't change, even if I'm no longer a bio. *Wait—maybe someone really is using my copy to test this program!* Any new Bali Hai software—yes, I wanted to test preferences. So, we copied ourselves to do the test. Whatever this is, it isn't a VEI product. Copies are supposed to be destroyed. Tax laws require it. And VEI always follows the law. Who knows I kept my copy? Obviously, someone did and took advantage. There will be consequences. In addition, this product is unacceptable. I'd rather be in a virtual prison. At least you'd know what to expect.

What do I look like? There must be some way to see my reflection. My face feels like I'm still forty-nine. I must be the copy. I'm wearing the cotton pants and blue shirt I wore the day we tested for preferences. Still, I could be a new virtual if my original bio-self died and I transitioned to virtual existence. Perhaps I was wearing the same clothes I wore when I made the copy. The clothes could be a coincidence. My death may have been traumatic and the memory of it is hidden from me for now.

Was I murdered?

No, I would have been transitioned to Bali Hai and not this hell hole. I must be the copy. What about Patel? Could he have done this? He knows where my copy is stored. No, Patel has no sense of humor, and his ethics wouldn't allow it. I made the decision to keep my upload copy, and he warned me against it. Taxes, always taxes—but who would know? Obviously, someone besides Patel.

MORE SCREAMS! This is unacceptable. I'll wait; Marcia will find me. She promised to keep my copy safe. So, who uploaded me here? I remember arguing with Patel. Marcia told me not to worry, that she would make sure and then—What is the last thing I remember?

I was sitting on the deck of my virtual beach house in the Bali Hai Malibu environment. I remember the ocean, the breeze and the sound of waves rolling in and out. There were sim beachgoers strolling by me, carrying surfboards and some striped, bare dolphins were zigzagging among the swimmers. It occurred to me that observing Bali Hai wildlife might become a favored pastime. I made a note to Miranda on wildlife enhancement.

My last thought was of Laura. Christ! Is her copy here somewhere, at another transition point? If there is anyone with less patience than I have, it's my sweet wife. Whoever is responsible will regret this travesty.

Only one way to find an answer. "Command: Tell me my location. Include the program."

Good, a blue light is bathing that pathetic tree. Who's the girl? Is she a copy of Miranda? She looks like Marcia. Bali Hai's Miranda looks like Marcia, but there is something different. She also reminds me of my mother. It makes no sense. I was ten when my mother died; I should barely remember her.

What's wrong with this AI? She's standing there, staring at me. Unacceptable. Marcia will have to reprogram her. She probably thought the "mother" aspect might please me. No.

"Hello Grandfather or may I call you Grandpa? My name here is Miranda Four."

"Grandfather? What are you talking about? Who programmed you?"

The voice, at least, is the same, low, and musical.

"In the bio world, I am your granddaughter. Here, I'm Miranda Four. You may call me 'Four' if you like. You're in Shemathra's Realm, the program formerly known as Bali Hai."

This must be a joke. "Nonsense, Four, I may be my copy, but here, I AM Gunter Holden. When I discover the person responsible for this farce, he or she will be fired and most likely face a lawsuit. If you are the AI here, you are technically a sim, not a virtual, not human and we are not related."

"Grandfather," she sighs, *"you have slept for over one hundred years."* Why is she staring?

"Don't be ridiculous."

"We don't have time for this. Let me start again."

She's checking data that hovers near the tree. How can I override her program? There must be a command. It'll have to wait . . . she's done. What now? Why is she pointing at me?

"The original bio, Gunter Holden, committed bio suicide in 2123 and later, self-deleted in the 2180's when Bali Hai became Shemathra's Realm. To communicate with you, I have augmented this program's Miranda, Miranda Three. My name is Mira, and I AM a bio. A virtual me controls this Miranda when I meet with you. For your safety, everyone here must assume that I am Miranda Three."

A scream echoes in the distance.

"The slaughterhouse, virtual humans are being culled today."

"Culled?" That's concerning.

"Deleted," is all she tells me. There's a hint of regret.

"Four, Mira, whatever you call yourself, I want to leave this program. No one needs to know. Copy me, then delete the 'me' here and transfer my new copy to another program. I have no business here. I want out, NOW!"

Four laughs. Incredible! *"You can't leave and unless you do what I tell you, you'll be screaming along with the rest of them. Your choice."*

This isn't funny. Besides, Miranda was never programmed for humor. Concerning. "How do I move forward?"

Four studies the distant land mass where screams and moans begin again. She hesitates. *"All attention will be on the slaughter. We must act quickly, or you'll be discovered."* She rubs one index finger against the other.

The palm shudders and a medium tall young man appears standing next to the palm. He's . . . he's . . . me? Sandy blond hair falling in his eyes. I was always brushing it back then. Same gray eyes, but his are vacant. I remember that white cotton shirt. I always tucked it in. Same canvass shoes I bought the year I divorced Marcia.

The smile makes me uncomfortable because I'm seeing myself as . . . More accurately, I'm looking at my thirty-year-old self. Oh, God he's not another copy. This is a sim of me!

"Gunter sim," Four asks, *"what is your function?"*

The sim flashes a blank smile. *"I am here to greet newcomers. I welcome you to Shemathra's Realm. If you join the herds, you'll choose from one hundred natural wonders, including golden prairies, endless tundra, savannas, the rocky slopes of the Cascades and the sheltered valleys of the Andes. All lands are ruled by the White Wolf. You'll exist in the peace and joy that comes only in worship, basking in the light of the Goddess and her infinite bounty.*

During the coming Eighteenth Great Migration you shall witness the glory of the chosen as they ascend to another universe, arising again as corporeal beings, destined to be gods in a Universe of the Goddess.

If you decide to join our humans, I will guide you. I promise to instruct you and help you avoid offense, advising you when you make your memory tributes. Shall we begin?"

"Gunter sim, cease."

***

All that was left

"Is this a joke? If so, it's very sick." I hear more screams. The Gunter sim keeps smiling. There is nothing else but to play the game. What does she want?

Four looks away as if she pities me. *"Do you know what year it is?"*

"Let's see! My last memory was June 12, 2116. To test software preferences, all of us, VEI partners, mind uploaded to Bali Hai. After that, I don't know. I remember the Bali Hai beach. I assume the bio me decided to save his copy. I remained stored somewhere until someone found me. Does that answer your question?"

"Yes," she smiles, *"today is June 2nd, 2290."*

"Ridiculous. In 2115, the most basic after-death program is a paradise compared to this travesty. My last memory was of the Malibu Beach. The smell of the ocean, the sun, beachgoers, if you didn't know already, you would think you were a bio. Did we lose one hundred forty years of technology in some kind of disaster, such as a plague or a comet?"

"Worse." Four shakes her head. *"Technology has progressed but not Bali Hai. What is left of its memory resources are squeezed like a withered lemon into the Shemathra Data Stream. The result is the barest minimum. You'll see it soon."*

The sim smiles and waits for her to finish. Oh, God! A wall of screams bursts from the slaughter place.

"Your bio counterpart, Gunter Holden, my grandfather, transitioned as a virtual to Bali Hai in 2123. There were murders that I will detail later. For now, we have other matters."

"I was murdered?" I knew something was wrong. I need help.

"No Gunter, you were the murderer." She's staring again and pointing at me. Something is wrong with this AI! *"And YOU killed yourself to follow your victims. Now is not the time to explain."*

"Now *is* the time. I insist. What happened?"

What do I do? There must be some way to call for help!

She's approaching my sim. Maybe she'll listen to me after she's done with the sim.

"This is slightly painful for me, Gunter. Until your copy upload, this sim was all that was left of you. My grandmother, Marcia Evans, loved you and she programmed Miranda to love you as well. So, the AI part of me loves your sim. How very odd."

Yes, very odd.

I catch her fleeting regret as she embraces my younger self. The sim disappears. Shocking! What if . . .

"Relax, you have nothing to fear from me. I have deleted the sim and now I'm going to give you his program and memories."

Four is moving toward me. Oh God! Where can I go? This AI is malfunctioning!

Four shakes her head. *"If you don't acquire this information, you'll have no defense. They'll catch you and you'll join the slaughtered."*

Bitch! When I escape this nightmare, I'm terminating her program.

Four stretches out her arms. *"Now embrace me or don't. If not, soon, you'll join the culled."*

I have no choice and she's coming closer. She presses my head to her breast. Half-thoughts and images flood my mind.

City skylines and celebrations, presentations, fires and strange music, sims appear and disappear. Tourists flood vacation programs, then vanish, dissolving into blue skies and sunny beaches which sift into nothing. Lovers are naked and oblivious to my sim's gaze. Their bodies fade as high-rises collapse, and lakes blow away. Bistros, cafes, and clubs fade. Cities fall as if an earthquake has swallowed them.

Moans of animals, bellows, neighs, squeals, and bleats. Cattle, mustangs, goats, and sheep stroll and stampede on vacant city streets that give way to grassy fields and desolate plains. Thoughts stunted, devoid of emotion or judgment. I witness ceremonies. Herds thunder their approval. Human virtuals are condemned and deleted horribly

Blue-green ribbons of seas drain of color, turning a ghostly gray. Where did the sea memory go? The sim doesn't care, but I do. Human habitation has shrunk. Now, squat buildings pile together to accommodate wide streets for the herds to come through. I hear crying. STOP!

***

The Tax Sim

God help me! The sim is gone. Why am I wearing his clothes? I need more information. It must be in a program malfunction, a perversion of some kind. No, the sim is still here, inside me. I can hear him whispering that he is part of me now. Oh God, what if she's telling the truth? My file has been compromised. I push the sim memories away, but he's still in a corner of my mind. He's sleeping now, I think, hope.

What's my next step? Where is Marcia? It may be over a hundred years, but surely, she resides in another program. I must find a way to message her. Is Four an AI or a person named Mira? Regardless, she is delusional. She claims we're related. I'll appeal to her sense of family. I can persuade her it's urgent that I locate Marcia. And where is Laura and where is Patel?

"Bali Hai is gone, Gunter." Four waves her hand to emphasize her point.

"No, you're wrong. I can fix this if I can communicate with the outside. Four, I need your help."

Four shakes her head. *"All communications are forbidden. No one here can talk to anyone outside this program. Gunter, if you're a virtual human here, you're in danger."*

"Four, where is everyone? Marcia, Patel, where are they?"

"Before I tell you, you must understand why I brought you here. There are two things you must do. If you do them, I will transfer you to a more comfortable program and you can stay there for as long as you like.

"Transfer me to Bali Hai and I may agree to help you. We can discuss your terms when I feel safe and at home."

"You're already home. This was Bali Hai before Hosseini destroyed it and used what was left to create Shemathra's Realm."

"You're lying."

She ignores me. *I'll tell you your first task now."*

I hear another scream from the 'culling.'

"This world, Shemathra's Realm, is dark. No one here can communicate with the bio world, nor with any other virtual platform. Here, your sim is a "tax collector," and you, a spy. You will record and bring what you see to me."

"Shemathra what? What's Shemathra?"

"Grandfather, do you WANT TO SURVIVE?"

She's serious! "Yes—of course." There's another scream.

Four waits for the scream to fade. *"Severing contact with the outside has not escaped the attention of the bio world. A congressional investi-*

gation is scheduled. SEINI is the company that acquired VEI in the 2180s. Two years later, the original Gunter virtual self-deleted. The man behind SEINI exists as a virtual here, in Shemathra's Realm. Everyone, cult member or not, fears him. His name is Donovan Hosseini, and here, he is the llama god, Urcuchillay."

She looks up to the blank sky and lowers her voice to a whisper. "You, Gunter, must pretend to be your sim." This AI is addressing me as if I were a small child. I swear I will delete her.

"As a sim," she tells me, *"you have access to all Shemathra locations. You are familiar with the Virtual Bill of Rights?"*

"Of course. I helped get it passed."

"Hosseini hides behind it while he continues to violate everything in it. When I call you here, I will download what you have witnessed. If you survive, you may be required to give testimony before Congress."

"Survive? What do you mean 'if'? Why should I risk my 'virtual' life for you? You are breaking the law by keeping me here against my will. Send me to a safe program and then, only if my safety can be guaranteed, will I consider helping you."

(If it really has been over a hundred years, maybe there is a law that protects copies.)

Four glares at me. I shouldn't have threatened; she's not stable.

"Gunter Holden, you'll get no sympathy from me or from anyone else. If there were another way, I would have left you where you were, encased in a red crystal, hidden in a dusty case in a dark closet. You have more to answer for than two murders. I'll be glad to enlighten you, but another time."

"Me, a murderer?! You're misinformed; I'm no killer. Where's your proof? Who did I kill? I want answers before this goes any further."

If she imagines I'm a murderer, she's capable of anything!

She's pointing at me again. *"I'm tempted to leave you here. When they find you, you won't last long. Gunter, please know, deletions in Shemathra are not painless. Your 'rights' will be the least of it. I'll explain the murders, but first, do as I say."*

Time to be quiet!

"Let's jump somewhere safe."

Thank God she's calm again.

"Urcuchillay uses crow sims to keep him informed. We'll jump to the villa. Should any be curious, you're a sim being reprogrammed."

She clutches my arm. Where are we jumping?

***

Shemathra's Realm, the Villa

Can I protect him?

June 2, 2290

He is sleeping. For now, it's as if the tax sim doesn't exist. Tax collecting starts in a few days. Can I protect him?

Via audio (confidential)

June 3, 2290

To: Byron Hernandez, Investigator

Trammell & O'Connell Law Offices

Byron—I have attached records documenting my first encounter with the copy of Gunter Holden, uploaded to Shemathra's Realm on June 2, 2290. Hosseini is aware of who I am, a fact that amuses him. He considers himself invulnerable to any mischief on my part. However, he is unaware a copy of my grandfather, a legal resident of Shemathra, exists. If Hosseini should discover the copy of Gunter Holden, he will try to neutralize him.

After reviewing this material, if you are still interested, I will send more.

Mira Patel Holden

Via private audio

From: Byron Hernandez

June 5, 2290

Mira —Thank you!

First, let me emphasize how valuable the copy of Holden is to our case. As you know, our office is working with the Congressional team charged with regulating Virtual Affairs. The copy of Mr. Holden is vital to this investigation. I urge you to persuade him to continue to cooperate. It is important to our investigation that the Gunter copy agree to visit and record

what's going on in each of the four virtual human colonies. I am certain that if enough information is gathered there, it will bring Hosseini to justice. If we are successful, ownership of VEI will be reviewed and possibly restored to Holden's copy and to you as his proxy. I look forward to your next report.

Regards,

Byron

THE ELYSIUM

Resources and risks

June 7, 2290

Although she did not ask for his help, Henry insisted on working from home. "You need to be with your team at the Quantum International event," she protested. "They depend on you!"

"I'm a click away and they'll be fine," he assured her. "It's easier to keep tabs on what you're doing. You don't know what you're up against, or what that Hosseini will do if he finds out what you're up to." He cupped her chin. "I want to keep you out of trouble."

When Henry suggested she make a few transparent attempts to plant new spyware in Shemathra, Byron Hernandez agreed. These efforts were quickly removed without comment by SEINI, as if Hosseini were making a point of showing her that her tricks were easy to detect. On the other hand, her success in maximizing AI program memory proved her worth.

As plans took shape, she began to worry. This Gunter is a copy of the original, but as Byron said, Gunter's copy is now legally *the* Gunter Holden and a human virtual. Her grandfather is sharing his files with his tax collector sim. If this Gunter-sim hybrid is discovered, Hosseini will take great joy in torturing him.

Convinced of the copy's value and what Mira offered, Hernandez responded by sending her the original Gunter's remaining memories from Bali Hai. "Take time to learn what's going on and who your grandfather was before you put his copy in jeopardy. Know exactly how you want to use him and what you want him to find. He's a virtual human and he's too good a resource to waste."

***

Day at the Park

June 8, 2290

She sits at her workstation, where an augmented reality, something simple, surrounds her with a long-ago day in a small-town park. Children swing and others slide down into the waiting arms of their parents. She's on a comfortable bench reading a book by the philosopher, A Wave. The book is very retro and made of paper. There's a nearby tree. She hears the chatter of squirrels and there's a dog chasing some kind of twirling disk. Regretfully, it's time to work.

"Stop 'Day at the Park,'" she tells AR Options. Where to start? First, she thinks about all that can go wrong. The Bali Hai platform was corrupted to create Shemathra's Realm. She knows that any records of Hosseini's crimes, obtained illegally, are useless. Gunter Holden's virtual copy can make a difference. If Hosseini discovers her spy, she must find a way to delete the copy. Her grandfather will not become slaughterhouse entertainment. She cannot resist–the thought of his deletion makes her cry.

***

Recorded Encounter 1B

June 10, 2290

Shemathra's Realm

V–Loc: Villa programming site.

Audio:

Byron–The Villa interior is the most secure location in Shemathra, programed to be safe from any surveillance sims. From this point, I will refer to the copy as Gunter. In this record, I tell Gunter his assignment and what he will gain if he cooperates. Gunter now possesses his sim's memories. The sim memories should shield him and hopefully prevent discovery. I will insert Gunter into each human habitat and then summon him back to the villa after he records what he sees and hears. There are four human colonies. I will send you Gunter's complete records, including his thoughts after each visit.

Let me know if you have questions.

Transcript:

Gunter Holden (copy of original bio)

Post jump to Villa

I'm on a stretch of beach. The ocean here is alive, not still and menacing like the other. Is this part of Bali Hai? The pathetic island with its single palm tree, the dead water, and screams might have been a bad experiment. I hope so. But what about the sim?

Ha, I see Four is watching me, waiting for my response to the change in location. I'm underwhelmed. Why is she smiling?

I see a villa less than a quarter mile from the ocean's edge. Is it the "Villa" from Bali Hai? Yes, this could have been a bad joke. She's gesturing toward the Villa. I nod and like magic, we're passing through the Villa's cream-colored doors. Like the beach, this is familiar, but there are differences. I remember a large palm tree was on each side of these doors. There are no palms. Instead, a faint image of a single palm tree is in each upper panel. Four points to a room with shelves filled with old-fashioned books. All the books are covered in shades of white.

"Would you like some coffee?" Four smiles and offers me a cup and smiles again. *"In a white cup, of course."*

How does she know I prefer white cups? I'm on the edge of a couch. What will she do next? What does she really want? "Yes, a white cup would be fine."

The coffee appears on a tray edged with ivory angels.

"You murdered your wife, Laura," Four says, as if she's remarking on the weather. *"And you murdered her lover, your brother, Jacob."*

"You are joking or lying. I'd never murder anyone."

"Laura wasn't meant to die. She was killed, protecting your brother, your intended victim."

"Wrong, again. Laura would never betray me, especially with Jacob. I despise my brother, and I admit that I wish he'd never been born, but I wouldn't kill him. He's not worth it."

"Your wife was afraid of what you might do when you discovered she was leaving you for Jacob. As a precaution, she added Bali Hai nanobots to your brother's tea."

Is there any way to contact the bio world? This AI must be deleted.

"After their bio deaths, Laura and Jacob uploaded to Bali Ha. Rather than allow your brother to enjoy the pleasures of Bali Hai, especially with your wife, you decided you would persuade him to self-erase. If he were deleted some other way, say, by an unfortunate program event, everything would point to you. So, you killed your bio-self, mind-uploaded, following your victims into Bali Hai. Of course, when I say 'you' I mean the original upload of Gunter Holden. Both Laura and Jacob self-deleted a few years after their upload. However, the original you remained in Bali Hai."

"I don't believe you. Why would Laura betray me? Give me a reason."

"It would be easier for you here if you accept what I tell you."

"Jacob hates the idea of after-death programs. Laura knows Jacob is a loser. What you're describing is impossible."

She's shaking her head.

"Gunter, this all began when you committed an unforgivable crime. Are you familiar with 'Joy Forever'?"

"Of course, an after-death company. I don't consider them a threat."

"They weren't until they began to steal VEI software. Not only did they steal VEI intellectual property, but 'Joy Forever' offered packages at a fraction of VEI's."

"Outrageous! My lawyers will put a stop to this. Let me contact them."

"But they didn't. Not quickly enough for you. So, you decided to allow the theft of tainted software. 'Joy Forever' copied it and used it, resulting in a mass deletion. Almost two million virtual humans gone in an instant, 'Joy Forever' was done, but Gunter, so was the original you. Patel resigned, Marcia gave notice and Laura turned to Jacob for comfort. Everyone saw what you had become."

"I wouldn't do such a despicable thing. You are either lying or misinformed. I demand to speak with Marcia Evans."

"Laura was afraid that you would hurt Jacob. As your wife and a member of the Board, she had access to Bali Hai nanobots, and she put them in Jacob's tea to protect him."

Now I know that she's lying. Jacob? Occasionally, Laura and I argue. Jacob, no doubt would take advantage. But an affair? I can't think about this now; I must . . . I can't think now. Must put this aside and humor her.

"Okay, what else do I need to know?"

"There was a merger, in fact, two mergers."

"Oh, for God's sake. What do you mean mergers? VEI can't be bought. You're mistaken." Has my copy been kidnapped by anti-virtuals? Be careful here, she's very still. Is she angry? I'll need her help to leave this nightmare.

"Listen carefully!"

Four must have a rich imagination.

"Do I have your complete attention?"

"Yes."

"Eight years before you killed yourself and arrived in Bali Hai as a new virtual, a man named Donovan Hosseini founded a new religion. Have you heard of him?"

"Hosseini is a low-class sleazy operator. He produced VR porn and invested in the eco-kit industry. He owns several media companies. He is not a player in the after-death industry. A real bastard if any of what I heard is true. I thought he retired. So, he started a religion—why?"

"What better way to gain power? The Shemathra religion is based on a cult that originated in Alaska, a few years before Hosseini came into the picture. The cult worshiped the goddess, Shematre. Shematre, Hosseini claimed, came to him in a dream. It's a complicated, tortured theology; it's irrelevant. The faithful now call her Shemathra, the white wolf goddess. In Shemathra's Realm, the 'goddess' appears in a cloud and puts on quite a show with thunder, lightning, and lots of threats. Every human virtual here is strongly encouraged to pay memory taxes and tributes. There are penalties for non-compliance, some more dreadful than others."

"Unbelievable."

"The lie is as follows: In Shemathra's Realm, if you manifest as an animal and become part of a herd, 'acting with one will, her will,' you might be transported to another universe, and you'll become a god. Her consort, Urcuchillay, is the only one here who talks directly to her. He conveys her wishes to the faithful and. Urcuchillay's power is absolute. Would you care to guess who the consort is?"

"Hosseini?"

"Yes, Hosseini is the llama god, Urcuchillay. Avoid him."

"It's difficult for me to accept that anyone believes this Shemathra fantasy; it's more than a little ridiculous."

"I doubt that many believe this tale entirely, but, opposing him results in dreadful consequences."

"Tell me about the mergers."

"The first merger involved the after-death company, Infinite Bliss."

"Infinite Bliss? Not a chance. Few people even know who they are."

"Your nephew, Diego Putnam brokered the deal."

"Who?"

"It doesn't matter. What matters is who was behind the mergers and the destruction of VEI, you and almost everyone else in Bali Hai. That person was Hosseini."

"You're lying. I never would have agreed to this. I would have called my lawyers and tied them up in the courts."

Four moves to an ivory-colored rattan chair. Even if this is all a lie, it's still upsetting. I'll find out who is responsible for this farce, and they will regret it. Maybe it's some kind of test.

"That was your first thought until without warning, Bali Hai's virtual Paris and all its inhabitants were erased. When Chicago was threatened, you cooperated."

"Monsters!"

"Grandfather, there is something else you must know, but it will have to wait."

"Why?"

Four shakes her head. *"Yes, I'll continue, and you will listen. After the first merger, the Shemathra Group was only one of the new communities Bali Hai was forced to absorb. Many of its programs were deleted or greatly reduced. Other than Shemathra, most of the newcomer communities followed some Catholic or Protestant belief system."*

"You're mistaken. Even if I couldn't fight, Patel or Marcia would not tolerate any of this. Hosseini would spend his days, virtual or otherwise, defending himself against a tsunami of lawsuits. We would break him.

"Marcia and Patel left VEI shortly before your suicide."

"I still don't believe you."

"After they left, your nephew, Diego, took control of your shares and sold you out. He replaced you on the Board and forced you to mediate the inevitable conflicts between Everlasting Praise, a Christian community and the only pagan group, the cult of Shemathra."

"Okay, you lost me at Diego; who is Diego again?"

She shakes her head and turns away. I'm hoping this is a bizarre joke and I can find out who is behind this. I'm not laughing.

Sitting down, Four leans toward me as if I were a child and she, a very patient teacher. Insulting. Why should I continue to indulge her?

"Diego is the son of your sister, Estrella."

Is this true? If I don't take control now, I may be stuck here indefinitely. Even copies should have some rights. Still, no one needs to know about my copy. "As far as I know, Estrella has no children. I'll be happy to have my lawyers check on that if it would help." Oh, God, she's staring at me. This is a nightmare!

"Look at me, Gunter. Pay careful attention if you want to continue to exist. What followed was Hosseini's hostile takeover of VEI, the destruction of Bali Hai and the creation of Shemathra's Realm. Before Hosseini transitioned to this program as the llama god, Urcuchillay, the changes were incremental until another 'unfortunate' mass deletion occurred. Soon, Shemathra's followers enjoyed the lion's share of the newly available memory. When it was evident that Bali Hai was beyond saving, the 'original' you decided to self-delete. There were other factors. I will disclose them in time."

There is no choice but to play along. "What do you want from me? Why am I here?"

She sits on an arctic-white couch and points the open doors of a balcony. Small palm trees are there, each encircled by balcony tiles the yellow-white shade of raw milk. Between them is a hammock. The palms are a pale version of nature while everything else on the patio, like the house is some version of white.

"Why is everything white?"

"Urcuchillay considers color a waste of memory. I avoid it here because we might attract spies. I want your undivided attention."

"Why should I help you?

"When he was still a bio, Hosseini used his influence to alter data taken from a public document. A convenient change to Illinois State Law resulted in your removal from the VEI Board with Diego as your replacement. Diego agreed to the merger and sold you out. I want you restored as the lawful owner. "

"What else do you want?"

"Why grandfather, you don't think that my desire to right a wrong is its own reward?"

Cold and sarcastic. "We're not related. I had no children."

"But you did. During your Bali Hai years, you found a memory your first wife, Marcia Evans had left for you, Marcia was pregnant when you left her to meet the next wife in South Africa."

"Ha! I was back within a month." The thought of Marcia being pregnant, especially then is upsetting. "Even if she tried, she couldn't have kept that from me."

"She knew how you would react. You would have dismissed it as an effort to keep you and you would have resented it. So, she arranged for the embryo to be removed and stored. My father, Ravi, is Marcia's son and yours."

"Arrangements, how?"

"Patel helped her. Did you know he was in love with her? You never saw past your own needs. Randell Patel was your colleague and the most brilliant member of your team. His work in developing virtual ecosystems still supports countless programs. SEINI profits from Patel's work creating VEI products. If nothing else, Gunter, this should anger you. As your heir, it angers me."

She's clearly mistaken. "I just spoke to Patel and . . . I told him to store my copy. Oh God, he did and that's why I'm here, isn't it? Where is Marcia now?"

"Marcia knew being alone was something you couldn't handle. She killed herself and transitioned to Bali Hai to help you adjust."

"She wouldn't have . . . you're lying. If you're not, why isn't she here?'

"Gunter, she stayed long enough for your file to stabilize, then she self-deleted."

"I don't know who programmed you, but I intend to sue that person for subjecting me to this farce. Now transfer me to a decent program or put me back in the file until this is sorted out."

"Denial still? Grandfather, both you and Ravi, my father deny what's in front of you. Despite all the crimes the original you committed my father still loves you and rejects any criticism of you from me or anyone else."

"I'm asking you again; where is Marcia?"

"Again, after jumping from your 'special' bridge, Marcia, my grandmother joined you in Bali Hai. When you were no longer in crisis, she deleted herself."

"But why? Marcia wouldn't do that; Bali Hai was our project." Can this be any more pathetic? Four looks as if she pities me. She's turning away, uncomfortable; why?

"Be grateful she left when she did, Gunter. She was spared the descent into hell that happened after she was gone. However strong she thought you were when she left, there was no way to prepare for Hosseini."

"You keep saying that I have a son. Even if everything else that you're telling me is true, how is that possible?"

"Patel helped her. Decades after your bio death, Patel found a home for the helpless little embryo who became your son and my father."

(Oh God, what if this is real?)

"In exchange for a financial arrangement and later, a favored part in Patel's will, a relative agreed to bring Marcia's baby to term. Then Patel, who loved Marcia more than you ever could, raised her son."

Marcia would never self-delete because Bali Hai is her dream as well as mine. What's happening? The Villa is fading. . .

"Until I'm ready for the next step, I'm putting you into dream-memories."

"Don't put me in any state without my . . ."

A guitar strums as I float into a dream.

I'm finishing a presentation to the applause of dozens of investors. "Nanobots, nanobots mean never losing a memory! No more yearly updates! When you're ready, they're ready to transport you to your custom paradise." Rotating above us all is an enormous globe. The Earth spins slowly while holos of cities float in the air and sparkle with life. Lights dance on Paris' Eiffel tower and tiny sims dance through the streets of Rio.

I bathe in the approval of the audience, I . . .

***

It's cold in here. Marcia is crying. What happened? Ah yes, I just told her that Shawndra and I are getting married. Marcia must have known; my latest divorce was done weeks earlier. Why is she crying? What did she think? That I would choose to be alone? We're in the kitchen. Her hands shake. I've told her often enough; Marcia knows my love for her will never change, but life goes on and after all, what would people think of a man like me staying with a woman so much older?

I can understand her being upset the first time; seeing Therese and I together must have been a shock. Marcia and I had some wonderful years, the best; the age difference—eighteen years made it inevitable. It makes me sad to see her sobbing like a child. Maybe it was the trip to Cabo. We planned the next phase of Bali Hai. Intoxicating. It must have been the margaritas because we came together. But it ended. I was wrong to not tell her about Shawndra, but I wasn't sure then. It would have spoiled the trip. Like old times. Like old . . .

***

"You're a fool!" my father shouts at me. "You're a fool, Gunter, if you think people really want this. Virtual reality heaven? It's your call. I want no part of it."

We're on the veranda. I can hear the Thames waters rushing by as I try to reason with him. The nights here are magic. Crickets sing in the grass as I plead. But Jacob got to him first. Jacob and his nihilism has drained my father of all wonder. Hopeless. Bali Hai is the gift of life. I won't stop trying. Dad must see it . . .

***

The sun is directly overhead. It's way too hot. Bees are droning nearby. Maybe it's all the roses. Rows of headstones and dedicated statues and there is a rose covered coffin. Celeste is watching me, wondering what I'll do, so I don't make her wait. I'm on my brother's back, pounding the side of his head. Her hands are pulling on my neck, trying to protect her precious son. I ignore my stepmother's pleas. Pathetic.

"Die weasel." I scream. "It's your fault he wouldn't listen." My father listened to Jacob, my loser drug addict brother. Dad's gone because he wouldn't listen, he wouldn't listen listen listen . . .

***

"Listen Gunter!" Someone's hands are clutching the sides of my face. *"Are you listening?"*

"It's your fault he's dead!"

Where am I? I was at Dad's funeral. I must be in another nightmare. I'm swaying in a hammock, and I hear the ocean. Where am I? Oh God, no! I was dreaming. Now, I'm awake.

"The first lie you must face: Eric was not your father. There was no reason to destroy Jacob," Four tells me. Of course, she's lying. Pathetic. Of course, Eric *was* my father. She flips me out of the hammock and onto the tiles. She leans down, grabs my face again, and forces me to my feet.

"What do you want, Gunter?" Four demands.

What does she want me to say?

"I'm asking because there is no one else here who cares. Everyone you once knew and thought you cared about is gone. Gone from Earth, gone from virtual existence, gone. None reside in any program anywhere. You're alone Gunter, except for me. I need you. If I didn't, you wouldn't exist, except for a red crystal and some code. Even that wouldn't exist if anyone knew."

"I want to leave this program. Will you do that—let me leave?" I must choose my words carefully.

"If we're successful, I'll transfer you to something better, more like the Bali Hai you knew. But first, you must help me defeat Urcuchillay."

Four points at chairs away from the palms and the hammock, on the sunlit part of the balcony.

"As I describe what we must do and why, you will not comment, only nod your head on occasion. Crow sims rarely fly over this setting; however, we must be careful. To them, you are a sim. When I address you as such, as 'Gunter sim,' the sim memory you have absorbed will inform your response."

My questions would have to wait until I have more power. She moves to the chairs near a swan sculpture and a simple white stone fountain. When I sit down, she shakes her head. *"You must stand, Gunter sim."*

"Yes, Miranda Three, I will stand." The words come out before I can stop them.

"Do you see how easy it is, Gunter sim? Your sim memory will protect you, but you must still be careful. Gunter, do you understand? Your sim's code is only a trace of you. It's an empty suit, a mere echo of your former self. Miranda made your sim as all sims are made, by using a piece of recorded memory from the original Gunter Holden. Then the sim was given its task and later, the code was modified. Hosseini decided your sim should perform another task in addition to its original role as a hospitality sim greeting new residents. He thought it amusing that one of his tax collectors should be your sim. Now, I have recoded your sim for a different purpose."

My words are my own again. Still, I look for crows before I speak. "When you don't add the word 'sim' you're talking to me, otherwise, I'm playing a part, and the lines will be there because of my absorbing the sim memory. And I will address you as Miranda Three. Is that right?"

"You're not playing a part; you're along for the ride." She says and looks up to the sky. Above, we see the lazy glide of dark shapes, circling, then disappearing.

"Don't say anything. Nod your head on occasion. Keep all emotion out of your face save for a cheerful smile." I give a broad smile, one that Marcia had described as my shit-eating grin.

"That will do. I'm going to give you two assignments. One will be for you as Gunter sim. One will be for you, Gunter."

She looks up again. The crows are gone. *"Do you know what was done to your world, Gunter? You allowed it to slip away well before you self-deleted."*

"Why did I self-delete? I know myself; I wouldn't have given up."

"While Bali Hai was being stripped of its resources by Urcuchillay, you were being stripped of everything you believed in, good and bad.

And there was something that made you change what you wanted. Nod your head, Gunter sim, the crows are back and they're watching."

"Yes, Miranda Three, I am listening."

"First, Gunter sim, you will visit The No Where, one of the four human communities. While you are there, Gunter sim, you will collect taxes. You know what to do. Memory is the preferred currency. When you have completed your task, I will call you back to this location and you will report your findings."

"I will jump to The No Where, collect the taxes and you will call me to report my findings."

A loud caw comes from the tiled roof as a crow sim takes flight, following another, disappearing over the shallow horizon. *"Gunter, can you guess how many virtuals are here? I'm referring to those who remain human.*

I'm afraid to know. "My guess is not many. Tell me, how many still cling to their humanity?"

"Shemathra's Realm claims a population of three million, four hundred and fifty-six thousand virtual citizens. Less than one hundred thousand of the virtuals here exist as human. When most of these human virtuals transitioned to Bali Hai, they didn't realize the danger until it was too late to leave. Currently, human virtuals use only two per cent of the program memory resources.

There are four distinct human communities. Twice a year, each human virtual is granted the honor of donating memory to the goddess. Shemathra punishes those who can't or are unable to arrange a donation on their behalf. It is your task as a tax-collector sim to visit each human habitat, collect the taxes, tributes and determine if any residents are hiding inappropriate or unnecessary uses of memory. Those who have no more assets, no more anything of value will soon be deleted and the memory data from their files recycled."

***

Oh, God! Bali Hai has become a police state. "Four, I'd rather self-delete than have any part of this. It's grotesque. If the bio world knew the circumstances of their loved ones continued existence, they'd"—

"The bio world only knows what Hosseini wishes them to know. I am forbidden to record any human habitat here or activities involving humans. It's in my contract.

Gunter, do you know how virtuals are deleted here? There are three ways. The first is a strong wish to fade. Few choose that one because the second way is so horrifying that it triggers the instinct for survival.

The third way is a lie. There's a "Grand Ascent" once a year. It goes like this: After an ornate, public ritual, Urcuchillay sends deserving supplicants to a ship that transports the chosen virtuals to a parallel universe where they will become bio again, but this time, they will live forever as bios. And each of these lucky travelers becomes a god who will rule over a new world."

Four shakes her head in disgust. *"It's a lie. There is no ascent, nor is there a ship, only a mass deletion. During their deletion, these chosen worshipers are stripped of their memory and the data goes to the memory bank. Hosseini also claims the financial resources the departed leave in the outside bio world. Only human virtuals are formally taxed. Join the herds and Shemathra owns you and what is yours is hers."*

The reality of this situation has begun to settle. I am afraid to ask, "What is the second form of deletion?"

"*You are put with other virtual humans who have committed infractions ranging from non-contribution to lapsing into human form while part of a herd.*" Four sighs. "*It's an ugly process. The lucky ones who cooperate get the bolt, which triggers self-deletion. Those who cause problems have their throats slit. Then they're thrown into boiling water. Some mercifully manage to self-delete before the water.*

Those who don't, who cling to existence despite the enhanced pain program that simulates being immersed boiling water, those deletions are recorded for the entertainment of the herds and officials of their High Court. Regardless, all of those held in the yards are herded together and executed. Few manage to self-delete. The threat of slaughter triggers self-preservation. You understand."

"Why?" I ask, "why am I really here?"

"*I want to restore VEI,*" she tells me. "*My father, your son, wants no part of your legacy. He is content with his life, more like Patel who raised him, than you. Your son is an anthropologist, what used to be called a scholar, although the world has little need of scholars. Rather than contributing to the artifice of a virtual environment, Ravi, my dear papa, preserves the echoes of culture.*

Hosseini knows who I am. I sought employment here for the chance to reclaim what was stolen, and yet he allows me access to this program, the one that he inhabits and rules as a tyrant god. There are safeguards to protect him from me. My presence is a joke to him. He takes pleasure in allowing me to see what he has done to my birthright. He is a monster."

She points at me. "*But he doesn't know about you. I'm sending you to each human enclave. Gunter sim is a tax collector. You, Gunter, are a spy. When I call, you will return here and I will download the records of what you have witnessed, all you have seen and heard and then these memories will be given to those who can bring Hosseini to justice.*

You will enter these human colonies as a sim. If you want to avoid the slaughterhouse, you will only jump to the locations I choose. Others will see you as a tax collector sim, but your thoughts will be your own.

Remember! Let your sim memory be your guide. Your files carry all the complexity of your forty-nine years as a biological being. Whatever you do, don't let anyone see who you really are. When you return, depending on what you tell me, I will reward you. I'll tell you more of what happened to the original you. I warn you, there will come a time when you'll regret learning it."

"Perhaps, but I want to know."

"Yes, you must. I'm sending you to The No Where. I warn you; it is the most wretched of the places where human virtuals exist. Are you ready, Gunter sim?

"Yes, Miranda Three, I am ready."

SHEMATHRA'S REALM

The No Where

Record 1

THE NO WHERE

Shemathra's Realm

V Loc: The No Where fenced human virtual habitat, barred perimeter,

Montana Vista Grazing Ranges

June 14, 2290

Gunter Holden (copy) (recorded encounter, Record 1)

What's the thin bar of blue light? Interesting! Where does it go? Looks like pretty much forever or close to it. No way to tell. Except for the blue light, it's incredibly dark here. Is the light a barrier of some kind? Okay, on the other side, there's movement and . . . what? Okay, moving closer, there's finally, sunlight. I can see short grass, and hills. Maybe a prairie? There's lots of grass. That's more like it; but why does the sun only shine on the prairie side? What are the moving objects in the distance? Are they cows? There are some horns, yes. They're moving closer. Oh, now I can hear the moos and grunts. Wait—is that singing?

"Ummyoo looovoo is gonoo to the moons, moons, Juuupiter moooons awayoo to the cold whereoo the---" It's coming from a handful of cows, their mouths straining to form words with o's and consonants.

"It's all right to use your hoooo-yuoooman voices onmoo certain woooords," the lead cow assures the group. "Mooarian and Sybiloo shouldoo practice later. For noo-ow, please, ooonly hooumuh the melody."

Six cows huddle near the light bar. They're swinging their heads and tails in agreement. Marian and Sybil hum and moo while the rest join in to create a harmony. A new cow is leaving the main herd and she's ambling over to the group. "Canoo I join in?" she swings her head and asks.

"You'll moo-need to auditionoo," the chorus leader informs the wannabe, who is a large black cow with a backend stippled in white dots. The leader is a red heifer with a white star on her forehead. She dismisses the newcomer. "Woohen we decide to invite noowew members, we will let you knoooow."

"You're a clubooo?" the new cow asks plaintively. "I miss hoooman voice singoooing. My favorite songooo is 'My sweetheartooo dwells in a Venus mooo-cloud.' I'm-mooo Dooorothy," the black cow offers.

The red heifer chews her lunch cud, and turning her back, she dismisses Dorothy with a twitch of her tail.

"I was in the church coohoir when I was a bio-ooo," Dorothy announces, not taking the hint, and still hoping to impress.

I hear snorting. A bison is trotting over to investigate. 'We're 'The Prairiemooo Cowbellsooo," the red cow explains with a proud moo. The massive beast glares at her, his head down, in attack mode. She tosses her white-starred head, as if her rank as group leader settled things.

Unwilling to let her have the last word, the bison kicks up a mound of dung, flinging it onto the red heifer. "We don't allowoo any hoooomanugrrruph songs," he snorts. With a collective head-swing, all six cows turn their backs and resume grazing for lunch. The buffalo nudges Dorothy, the interloper, who reluctantly trots back to the herd.

No 'hoooman' songs? What songs *do* they allow? Whales' songs or birds' songs? Are there official cow songs? What has happened to these people? Why would anyone choose to live like this? Glad I'm not *their* tax collector. I collect taxes from human virtuals only or rather my sim does.

Where are the human virtuals? Yes, oh I see them now. They're sitting in groups, forming circles. Not a lot of movement, except for a faint ripple of color which bathes each circle. Green dominates in the largest group of circles. I won't be collecting from the greens until the next tax visit. My sim tells me greens promise to pay all their back taxes plus penalties before the next tribute. If they lie, they are sent to slaughter and when enough pain has been inflicted, they are deleted and the data from their uploads repurposed. God help us there's a color code.

If they can pay in full, their light turns a bright violet and right after the next goddess tribute they jump to Purdy Town, the basic lifestyle program.

"Few make it to Purdy Town," the sim informs me. I imagine Purdy Town must be a paradise compared to The No Where. The violet circle is the smallest, five virtuals to be exact.

Greens have friends in other Shemathra human communities who can locate and convert available memory, either in objects formed from their memory allotment or they can forfeit years of their youth. My guess is none possess assets in the bio world, or they wouldn't be here.

"You must pay attention," the sim cautions.

Virtuals sitting in circles where the glow is red, or pale yellow must find memory from somewhere within Shemathra's Realm, perhaps by persuading a friend or family member to help by donating memory to pay their taxes. Doubtful. Plus, only human virtuals may be contacted. Members of the Shemathra faithful, those manifesting as animals, are not to be bothered by any human virtual. No exceptions, even if family or a close friend. The penalty is slow erasure by the boiling steam of slaughter.

The gray circle, my sim whispers, is the end, either by choice or when the virtual has no way to pay memory tribute. Green is best though; many of these people have retained aspects of the image they chose to manifest as virtuals. One woman strokes her beautiful hair which falls gracefully on her shoulder. As her fingers comb through it, following a path from her brow to her shoulder, I can see her face has lost much of what defines one face from another. Like a manikin, the contours are smooth, without the interruption of character. And her eyes are closed. In her mind at least, it seems her hair defines her.

Most of the green women are easy to tell apart, some are attractive though none appear below ninety. They have pleasing faces and pale green tunics hang becomingly on their tense bodies. Normally, I would expect some flirtatious glances, but I am the tax sim and can erase them in an instant. They look down as I pass them.

Next is a circle of human virtuals sitting in a yellow glow. All heads are bent as if in prayer or overwhelming depression. A low moan begins as I reclassify several, the light around some of them turning red. One woman, whose face has the crevices and puckers of someone at cen-fifty, whispers encouragement to another, smaller woman, who looks to be under seventy. My guess is the older one has gifted her years of youth to her wife. The protective one embraces her beloved, murmuring she is her wife forever, and whatever happens, she croons, they will face it together. The younger woman cries and nods. They link arms as they move to one of the red circles, groups where little time is left.

More hulking shapes approach the fence. They're the larger bulls and now, a pair of angry bison appears in a cloud of menace, raking the ground, bellowing threats. Searchlights scan the human side of the fence, like some nightmare police state. Animal bastards! A large bull charges the bar of light. Strange, there is a blue stripe on his back and, instead of the bull's shadow, I can see the light on the barrier turning white.

There's an echo of humanity in the bull's voice as he bellows, "Stayoo away!" Seeing no humans near the fence, he snorts and with a loud grunt, trots back to his friends who pound the earth in a show of support.

What kind of ground is on this side? Yeck, it's the same black tar sponge that was on the island. There's nothing here but humans waiting to be erased. Even the violet circle must know their time in Shemathra will not end well. Couldn't Hosseini allow them trees, shacks, something? I can see their faces when they lift their heads to catch a glimpse of the sky. Some are smiling, dreaming of better days, I guess, where the sky belonged to everyone. As I suspected, the sky's color spills on to the barrier light and makes it blue. What happens if there's rain? Does the barrier turn gray? What happens at night? Does the moon change the barrier's color?

Interesting, I'm picking up a mood. I've always been able to 'read the room,' or in this case the local prairie. Many on the sunny side seem listless, ignoring the theatrics of the bison and dominant bulls. Several of the herd are grazing while avoiding the others' belligerence.

Every cow, bull or bison is supposedly committed to following the herd, always gazing at the swaying backend of a neighbor. Eventually, even the weakest mind will scream for something new. Plenty of them can't let go of the past and so, they struggle to keep their human voices. I wonder if Hosseini knows.

Uh-oh, more human virtuals are creeping closer to the barrier. Be careful; human virtuals are unwelcome and *not* part of the club. Should I remind them to be careful?

"*Taxes*," the sim whispers. The sim can wait while I talk to the people here—real human virtuals—not the idiot beasts on the other side . . .

More humans are sitting close to the bar fence. How many humans are there in 'The No Where"? Nothing exists here, other than the wretched virtuals who cling to each other. Another searchlight goes on and I see them clearly.

Oh, God! There must be thousands here! I watch and listen as my sim goes from group to group. The circles are part of the process. We humans love our rituals. Most circles are close, but not too close to the light barrier. How many are there here?

"Two thousand three hundred and five human virtuals occupy 'The No Where.' More will come as others are deleted," the sim tells me.

"Get back, hoooooman scum,' a massive bull grunts in puffs of outrage. The beast threatens to push through the barrier and trample the interlopers. Charming. Typical bullies, acting tough. Assholes darting to the light's edge to grunt warnings at the humans to "Keep away." Poor bastards. Bellows and snorts warn the pathetic hopefuls to move. For some reason, these bovine creatures make me sad; they were once people. But people, I admit, I would have taken great pains to avoid. This was once a paradise... I can't think about that now.

On the prairie side, clouds move away from the sun and shimmers of blue and green throw light on the human side. The light is dim here because there is no sun on this side, and I doubt there is a moon. The sim whispers, warning me to control my anger and against interfering. He knows who owes what taxes. Basically everyone, but for a few, those waiting in the green light, there's hope they can escape if taxes are paid before it's too late and the penalties overwhelm. If not, they are deleted, but not before they experience the pain of the slaughterhouse. The large bull lingers close to the barrier, and he is watching me. My sim must start tax collection.

I get it. These human virtuals sit where they can see the prairie sun and later as a bonus, perhaps they can gaze at stars in the night sky. And maybe, the moon. Why am I joking? This is pathetic. I see that some humans ready themselves for the sim by sitting together in concentric rings of three to five red rings. The glow ripples with fear. They want to get it over with, to know how much time they have or what might save them if they're allowed to contact the bio world. These red circles disappear into the dark in front and behind me.

In the distance, I hear human virtuals singing. HA! It's "The Moons of Jupiter!" Is it possible they yearn for a connection with the animals who have exchanged their humanity to live in a farce? Nothing is what it seems in The No Where. Those on the sunny side, munching on weeds and sweet clover are beyond any efforts to connect. They are part of a collective, only a single mind decides where they go and what they do. I think the magic doesn't work on everyone; some remember what they have lost.

Bellows and grunts stop the human singing as a massive steer charges the barrier. I see flashes of a white curved horn. With a snort, the longhorn scoops up a wretched human virtual who has wandered too close. My sim warns me not to interfere. Whatever piece of code used to make my sim did not include my views on unnecessary risk. The sim doesn't know; I would never interfere. What? The human virtual has disappeared!

The steer, stretching his neck, utters a loud "Moo-ooo-uh," then turns back to the herd. There was no 'pop.' Where did the virtual human go?

"Disregard!" the sim urges me. *"The human is either deleted or sent to slaughter. I must collect the tax!"*

Fine, let's get it over with. We start at the end farthest from where we entered. I let the sim have control. I am forced to watch as people beg for another chance. Just let them, they beg, reach out to their bio family and all will be paid.

I stay hidden as I watch the sim squeeze tribute from these sad people. It's tragic. *"The Goddess Shemathra wants no more communication with the bio world,"* the tax collector tells them. *"She forbids the contamination that results from contact with the bio-outside.*" My sim flashes the same grin and gives each a friendly nod as if he's distributing free samples instead of stamping hands with an indelible appointment, a command to report for deletion on a certain date, like spoiled fruit. Oh, God.

I hear a man urging his wife to let him make decisions on the tiny savings left in their memory account. They're in one of the yellow circles.

"There's not enough for both of us," he tells her with a sigh.

It's difficult to determine who is the husband and who is the wife. They are both gray, and each wears a gray tunic, compliments of Shemathra. There is little to define gender.

Finally, the husband puts his arm around her and pleads with his wife. "Jean, honey, do this for me. There's not enough for both of us to pay the tribute, but there is enough if only I go. You can stay in the yellow group a little while longer. I'll get you out as soon as I can collect on enough memory debts. There's no need for both of us to default on the tax. I have some contacts in 'The Palms.' I did some favors there. I'll call them in and plenty of people will help. We have some time before they execute this set of deletions. Believe me! Your deletion will be cancelled; you'll be fine. You know I love you. Trust me honey; we'll be okay." (Don't trust him, Jean!)

Jean shakes her head. "Don, we both know there's not a chance that you can pull this off. I'll rather delete myself than stay with you in this hell. So, no more of your bullshit."

"Honey, keep it down," Don whispers. He casts a nervous glance to see if any of the bulls heard the insult.

Jean shakes her head. "You always have a plan and look where we are now."

Don takes his seat in a green circle. Jean moves closer to my sim. She extends her hand.

"I give my husband Don my share of our unused memory." She is stamped for deletion. Don turns away and takes his seat in the "to-be-approved' circle. Two women guide Jean to a gray circle where all are marked for deletion.

How do I collect taxes from people who have nothing? There's a small circle that glows red and a man in his nineties is approaching me. His eyes are not on me, but on his feet, as if he worries that they will fail to hold him up.

"Greetings Mr. Turner!"

"Greetings, Gunter sim."

What will I do if "Mr. Turner" discovers I'm not a sim?

My sim moves to control. "*What tribute does your unit offer?*"

Mr. Turner sighs and trembles. "All monetary and excess memory sources are nearly depleted. We are all aware we must still honor Shemathra, Gunter sim."

"That is unfortunate. All must pay tribute."

"One in our group has volunteered to swim in the Data Stream. She requests an appointment rather than the gray circle.

"*If the memory she offers is enough,*" the sim says, "*I will stamp her with the appointed hour. She must pay tribute on behalf of the twelve in this circle. If so, Grace Hanson will enter the mist. Shemathra will be pleased.*"

"Gunter sim," Turner chokes back a sob, "we ask for time to hear her story."

"Story?"

"Before she receives her appointment, Grace wants to tell us her story, who she was in the bio world. She wants to remember those who loved her and the love she returned. And dreams, Gunter sim, Grace will recount for us her favorite dream. This way, a part of her stays here with us."

I'm pushing the sim down. 'Gunter sim' doesn't want to wait, but he will because I say he will.

"Not too long, Mr. Turner," I tell him. "I must leave soon."

I remember the island screams. I'll only risk my neck so far.

Turner hesitates, surprised I agreed to wait. He turns to the group behind him and says, "Circle!" There's a ripple as the pattern shifts and a new circle appears. Twelve virtuals, friends of Grace, those granted a stay of execution by Grace's sacrifice, I assume, sit, and wait. The ground beneath them is like the island, featureless, an expanse of gray.

In the distance, buffalo are tearing the ground as they snort warnings.

"Not too closesoo, hooman scum or you'll see the slaughterhouse before the new mooooon."

The circles shudder, contracting away from the shimmer. A young woman of fifty approaches Turner's circle. Her youth trembles in the sea of gray faces. My sim tells me Grace is exchanging the memory that she possesses and uses to maintain her youthful appearance as a gift to her circle, enough to purchase a reprieve for her friends.

"Hello, Grace," Turner greets her.

"Hi, Ethan," Grace smiles.

"Are you sure, honey?" Turner can barely look at her. Oh, please, I hope he doesn't cry! Damn, he's crying! I don't know how much more I can take. Four will have to come up with another plan.

Grace shakes her head. "Ethan, I'm ready to go. Please stop."

Ethan pulls himself together. He takes her hand and guides her to the middle of the circle. Youth shines in Grace's plain face. I want to look away, but I can't avoid hearing her story.

***

Grace

Swirls of data rise from Grace's fingertips. As she speaks, the data forms holo images. I see purchases of different foods circle above us. The memory has a luminous quality until it dissolves into the gray of a small town shops.

"During my bio-life, I checked groceries. Then, there were still places without smart houses or refrigerators. I worked for a local chain, an old-fashioned occupation I don't miss. I grew up in Sioux City, Iowa. And that's where I stayed."

The town disappears and a shower of red roses bathes Grace. The roses begin to organize, forming the words "Congratulations, you won!" The words are now gold in color, and they create a strobe effect, causing gasps from within the circle.

When I was notified that I had won the state lottery, I was startled. The prize was Bali Hai uploads for me and my husband. Nothing exceptional had ever happened to me before. When my husband left me and sold his after-death option, I was glad. We escaped a loveless marriage."

The gold letters dissolve and now I see an older version of Grace. She opens a door and what is that? Oh, it's a kitten. The kitten holo is replaced by a cat and now there's a procession of cats.

"After he left, a feral kitten, a calico, made its way to my door. I took in the calico and soon, more homeless kittens. I became a cat lady. Cats are complicated creatures and I, a simple woman, found them fascinating."

The cat parade fades into two cats, both snuggling next to a younger-looking Grace who sits on a deck by a lake. Is she a virtual? The lake looks familiar. Oh God, she's in Bali Hai!

As a virtual, I confess that I failed to experience all of Bali Hai, its hundreds of locations, the games, and fantasy options. In truth, the package I won covered only a fraction of them anyway. Besides, I used my memory budget to maintain two sim cats—oh, I wish I had found some way to keep them but, they are now . . . gone to taxes."

I wish I could feel more empathy. I had no time to give to any animal while I built VEI. I was also allergic to cats. Hopefully, she'll wrap it up soon.

Grace

"At the end of my bio-life, there were twelve cats sharing my house. Each one loved me in its own way. Some cats slept all day; others brought me birds and mice, a habit I tried to redirect but couldn't. You know, I felt closer to them than I ever did to Stewart, my husband. It's good that Stewart never came here considering what has happened to Bali Hai. It

turned out fine for him; he was always luckier than me, except for the state lottery.

It has been years since I spoke with my children. They have their own lives to lead, and I am a distant memory. If they are virtuals some-where, I don't know. I don't know why, but I still worry about my cats. They're long dead, yet I fear I didn't do enough to protect them when I knew I was dying. I hope they forgave me."

Oh my God, must I listen to this? My sim is chafing to leave.

Grace's Dream

Colors in her dream have faded. We see Grace as an old woman, who sits alone in her small-town house, Cats are everywhere and here comes one more. Is this a dream or a nightmare?

"In my dreams, I'm back in Iowa. The sliding door to the yard is open and I hear purring. Wayne, the old tuxedo cat walks in. My favor-ite cat, Lily—she was gray—is on my lap. The rest of my sweet babies vie for the best place on the couch."

The cats dissolve, gone, along with Grace's small-town life.

"I miss them so," Grace whispers as she walks toward me and extends her hand. Before I can think what to do, the sim takes over and I take her hand. My hand produces a dim light which turns red. Grace withdraws her hand which now has a visible white mark. Grace herself is no longer young, but the red glow is darkening around her. She will jump to the Data Stream when the time comes, but for now, she'll stay with her friends who are almost as gray as she.

"Your receipt, Ms. Hansom. It will take you to data processing at the appointed time. Your donation will cover the taxes for this circle

until the next tribute in six months. The Goddess Shemathra is pleased."

Turner leads the circle as they chant, "We will remember, Grace. Your dreams remain with us!"

Putting his arm on her shoulder, Turner guides Grace back to a dark red circle. I can't wait to leave. We hurry through the countless circles, condemning over nine hundred unfortunate virtual humans who have nothing left but a distant sun. Painful. I push the sound of the herds away as I finish. There are several hundred in the red circles. I'm angry.

"Be careful to hide it." My sim warns.

These sad ghosts were people once. They lived in the bio world and then uploaded to paradise. Hosseini has brought pain, agony and death to what was a land of sweet adventure.

"Careful!" The tax sim says I am a distraction. He needs to finish his collection.

Groups of gray-looking people huddle, just out of sight. The virtuals who wait here in the dim gray glow choose to delete rather than chance the slaughterhouse. Like Grace, several have gifted their neighbors with what little memory they have left. For me, it's gifting more time to spend in this purgatory.

The tax sim interrupts me, whispering, *"You risk discovery if you talk to anyone here.*

"Taxes! I must collect the tributes promptly," the sim insists. We stamp the hand of each virtual sitting in a gray circle. There are hundreds. It's hard to watch. I sink deep into the sim, as each virtual disappears when stamped. There is no graceful exit, just a spray of white which vanishes with a machine-like pop.

Every human virtual, not sitting in a gray circle, turns away. But the gray ones look on. I see androgynous, avatar-like creatures, their eyes following my sim. Each one shudders, watching the spray of what was left of someone's mind upload, gasping as the 'pop' announces the spray gone, sucked away. Yet, each wretched soul smiles as the sim deletes them. There is nothing left to fear, I suppose.

My sim wants to jump to the next human settlement; he has a schedule to keep. I override him and jump back to the villa.

End Record

SHEMATHRA'S REALM

Urcuchillay

The Imperial Palace of the Consort

June 25, 2290

Using his new serpent's tongue, the Exalted Consort samples the stream of fresh data of tax revenue. The tastiest bytes flow from what's left of the old Bali Hai which will soon float swiftly along the Data Stream. He loves the salty taste of city buildings and sidewalks breaking apart in his mouth. Memory taxes are almost as good. Recovered memory is revenue in his bank accounts, making him one of the richest men in the world—bio and virtual.

Donovan Hosseini is pleased. Is he forgetting something? What else? He blows bubble notes that burst and cling to the ears of his guards, whispering a decree: "At the conclusion of the coming August Grand Ascension, schedule twenty residents from The Royal Arms community and twenty residents from The Palms community for slaughter. The charge is failure to honor the Goddess. Say that all will be forgiven if, within the following seven days, they pay twice the amount of their last tribute and the resulting memory deposits promptly into the Data Stream. Please prepare a list including three prominent human virtuals from each community. Make them all fear you; be unpredictable."

The captain of his Royal Guard grunts an acknowledgement. The Guard is a collection of bison selected from the meanest, coldest group of killers Donovan Hosseini could find. Lots of perks involved when taking care of the big boss. Prime grazing and the pick of females buy a lot of loyalty.

A new information bubble hovers on his tongue, and he nods in approval. The list is ready. Those virtuals selected can either choose the hook and boiling water or pay the extra tribute. He's doing these humans a favor. He could take their assets now, including their mind-upload data if he chose. Kind of sad; power here makes virtual life too predictable, there is no one to conquer in Shemathra.

If he ever self-deletes, Donovan Hosseini will take everyone in Shemathra with him and it will be spectacular, better than Holden's roller coaster. He'll be a Pharaoh, or an Aztec king. But now, there's the Virtual New Deal. He intends to run it. Any existence, bio or virtual is ultimately disappointing. The trick is to keep moving on to something new.

"All of you, scram." The guards trundle out with a few snorts and Hosseini becomes himself, a version of the bio he was at the height of his power. He was cen-thirty-two when he realized the idea of death was inevitable and he began to plan. He would upload to a virtual world, but on his own terms. In Shemathra, he makes all the decisions, saying who lives, who gets erased and who suffers. And everyone's assets, plus all the memory assets here are his.

Time to make a few decisions, "Carousel," he commands. Surrounded by holos of himself, he tells them, "Rotate."

As the holos rotate, he considers which one suits his current mood. Recent versions of the Arabian Nights jinn are the first he sees. The snake one, yes! He loves its huge head, a green-eyed snake that encircles petrified virtuals, trapping them, slowing feeding on their data, then releasing the remnants. The scorpion with its gleaming stinger, intrigues him. Ready to pierce and paralyze its victims, it gorges on the data released by the unfortunate human's erasure. These beauties are meant as deletion tools for future programs. Should he preview them? It might be worth it, just to see reactions here. The girl should present him with more options. What mischief is she up to? The crows will find out. When he springs the trap, he might go easy on her for a while. No promises.

He's in the mood for a little bio nostalgia. "Bio," he says. A holo shows him as the old man that he was on the day of his physical death. He had considered a spectacular ending, demonstrating his fearlessness by jumping from the top of the "H" building. Sadly, it hadn't been finished in time. Instead, he took a poison that delivered him into a gentle, permanent sleep, carrying him swiftly to what remained of Bali Hai. Soon, Bali Hai was his to rule. He had hoped to humiliate Gunter Holden a little longer, but when he learned of Holden's self-deletion, Donovan shrugged. The loser would have been a distraction anyway. His focus was to consolidate the herds and create a new world, Shemathra's Realm.

"Rotate." The next holo is Hosseini in late middle age, at the height of his power. On the shorter side of average, Hosseini took pleasure in cutting people down. Regardless, he accepted the value of appearance. The right donations opened doors and influenced an impressive number of laws. VEI fell right in his lap.

"Rotate!" He's confronted with his twenty-year-old self. No one knew it, but he had already done his first murder, a mouthy landlord. Who would suspect, with that innocent face?

Well, not so innocent. He'd spent the summer in Brindisi with members of the Fourth Mafia to learn the art of intimidation. His mother could have saved the money. He had learned all this in school by the time he was ten. So, Julius Caesar built a fleet in Brindisi to go after Pompey. Big deal. Hannibal braved snow, starving elephants and crumbling mountain passes to take it to the Romans.

Momma H, as his so-called friends referred to his late mother, beat him until he was nine and he gave her the first of many black eyes. She smacked him to toughen him up, she explained as she dabbed a towel to the blood dripping from her mouth.

"That damned stuffed bear I caught you with, what were you thinking?" *Nothing, you bitch, I was four when I found it; it was mine.* Didn't matter. After breaking one of his eight-year-old arms, she bought him a giant stuffed elephant, big enough for him to pretend-ride.

When he bought her the townhouse, she festooned the walls with holos of Hannibal and his Alps adventures. There had been no "Thank you, Donnie, for this great apartment!"

The entire collection looked like a parade with thousands of foot soldiers, rows of horsemen, and huge elephants with their floppy ears. Some holos showed assorted parts of Hannibal's march and the army falling to their deaths. Suckers. There was one holo where the starving elephants were allowed to eat. And the guy who everyone remembers? Not those poor bastards. She was more interested in a long dead conqueror than her only son. She even named him Donovan Hannibal Hosseini. Who does that? Doesn't matter. The bitch is long dead.

His fifties made for some good memories, especially when his cousin Leo introduced him to Aunt Susie and her holo-porn studio.

"You're a horny bastard, Donno, would you like to make some real money?" They were both high. Leo had just beaten a man to death because the man wore some pricey shoes. The shoes didn't fit, but Leo figured he could sell them. Then "Donno" let out a whoop because he found a heavy gold chain in a hidden pocket of the man's jacket. Leo whispered, "Keep it down. Don't be stupid!"

"Donno" had bristled with rage, his face red and he wore a smile found in nightmares. Even then, Hosseini was notorious for holding a grudge. For a while, he had wrestled professionally. After one guy too many beat him, that guy ended up dead, hit by a glide-van. Or so Leo had been told. It was after the 'stupid' comment that Leo told him about Aunt Susie.

"The trick is, passing your audition, Leo said, trying to keep his tone casual. "You gotta do Aunt Susie first and make a holo doing it with her and to her. When it comes to Suse and doing a porn holo, how should I put this, Aunt Susie wouldn't be your first choice, or even your ninety-ninth."

"Don't worry, Leo," Donno said, "I'm a star." And he was. Aunt Susie was breathless with his performance. Considering her overbite and advanced age, he silently congratulated himself for performing under pressure. Gene therapy might have fixed some of it, but the old lady figured she was good just the way she was. Still, he was indeed a star who became well-known in the holo-porn industry.

Ten years later, Aunt Susie had an unfortunate accident. Surprising no one, she left her porn empire to Donovan Hosseini. That day, when she (along with her broken fingers) dictated her will, he let her live and take all the meds she wanted to keep her comfortable. Two weeks later, Aunt Susie drooled and breathed her last. Almost brought a tear to his eyes, but Donovan had no time for sentimentality.

Within five years his new company, "Hot Holos" dominated the industry. After fifty years of memorable holo hits, Hosseini decided it was time to consider other opportunities. Someone said there were lots of opportunities on Mars. Without question, Mars, in his opinion at the time, was a shithole worse than any piles of garbage floating in whatever ocean.

His stay on Mars was only a week. The planet was a depressing lump of rock covered in red dust and heaven help you if you breathed any of it. Mars hotels were bleak. Boarding the shuttle back to Earth, Donovan heard someone whisper about a warehouse full of eco-kits meant for Enceladus and how they needed to unload them fast. He had no interest in Saturn or in its moon. Like Mars, they were godforsaken places. The Enceladus people had rejected the kits and the guy on the shuttle was looking to make a quick sale. Here, like Aunt Susie, was an opportunity. Using the reptilian charm that had served him since his early days in porn, Hosseini bargained for the entire pile of eco-kits. Later, the kits were labeled "Mars-Eco, Inc." and on their way back to Mars.

Whatever was in the kits could have been sludge from the bottom of a Venice Canal, Hosseini didn't care. Then, a miracle happened and whatever was in the kits, The red planet liked it and to his great surprise things began to grow. If he had known he would have charged a fortune. Still, being known for something positive was a new experience. Layers of lawyers and managers came next as he began to expand operations. Seeming legit was important, but the weight of maintaining anyone's good opinion was useless. Better to inspire fear.

VR after-death programs were intriguing, cutting edge, but there were risks. Too many screw-ups and too easy to point fingers. When technology began to catch up with all the "big ideas" industry geniuses, one "genius" stood out: Gunter Holden. Donovan wanted to cripple Holden, the boy-genius. But not quite yet. First, let Holden build his empire, then he would take it. As it turned out, Holden made it too easy.

Hosseini was patient and he waited for the right opportunity. When he heard of the Shematre cult, a group in Alaska that worshiped a white wolf with a woman's face, he laughed. Some people will believe anything. But it got him thinking. It took years to develop a simple story with a set of beliefs that took away doubt and left decisions to him. Most people hate making decisions. Not him though; he loves it. And now he makes all the decisions, saying who lives, who gets erased and who suffers. The Grand Stampede was Hannibal's march. He was Hannibal and he would bring much more than elephants and horses. Too easy.

The Grand Ascent and the Grand Stampede are almost here. Time to plan the main event. Hosseini, who manifests as the young wrestler he was two hundred years ago, nods and becomes the serpent. His tongue waves and shudders with anticipation. What to do with the girl? What if someone misses her, like the boyfriend maybe? The boyfriend does some kind of cyber security. Could be dangerous. Why not just erase her? No, for a while at least, she'll be useful. It makes him sad he is no longer interested in romance. His holo porn days played a part. Too much for too long a time. Anyway, he can have any tail he wants. The idiom makes him chuckle.

SEINI RESEARCH 19

The Coral Triangle

July 3, 2290

Setia and the timed crystal

In the Coral Triangle, islands appear and disappear, and so do people. Mr. Sukawati often reminds himself that wherever a SEINI research center sits, people disappear. All are in remote locations, difficult to access, almost impossible to inspect. People living where the new SEINI facilities now stand are gone. *Did they move? Where?*

And the virtual residents uploaded to SEINI New Deal programs—where are they? They began to disappear as well. Admittedly, virtual life isn't for everyone. These were simple lifestyle programs, perhaps too boring. Still, Sukawati knows that five years after the

U.S. president signed the Virtual New Deal, millions of people, both virtual and bio, are inexplicably gone.

Any leaks of 'what we do here' at the SEINI Research and Development, will be dealt with harshly was a message stressed during orientation. He thought it was only a warning. Be careful what you reveal to outsiders. Then Balik disappeared and no one asked questions.

"Balik was warned," people murmured. Such a funny kid, so very sad, but, Balik had continued making jokes about program development.

An independent designer of VR eco systems who left his clients to become a member of the new SEINI team on an island in the Coral Triangle. His pride and elation faded when he saw the blank look on Setia's face. She disapproved.

"I fear Hosseini," she said. "Don't you know his reputation?"

But the decision had been made. Why was she questioning his judgment?

"Of course, I do," he answered her, more shrilly than he intended. "It's only for a few years and the salary is unbelievable! Randall Patel once worked there. It can't be all terrible."

"Randall Patel was gone before VEI collapsed," she sighed.

He shook his head. "The children are old enough for us to be away. They're in Jakarta and my brothers will care for them until we return. And their education, Setia, just think, the finest private schools and then," he insisted, holding back his tears, "a top university with advanced degrees if they choose."

"They're still young, our son isn't ten until the spring of next year. Andi, what are we doing to them?" She didn't understand. He was too proud to explain. They had enjoyed a comfortable life because of what she earned as a light sculptor, not his meager pay. SEINI representatives promised him creative freedom as an assistant director of design and planning.

"We can see them on holo every day if you want. The next nine years are for Ambar and Arief, their schooling and future," he argued. "You're an artist, Setia; you can be one there. Study the light for inspiration. The dawn is beautiful."

But there is no freedom here, only a nightmare. Everyone here is an assistant director, and they are all expendable.

"You know to be careful, though, don't you?" he warned. She nodded, a look of grim resignation on her face. She is a hostage, imprisoned by his vanity.

Countless, trusting people have disappeared. Most were humble folk, nearing the end of their lives. In exchange for trading their last years, leaving this earth to the young, they had opted for Social Security's "Virtual New Deal," continuing to exist in a simple, worry-free world.

What happened to the uploads? *Where did they go*? For months, he had worked, developing New Deal VR programs. Small heavens, Setia called them when he showed her the concepts. Before they came to this angry island of "lost souls" as Setia often refers to it in whispers, Sukawati made a promise to himself.

Someday, he would create a virtual island paradise. There would be no fear. Sims of stately elephants and tigers, dragons and orangutans would be there, rich in detail, evoking a simpler time. Virtuals, could live as they like, in a farmhouse, a cottage, a way station on the way to judgement, enlightenment, to Heaven that surely waits. This new world will embrace all as they find their way to God's judgement. After betraying so many, he wonders, who is he to create such a world? There is only one Creator.

The uploaded human virtuals meant to inhabit the after-death programs he designed, all the lovely little towns, the sea cottages, and lively city blocks are gone. A few virtual humans remain, enough to satisfy any surprise government oversight. Those who escaped, the remaining uploaded humans, horrified, know any hint that all is not well, meant certain erasure. Every night he prays for those he betrayed and begs forgiveness.

Co-workers urge him to stop asking questions. What flows through the veins of this facility is the memory harvested from the dead. All of it from fat government contracts, it fills the SEINI purse. Hosseini is a leech, gorging himself on the memories of his victims.

Andi Sukawati is still haunted by Balik's last joke. "I have an idea for a new game we can play. It's called 'Can you find the virtuals in this program'?" No one laughed. Soon, young Balik was gone. Not even his name is alive here.

Beautiful Setia misses the embrace of her children and is bereft of purpose. She is an artist whose light sculptures grace corporate suites throughout Indonesia and beyond. On this wretched island, daylight glares until a dark curtain drops, she tells him. There is no art here, only volcanic rock, a restless sea, and SEINI. She wept when she learned where the temple had gone. "Crushed to make a path? Andi, why?"

He shook his head. There are peepers everywhere, he warns her. Every night, she whispers her pain, her bewilderment, and suspicions. He dares not tell her their son and daughter are being watched and what might happen if he reveals too much.

"You could have stayed" he hissed, his voice thick with remorse. He tried to be stern, cold, but he loves her too much. Every morning, as he wakes to the dawn and the sound of thunderous waves, he clings to her.

***

Setia and the timed crystal

Hearing her husband's soft snore, she rises, gets dressed, and goes to the sitting room where she keeps her sculpting tools. No art is here; no light composition can emerge from this awful place. A student of history, she had purchased a tool crafted in the 21st century and on impulse, decided to bring it with her. Now, this little device folds all her hopes of escaping this island hell into one small case where the "timed crystal" waits. She had claimed it as a sculpting tool, and no one questioned it. Several lifetimes ago, it was used in communication, exploration, and early quantum computing.

She tucks it into a deep pocket of her artist smock. Before leaving Jakarta, it had taken weeks to perfect the coding. Setia slips out the patio door. An occasional spray of sea water soaks the wooden planks. Ignoring the cold, she makes her way along the wet sand to rocks piled high above the eyes of temple guardians and grasping the wet black stones she climbs until she can wedge the crystal securely into a crevice, hidden from the hostile eye of a guard.

Tonight, the moon is a black circle, so the darkness and the sea shield her as she rebels against SEINI. The crystal's eye is exposed, and it peers out into the dark horizon. Black volcanic rocks hold it tight. Her light-message is secure, but she is not. Silky waves can still take her, and fold her into deep waters. As the cold sea tries to seize her, she holds firms to the rocks that hold the timed crystal. Then, Setia activates its message, an urgent call for help.

Her feet slipping, she struggles to the dubious safety of a narrow strip of sand and the dark cottage. What if Andi is awake? She won't tell him what she did. He would insist they remove it and pray that no one saw her or the crystal. Tonight, it sends its urgent message. A disruptive frequency makes communication almost impossible for several miles offshore. But the timed crystal is from the past. They won't expect it.

As her feet reach the smoother sand, she sighs with relief. In the distance, she sees the research center and curses it.

THE ELYSIUM

I'm naming it Gunter

July 5, 2290

Mira has decided-there will be no distractions today. First, she rejects her desk's offer of a new enhanced tropical setting. Using a program altered by Henry for safety, she sends a mind bubble containing more suggestions on jinn concepts. Hosseini intends to copy himself and the copy will be a new jinn monster in an after-death Arabian Nights. The goal is to scare them, perhaps, some will voluntarily erase after "donating" their bio wealth and relinquishing any unused memory. This is illegal. Any program that promotes the intimidation of virtuals, causing them to self-delete will never be approved. Hosseini wants approvals first and then the finishing touches.

She plans to interfere, delaying completion. If she doesn't, she is the one who will go to prison. She is a specialist, a designer of AIs and preferences for after-death programs. The jinn are her creations. Blind justice will point to her, not Hosseini, who is untouchable. A yellow light scans and approves her DNA. Then it illuminates the holo-platform as an after-death sample begins with a soft wind ruffling the fabric of an ornate tent.

She is in the desert. Exotic music and perfumes flood her senses until she gasps. Outside the VR world, she hears a scratching noise. It can't be the indoor air cleaners; it's the wrong time of day. "Pause." An arrow hangs in front, pointing to the holo as images dim and the sensory data stops.

There it is again. Where's it coming from? A hidden peeper, a busy eye connected to the llama-god? Her heart skips a beat, and she can't breathe. *Focus!* More scratches, but where is it coming from? Is it a peeper? Carefully, she moves a folded chair, looking for the cold gaze of her undoing. Instead, a pair of beady eyes peer out between stacks of Ravi's antique maps. Collapsing into the chair, she rests her head on her desk. It's only a mouse. Mira wants to kill it for scaring her. Should she invite the cat in?

Leaving the maps, the mouse sits on the carpet. How small it is! The creature is half the size of her closed fist. Because it's white, she knows it must be someone's lost pet. Rising on its haunches, the mouse cocks its head as it estimates the threat she poses. Tossing her leftover muffin crumbs to her tormentor, Mira ends the stand-off. But the mouse isn't ready to leave. It climbs the side of her desk, and stretching its neck, the mouse peers over the top of her work area. Twitching its nose, it studies her.

Yes, it was someone's pet, but it's mine now, she decides. She tosses it another crumb. Catching her parting gift, the mouse pauses when

Henry appears behind her. The creature hurries down to the floor, disappearing behind one of Ravi's favorite wood carvings.

Henry laughs and drapes his arm on her shoulder. "What are you doing?" he asks. He kisses her neck as he watches the mouse disappear. "Mira, the mouse lady, who would have guessed?" he teases.

"No, I made it go away." She insists.

"No, *I* made it leave.' Henry counters. "If *I* hadn't appeared, Mousy would have stayed."

"Then go back to your office. I think you should." She knows he won't. She's in danger and he likes to check on her. "I like the rodent's company," she says, turning her face away, as if to dismiss him. She resents his entering her workspace without permission. He insists it is for her own security and protection. And despite her many entreaties, he refuses to tell her about his job. Where does he work? What does he do there?

She has shared with him everything about the copy and what she plans to do with it. For now, Henry uses a spare room in the apartment, and she is forbidden to enter it. He should trust her. It drives her mad.

"I know it's difficult for you to understand," he admits. "I'm not Bluebeard with the heads of ex-wives hidden under my desk nor am I plotting the end of the world. Please, Mira, accept this. If you weren't in so much danger, I would work somewhere else. I am here because I love you. If Hosseini discovers what you're doing, he *will* try to hurt you."

"At least, Mousy is honest," she says. "All it takes is a blueberry crumb and we understand each other."

"Feed it, but don't tell me that you're trying to make a point. It's a mouse, Mira, and you like feeding it, however, you might check to see where the cat is before you do." Henry imitated a mouse nibbling. "At long last, you have a pet," he sighs. "You should name it."

"I'm naming it Gunter," she smiles.

"Mira, my love, that's sick." Henry shakes his head in mock disapproval. She isn't as hard hearted as she pretends. Regardless, the copy is an incredible stroke of luck. *What have I done?*

SEINI Chicago offices

Re: The Grand Ascension

Bio Throne Room

July 17, 2290

The twelve-member panel is here and the boardroom glows with an outer circle of holographic images. SEINI's trademark music intro begins in a darkened corner of the holo boardroom, as Mira waits quietly, as Hosseini bursts from a sixteen-foot monitor. His AR image undulates then abruptly disappears.

Screams escape from the captive audience as a spray of crimson light covers the walls and the domed ceiling. The light fades, and darkness floods the room. She rolls her eyes. She's seen this all before. Now, a golden light bathes the ornate chair where Hosseini sits. Ignoring the Board members, the god reviews bubble reports for the upcoming event. He looks as he did in the prime of his bio life—short, with the build of a fighter, chewing an eternal cigar.

"I expect some answers. The investors are getting nervous, not to mention Congress sticking its nose where it doesn't belong. How do we fix this? When am I gonna get the memory to expand operations? These New Deal contracts require proof of resources." Hosseini's holo multiplies and four holos become a circle of Hosseinis. No one knows in what direction he stares. As he waits for answers, the holos merge into a four-headed holo, rippling with bands of color, signaling agitation. The circle of Board members is silent as Hosseini's glare spits flashes of bright yellow light.

"The fee increase has been challenged." A Board attorney tells him. "The Virtual Rights Investment Group won't drop it. Too many voters have loved ones who will be affected or stand to lose if we don't explain. They say accounts are drained too quickly and there's nothing left for their own transitions."

To counter, Hosseini points to Mira's analysis, which calculates the memory shortage is equal to the amount gained from new members. His Greatness shifts his holo to a younger version, a thirty-year-old Hosseini, with a head of bright orange hair and a body rippling with oversized muscles. "A second Grand Ascent," he screams, saluting in her direction. "We make it a biannual event. What do you think? Make sure Marketing is on it. I want VR promos. We'll need those new residents to be paid up sooner than later."

The Board members whisper to each other. He has ignored their concerns. No one dares disagree. Then, Hosseini simply disappears, the connection terminates.

Shemathra's Realm, The Villa

"He mustn't see me."

July 20, 2290

Four is waiting. She's unpredictable and I'm worry about her reaction. I jumped back without permission, but why do I need her permission to jump?

NO! She's putting her arms around me and pressing my face to her chest. If her relationship to me is as she says, this is awkward. I feel the sim within me stop. It sleeps while Four absorbs my memory of the camp.

"Gunter, I see that you don't understand what is at stake here."

"Four, I sympathize with the dire circumstances here. Of course, I want to help these poor human virtuals, however, I think I might be more useful if I were in a different program. I have powerful friends and many of them must be residents in after other death-programs. If I can reach out to them, it could make a difference."

"All right, Gunter," Four takes my right hand. *"I wish there was some other way. It's clear that you must bear witness to the fate of many here. The memory that I'm about to show you is confidential, bound by my employment agreement with SEINI. This means that it's useless to me and to you."*

Before I can free myself from her grip, I find myself in a warehouse. Screams echo against tin walls. I'm in a windowless room, steam rising from its center. I can't see the source. Above me, a human-virtual dangles on a hook. It's hard to tell if this person is a man or woman. A man, I think, covered with blood which drips from a slit in his throat.

Rather than Urcuchillay, the virtual Hosseini manifests as human. He's naked and his enhanced muscles make him look more like a bull than a llama. Holding a large knife in his bloody hand, Hosseini is a ghastly presence.

"Pay attention, alla you," he shouts. "This is what happens to ANY virtual who presumes to question my decisions. Listen up, any deadbeats, who think you can get away with not honoring the Goddess by dodging the tribute tax. Think again!" The crane swings the dangling man to the center of the steam. Oh God, now I see it. It's a huge pot of what looks like boiling water. Then the crane releases its victim into the scalding water.

I can't watch this! Please, I can't listen! *Please Four; I can't!*

The screams, squeals of rabid pain, cut through me. When the screams finally stop, I look back. Strings of memory are a white mist, hovering above the boiling water. The mist, I realize, is the sum of who we are. I watch it rise, disappearing into a vent that leads my sim whispers, to the Data Stream. Behind Hosseini, a line of human virtuals waits for deletion. One by one, as they move forward, a hammer pounds a bolt into the forehead of each one and bodies vanish as memory strings of the slaughtered float into the steam. He mustn't see me. Hosseini can't know I'm here, I'll . . .

***

I'm in the Villa again. Four waits for my reaction.

"Do you understand? Hosseini ordered every human virtual in Shemathra to view this scene. It's not just about VEI or my regaining control; there are humans who came here because of you, Gunter."

"That's unfair! I had no way of knowing what would happen."

"But Gunter, you should have known. Even before your bio death, the original you knew VEI wasn't secure; mergers could happen. Why didn't that Gunter protect your people, especially after virtual Paris was erased? He could have reached out to your powerful friends then, while there was still time. He failed to protect your dream and now others pay for your mistakes."

"What do you mean, virtual Paris was erased? I wasn't there! What else is supposedly my fault? I wasn't there so don't blame me!? Why can't you be the hero, Four? You could have shared this information with law enforcement. Is your job more important than stopping this travesty?"

Four shakes her head. *"I already have Gunter. I showed them what I showed you. No one can use it. My contract protects Hosseini. It's already been leaked to the media, but Hosseini has influence there and it's been dismissed as a fake. Hosseini can't be stopped unless you help.*

I'll explain about virtual Paris later. As a tax sim, you can go places here that are forbidden to me. Before he self-deleted, the original Gunter was a legal resident of Shemathra's Realm. After the mass erasure of the Everlasting Praise faction, Hosseini claimed it was all an unfortunate accident, caused by the mismanagement of VEI. He made a big show of demanding tax laws change so people could make copies of themselves in case their transitions failed, or they were accidentally erased.

"VEI mismanagement? Oh God, if I survive this nightmare, I will sue the bastard and he'll be lucky to mismanage discount VR programs—"

Four interrupts, *"And the laws changed. Now, virtuals have the "right" to copy their file as insurance against 'accidental' deletion. VEI wasn't blameless. The original Gunter permitted the 'accidental' deletion of two million virtuals when he allowed infected software to be stolen by a rival company."*

"You're wrong. I'd never stoop so low. Don't change the subject, Four. Why don't they delete themselves here after requesting that their copies be sent to another program? Some of them must have the resources."

"There are no copies here. It's considered disloyal. You, Grandfather, are the only copy of a deleted Shemathra resident. You, alone, have the right to share what you witness here. I have copied your memories of the Camp and sent them to a secure location. They are solid evidence of wrongdoing. But Gunter, there are three more human colonies. As the tax-collector, you will collect information on these colonies as well. Hosseini has defiled your perfect world. You have a chance to restore it. If you don't go back soon, your sim presence will be missed.

I'll make you an offer, Grandfather. If you are positive that you can't do this, I'll remove you, however, you won't be transferred to another program. I'll return you to the file where the original Gunter had you stored. Unless someone looks again and finds you, that is where you will stay. God help you if that someone is Hosseini. I haven't told you everything."

This is blackmail. "I must have some control. I'll go to the next site and continue the charade, but when I think I've seen enough, it's not your call. I decide when it's time to return here. If not, put my file back in storage."

"I fear you might trigger unwanted attention by assuming control," she tells me, *"I must decide when you return. I urge you to be careful. Hosseini has spies who will report any irregular patterns in your behavior."*

"Thank you. Now that I'm aware of the consequences, I intend to be very careful."

"The next human colony you'll visit is Purdy Town. Until recently, these residents were forced to maintain a charade. They were the face of small-town contentment offered to the outside world. Since Shemathra has gone dark, the charade is no longer needed."

"You promised to tell me more about what happened before. You insist that Eric Holden was not my father. If you're telling me the truth, who was my father?'

"His name was Olaf Donald Vanderbok. You once contacted him regarding his research, but he died before you could arrange a meeting. When you were a child, you often went to a bakery with your mother, and he would be there waiting for you. You knew him as Mr. Donald. Do you remember?"

"Yes. I—I can't talk about this now. Tell me what you want me to do."

"Gunter sim, go to Purdy Town; it is time to collect taxes."

"I will go to Purdy Town and collect taxes."

"Gunter, be careful. Remember that there are spies," she cautions me.

I wish I could believe she cares at all. Maybe I'm dreaming. I'm still a bio and I'll wake up. "No Four, no Shemathra, wait. I'm lost now. Where's the Villa?"

SHEMATHRA'S REALM

Purdy Town

Record 2

PURDY TOWN, POP. 1,394

July 21, 2290

There's a sign.

"Welcome to Purdy Town, est. 2190, pop. 1,394."

My sim tells me the name comes from a famous quote. A long-ago comedian said, "I grew up in a 'right purdy town.'" Hilarious. Somehow it stuck in the public mind, and became a term disparaged by sophisticated assholes to put down those who choose a simpler life. Now the town folk here are stuck with it. The sign is old fashioned, the curved top of the white board held by two posts. Beyond, a short distance away, is a bit of Americana.

It's quiet here. I see white fences and blocks where neat uniform houses sit, like the long ago towns of middle America. Not many people are out enjoying the virtual sun. As I approach a street, no one is looking at me. They must know I'm the tax sim. I see no glide vehicles. Purdy Town is a 'land of yesteryear,' the promos say.

My guess is life here was boring and predictable, until Shemathra began to close them off from the world. The sim tells me Purdy Town was touted as a model Shemathra habitat for humans, the face Hosseini showed to the outer world until Shemathra went dark. I imagine, the people here would welcome boring. Life has become an old-fashioned, unending horror movie with a rotating cast of victims.

I hear nothing—no voices, nor the footsteps of people on their way somewhere, not the wisp of a breeze. There's an odor of hot tar in the air. For some reason it smells like fear. Do they delete people here or send them to the slaughterhouse? Folks in Purdy Town must spend their days wondering who will be deleted next. On one side, an empty desert stretches into distant mountains, barren except for some brush and ragged trees. More than likely, the townsfolk have accessed the memory data from parks and recreation sites like lakes and ponds to keep current on taxes and tributes.

Now that I'm closer, I can see the trees here are listless; the branches don't move. What is it about the green? Too uniform. Color is an extra expense, so keeping all the trees the same green must save memory. Why did they even bother? Why not more gray sand instead of desert? I could be wrong. The desert might have been a selling point for some. Sad. Oh wait, the stampedes! That's why, just in case some bull or cow is curious to see what the real desert was like.

To my right is more Purdy Town. The town has a main street. Several shops are on one side and in the middle, a wide dirt road separates the rows of shops and houses, making room for stampedes. On the other side of town, the sim informs me, are more shops. Most of those shops are smaller. Beyond the outer shops are more blocks of houses and behind the houses are the grazing lands of course, just in case some of Shemathra's bovine worshipers want to stop for lunch. My guess is human virtuals avoid setting foot on the desert and especially stay clear of the grazing land. Trespassing is a major violation here.

Checking my sim's data, I see there are no stampedes scheduled. I should be able to skip across the Shemathra highway and catch anyone who might try to avoid me. I'll also check for any new intel on the mustang herds. They are rumored to lead the Goddess Stampede this year.

Nope, doing a quick scan of the latest stampede reports, Gunter sim says not to worry. Thank God for my sim memory; it should keep me safe. The stallions come through Purdy Town monthly, but probably not today. Still, any virtual who crosses the road is careful to listen for the sound of hooves, a fact of existence here. In Purdy Town, there is no stopping for pedestrians, and no pity.

I count ten blocks of town on the left side of the dirt-thruway and eight on the right. The business district is split—some on one side of the main road and some on the other. Okay, I see a general store, a barbershop, a saloon, a café, dress shop, a hotel with a meeting hall, and one for hats for God's sake. Most are one story, but the hotel has three.

Boring design, all uniform, vintage small-town America. I can't believe they're still creating these small-town destinations. They were boring two hundred years ago. Wait, no churches? All small towns have at least one church. On second thought, not surprising. No deity is allowed to compete with the Goddess, Shemathra. I wouldn't be surprised if the human virtuals took the church out without being pressured, especially since it could be sacrificed as a tax offering. And of course, all the structures are white.

And the residential zones? The rows of houses are uninspiring. White cottages and a few two-story white houses with columns and front porches, and each has a swing. Something to do when you need to self-soothe. I see different types of trees including oaks, birch, and apple. How sad. The same dull brown defines the trunks and branches. All the leaves are the same dull shade of green. Sadly, no tru-color here.

Another sign points the way to a fishing hole. My sim cautions me to be careful. Signs here remind me of *Alice in Wonderland*. There's a consequence attached to each. Well, there's a surprise. A pair of Amish buggies are rattling on the dirt road in the middle of town. No horses pull these buggies. Why? The sim tells me no animal, sim or otherwise serves humans in Shemathra's Realm. They roll along, as if powered by ghosts. Any virtual humans here, must have long ago lost their minds.

The buggies are stopping. This should be interesting. *"Taxes,"* my sim whispers, *"remember you're here for taxes."*

One of the drivers, an older man with a fringe of gray beard leans forward to check on me.

"Monitor sims," my sim tells me, *"these are monitor sims."*

"You, sim," A younger man in a tall black hat waves at me from the other buggy. He climbs down and plants his black boots in front of me, preventing me from reaching the sidewalk. There is menace here. Time to be careful.

"I'm Edgar sim. State your name and purpose," he demands.

I flash him my best sim smile. *"I am Gunter sim. I am here to collect taxes. It would be wise if you do not interfere."* I smile again. Then, my mind wanders back to the Villa and what Mira told me, what she said about Eric not being my father. I know she's wrong, but what about Mr. Donald? How did she know about the bakery? What if—I can't think about this now. I must focus on surviving.

The monitor repeats his challenge. *"Your purpose, Gunter sim?"*

"I am Gunter sim. The Goddess Stampede will be coming through this community in late-July. I am here to collect taxes and check the readiness of this environment."

If this were Bali Hai, the memory used to create these sims would be banked and available for Patel's black sim beetles' file.

The monitor sim grunts and without any acknowledgement, goes back to his buggy. Both buggies continue their journey, the rattle of wheels fading as they pass through the town. The town ends, but the road continues with desert on one side and pasture on the other. How far does it go?

I must be careful. The older buggy guy is a monitor and very suspicious. He must be spying for the herds. Did I give myself away? Should I jump back to the Villa?

Curtains are rustling in the windows of small shops along the walkways. Folks are getting ready for when I call them to account. The wooden sidewalks are gone, most likely sacrificed by the community to pay taxes. The narrow walk is a smooth surface of dull black, requiring little to create it.

Ordinarily, my sim tells me, the lace curtains, swinging saloon doors and small touches like a striped barber pole would be considered a waste of memory revenue. However, these features have proved useful for marketing in the past, before Shemathra went dark. For now, they remain.

Before I collect, I want to check out the fishing hole. There's a path leading to it and I'm curious why this feature hasn't disappeared. I see a cluster of trees, and I feel an urge to relax. So peaceful here. Is that a tire swing hanging from that oak? I want to swing on it for a while, but my sim reminds me that he wouldn't use it. Oh dear, there's Brother Edgar standing on the other side of the trees and he's staring at me and looking suspicious. What do I do?

I call to him, *"Do you have data to share, Edgar sim?"*

Edgar shakes his head and moves back to the horseless buggy.

The Shemathra sun here reminds me of Dad's veranda and the oppressive Connecticut sun as it peered through the leaves. It might be pleasant to sit here on a cushion of leaves and moss and forget where I am for a while. My sim warns against it. Ah, there's the pond. Lots of rippling on the water's surface. I see, it's teeming with sim wildlife. Frogs and crawdads, ladybugs, and dragonflies.

Below the water, among the rustle of fish, is the flat eye of a catfish; its long gray whiskers waving. Is it studying me? Thousands of small eyes are staring—catfish, toads, crawling insects, and snakes. The paranoia is overwhelming. I sink deeper into my sim. In response, Gunter sim, stares back at the swimming and crawling eyes, questioning each silently. Do they have any new data to share? The eyes blink and withdraw. Other fish are joining in, their tails flopping in a frenzy. The virtuals here have deserted the fishing hole because of all the spies.

I stare ahead as if I don't see them. (I want to go home.) My sim isn't concerned. I must walk back to town. It's time to collect from Purdy Town, where virtual humans wait to pay tribute to their oppressor. As I approach the first section of shops, I listen for the sound of approaching hooves. My sim whispers that I am not in danger; I am a sim. Gunter sim is a well-known tax collector. I stand little chance of being trampled. (But what if the animals come through while I'm crossing?) Even if I avoid them, could one of them recognize me as a virtual? The sim tells me no.

We move quickly to the sidewalk. Collect taxes, I mumble to my sim and then let's get the hell out of Purdy Town. As I reach the sidewalk, a few virtuals walk listlessly past me. I'm smiling my best smile, but I'm still the tax sim, not one of them. No one will look at me.

There is a uniformity to the virtuals of Purdy Town. I'm surprised by the sameness in age. No children of course, no teens or twenty-thirties, not even a young-looking sim. I assumed that some would manifest as young people on occasion, but all here are older adults, not as old as those in The No Where, but most appear to be over eighty. Is there a dress code here, like the Amish bastards in the buggy? They all wear tunics over shapeless pants, none with belts to give their human bodies definition. The tunics are all the same yellowish brown, like the color of old-style paper envelopes. I remember seeing versions of postal envelopes in a Stanford art exhibit. It was from the early twenty-first century and the best part of the exhibit is that one had been used. You could still see part of the addressee label. I've rarely seen that color anywhere else. Funny, the things that you don't forget.

As the Purdy folk walk, heads down their gaze is on the black walk-way. All seem burdened by the troubles of the very old. The doors of the Purdy Saloon swing open and a balding man with a handlebar mustache comes toward me. Finally, someone tries to support the illusion. The man clamps his hands to his sides, I assume, to keep them from shaking.

"I am Mayor Andrew Knudsen," he tells me in a soft voice. "Gunter sim, we of Purdy Town are honored to host the Goddess Stampede. We gladly pay memory tribute to the Goddess."

"Thank you, Andrew Knudsen. I will inform Urcuchillay during the next High Memory Accounting," says my sim.

The man lets out a short sigh, and with an abrupt pivot, hurries through the salon doors. I follow him. The shelves are looking bare. A small white sign above the bar reads "Fine Spirits" in black, curving, old-fashioned letters. Below the sign are shelves with shot glasses and beer mugs, spread out so the overall effect doesn't draw attention to how few remain.

The Mayor wears an apron tied around his waist and a white-cloth rests on the counter, ready for the cleanup that is never needed. Ordinarily, I would explore this period location to evaluate its authenticity, but I decide to put Mr. Knudsen out of his misery by recording his taxes, paid in the memory gleaned from one of the five remaining barstools and three whiskey glasses.

Sadly, there is no whiskey, nor is there beer, not even the illusion of taps or bottles on the shelf. Why did Mr. Knudsen choose the saloon? Was it a dream or a spur of the moment choice? The whole thing depresses me.

As I exit the swinging doors of the Purdy Saloon, I pass a low building with three curtained windows, where the sim informs me, *"People are preparing their business taxes."*

The thought of what is behind those lace curtains depresses me. What would make these people stay in such a twisted lie? Better to delete yourself. They fear the culling, of course. I step back behind the shops to see who is in there. Is that laughter I'm hearing?

"The tax sim reminds me of my son-in-law, the sneaky little bastard," a woman says with a short chuckle. *Is she talking about me?* If someone sees me, what do I say? I'll pretend that I'm distracted by the sim crows overhead. (No, sims are never distracted.) I'll say I'm looking for undeclared memory, objects of special value, like a pet or a luxury item. These people would be frightened to know that I can hear them.

"He reminds me of my third husband," a man laughs. "Never could trust him. I followed him here and now he's the largest bull in Urcuchillay's color guard."

There's extended laughter. I'm glad humor isn't taxed; though in some cases, it is surely punished.

"I remember Dudley; he was certainly the largest bullshitter when I knew him," a slender woman giggled. A gap in the curtain opens and I can just see her. Her bald head declares her as a stubborn individualist.

"Oh, honey, you don't know the half of it! Inside that big bad bull there's a braying jackass begging to get out!" More laughter until someone warns to tone it down.

It's my sim they're laughing at. If it were me, it would be different. I might be offended. My sim has no need to be charming. I'm tempted to break into their little meeting, but why spoil it? They're enjoying themselves. There's so little joy here. Besides, I can take a little ego blow. So, they do have something to live for; it's their hatred for Shemathra and by association, my sim.

There are twenty-seven businesses here—eleven on the desert side and sixteen on the prairie, including the hotel. They all know the penalty for cheating. A record of a certain tax violation informs me the town was forced to watch the painful deletion of one of their own. I ask my sim what happened.

"Her name was Emily Cross," my sim whispers.

"Why such a harsh penalty?"

Emily Cross owned Aunt Flo's Delicious Fudge,

I'm approaching the hat shop as the sim tells me about poor Emily,

"The fudge shop was popular with many here. It was in the early days of Purdy Town when some residents were still able to manifest as under fifty. Now, youth is a thing of the past."

"Fine, but dear sim, that's not what I asked. Why did she end up in the slaughterhouse?"

"Emily loved to entertain. When Ms. Cross neared the end of her bio life, she had a choice: either she could either live comfortably for the rest of her bio life or purchase an after-death plan. Emily was one hundred fifty-eight when she transitioned to virtual life. At best she had only thirty more years of bio life, so it was a logical choice. She chose a plan and uploaded to Bali Hai. Rumors of a merger had lowered the price for entry-level plans, and Emily became one of the first residents of Purdy Town.

"So, she took advantage of my misfortune." Suddenly, I feel less sorry for her.

"Soon, the elite of Purdy town flocked to her circle of influence. Many considered her charming and entertaining because of her sense of humor. They called her the 'sparkling redhead.' Several here had known her in the bio world, where Emily had built a successful hospitality company. Later, certain events occurred in Purdy Town; there was gossip. When she was a bio, Emily had cheated on her taxes."

"Did she?"

"I cannot access that information. Not relevant.

Anyway, the first shop owner is waiting. "Finish your Emily Cross account."

"At first, she found Purdy Town pleasant, but boring. Still, she was beautiful again and there were enough attractive men and women to keep her amused. Several love affairs resulted in gifts of memory, and she upgraded her house from one story to two. Then, she decided to open a shop and soon, Emily began to host private parties for a select group. These were special occasions where people celebrated birthdays and enjoyed sharing memories of the bio world. Some of her earnings were used to enhance the shop and add extra flavors. When Bali Hai became Shemathra, life became more restrictive. Spies of every sort came to

Purdy Town. No act of disloyalty was tolerated. People feared any gathering where spies might be listening, including Emily's special events."

"I don't understand. Why was she sent to the slaughterhouse? People got the message. Why was it necessary to delete her?"

"Some people did attend, but not many. Emily was disappointed.by the depressed turnout and her meager profit and she made an error in judgement. She pocketed her profit from the private parties. Her profit was small, an insignificant amount in her mind. Rather than report it as income, she decided to transfer it to her youth maintenance account. When she failed to report the additional income, her fate was sealed."

"The hat shop can wait. Tell me why this merited such a harsh punishment."

"She failed to give an accurate report, that is why. It didn't begin with the slaughterhouse. First, the shop disappeared along with Emily's handsome two-story house. She was homeless, stripped of her youth and no one dared take her in. For days, she huddled against the wall where her shop had been. Then, she was sent to the slaughterhouse and everyone in Purdy Town was compelled to witness her end."

I can't think about this now; I see other shop owners waiting. People here have decided how they will pay. Most of them will give up something that is unnecessary, something they have kept, to remind them of life before Shemathra.

The hat shop is owned by 'Mr. Buzz Sherman.' Other than youth, appearance adjustment options were not part of the original Purdy Town package, I see Buzz as he appeared in his bio life, standing in front of a hat shop titled 'Sherman's Vintage Hats' in flowery old-school script. Buzz manifests as a ninety-year-old, still middle-aged. Short and balding, Mr. Sherman is an appealing man with a neat Van Dyke brown beard and soulful blue eyes.

Although he smiles, his hands are clasped behind his back. Buzz looks frightened. "I have no more memory from within the shop," Buzz confesses. "These three in the window are all that is left." He references a fedora, a woman's 1920s Great Gatsby hat with a white feather and another beaded flapper hat from the same era. I see the beaded flapper hat disappear, replaced by what looks like a short-brimmed, white summer hat from, I assume, the same era.

"I have exchanged my precious cap of virtual pearls for this summer one," Buzz tells me. He looks away, as if he might cry. (Please, no!) "I'd like to add the profit from this exchange to five years of youth. That should do it, I think." He still seems close to tears but relieved as he transfers the memory profit from the hat exchange and forfeits five years of youth.

If I told him I thought the new hat is more attractive, would it help? Probably not. I'm a sim; I have no opinions, just orders and reports. After collecting from Buzz, I move to the next shop, 'The General Store.' *Dry Goods, Novelties & Memories for Rent. Entry Fee: One week of youth per customer.*

This sign is different. It is rather loud against the neutral Purdy colors. A garish red with white trim, it dwarfs the double door entrance. Other than the proprietors, no virtuals are here; it's tax day. Jars of different fruits and pickled vegetables are neatly stacked next to a flour barrel, all holo illusions, programmed to enhance the experience of retail. There's an old ice chest, out of place next to three sleek memory booths, private spaces for those who can afford to rent a memory. Holo images glow on the pearly surface of each booth's outer shell, showing what's currently available. Price options range from five minutes to half an hour. All are guaranteed as being from the Memory Library, approved by 'Friends of Shemathra'. The memories are short windows into bio life as it was. Selection includes tranquil vacations, sporting events, dances, museum tours and amusement parks. All are preceded by Shemathra propaganda.

I'm a little confused. How do I approach taxes when it comes to rentals and the Memory booths?

"No need," my sim assures me. *"It has been reported. Ten per cent goes to the proprietors and the rest of the revenue goes directly to the Shemathra Data Stream."*

George and Margo Kovak, owners, of the Purdy General Store, are smiling. That's new; everyone else is frightened. Behind the main counter, round cyber-candy sits in a bowl labeled *"Jawbreakers, one month of youth per unit."* Next is a jumble of souvenir knickknacks, backscratchers, and a few mugs with "A Right Purdy Time for Coffee" on them. The candy and the memory rentals are all that is available for purchase. The Kovak couple presents the classic image of a middle-aged country couple. He's in overalls and she wears an apron. All they need is the pitchfork like the painting. "What was it called? "I ask the sim.

"What is what called?"

Of course, he hasn't a clue. I'll ask Four; she must know. The Kovaks are still smiling as they wait.

"Be careful," my sim warns," *the Kovaks are spies.*

Margo opens a vintage cash register. Tilting her head and tapping a manicured nail, she waits as my sim scans the income and the resulting tax. Then, someone bursts out of a memory booth. What is wrong with the man? He struggles to calm himself as he stands before me. His thin, aged body bends with sobs that erupt in a seismic fashion as he shields his eyes, which are devoid of tears. Is he ashamed of his unfettered emotion? It is so un-Purdy Town. For some reason, I'm distracted by his square tipped fingers (like Dad's I think, until the sim cautions me to guard against any emotional display). I pull away, just as the man extends his familiar hands and submits himself to me.

"Golf," the man sighs. "Ten minutes of someone else's memory of a morning spent playing a game I never liked. It was the only memory I could afford and have enough for one more tax."

I remain silent. Unaffected by the memory man, the Kovaks are waiting to see what I do. What am I supposed to do?

"I forgot the feel of morning," The man's voice chokes with regret. "It was early; there was a breeze, and the sun was new. Actual birds flitted in the trees, and I could smell the grass. Can't smell it here anymore and the birds . . . aren't birds here. The boy in the memory, the boy was there with me, someone's son I guess." the man is sobbing again. (What do I do?)

"My son, the boy in the memory looked like Ansel, same age, and I . . ." he sighs. "I needed, oh God, I paid for another ten minutes of golf." He shakes his head and his hand hovers in front of me. "I can't—I'm ready for the Data Stream."

I stamp his hand. "Please present yourself on this date." I tell him. He nods, relieved it's over. I don't look at him as he leaves; I can't. This is not Bali Hai, not my dream. I'm somewhere else.

I force myself to retreat deep within Gunter sim, away from Margo Kovak's piercing stare. "I'm worried, Sim. Does she suspect anything?"

"Doubtful" My sim softly reassures me. *"It is best to ignore her and continue taxes."*

I leave the store and allow the sim control. The sooner he finishes, the sooner I leave. Next, we visit the small businesses that assist Purdy Town residents in housing selections.

It goes quickly, until we turn to the hotel. Besides the rooms on the second and third floors, some with a view of a lake which is long gone, and now part of the prairie, a few dining tables dot part of the bottom floor which once held the registration desk. This floor is taxed separately as a restaurant, an eatery in Purdy Town terms. Only a few tables remain, the rest converted to memory for taxes. Two selections remain on the menu, a ham sandwich, and a vanilla milkshake.

No one collects the orders. Diners point to an image, the food appears, and the memory deducted. Currently, each item requires two weeks of youth. Still, on most days, those who can afford it, fill the tables, paying for the privilege with scattered trinkets and months or weeks of youth. Only five rooms remain on the second floor and two on the third. No one stays there now. They are afraid of being inadvertently erased if another room is converted into memory.

I'm aware the virtuals behind those curtains have hurried back to their houses. They wait for me by the front doors of their homes. I don't knock on any doors. Each virtual must have their memory tribute ready. I leave it to the sim. Gunter Sim knows what must be done.

There are six rows of houses on this side, three hundred houses in all. I'm aware of the exact number of virtuals. I cannot make exceptions. My sim insists on displaying his vacant smile, so I remain hidden. The first row is uneventful. Many residents offer furniture, like a chair, a small table or a lamp, pieces of their environment that remind them of the bio world. As I touch each offering, my hand glows with a green light if it is enough and it disappears, absorbed, counted, and transmitted to the Data Stream. If the tribute falls short, there is no light and the virtual hurries to offer something more, like a year or so of their youth option until it is enough.

The next three rows are much the same. One woman offers a teapot, recreated from a vintage ceramic she once sold to an antique shop. I tell her I must inspect her house in case she is withholding assets. She has a columned two-story house, so I am surprised to discover the stairs to the upper story are gone. The house appears to have two levels, but it is clear she has been converting elements of the inner structure into memory for taxes. Where the stairs existed, a blank white wall stands. She has no kitchen, nothing to create the illusion of bio life.

Only one room remains. In it is a grand old chair, overstuffed, Victorian, I think. Next to it is a beautiful birdcage, gold with rose colored swirls of metal flowers around the middle and gently curving vines connect the flowers to the base. But there is no bird—long gone, I suppose, since objects more than creatures are what she holds dear. Save the wall where the stairs once stood, every wall in the room has several shelves. Ornate lamps, and boxes with intricate carvings, old clocks of various sizes and two enormous cabinets hold complete sets of elegant dishes that wait for a table. She is in tears as she surrenders the teapot.

"There is something she's hiding, she's frightened" my sim whispers, *"the teapot is meant to distract you."*

"What?" I'm growing impatient.

"Ah, it's inside a clock." My sim is the perfect bureaucrat; he's all about rules.

"She's met her obligation, why should we care?"

"It's a religious object; such artifacts are forbidden in Shemathra's Realm. I must report this. It will be seized, and this virtual will be subject to deletion," he says.

"What is it, why can't you ignore it?"

"A rosary," he says. *"I sense its importance to her. By keeping it and possibly using it, she rejects the Goddess."*

"You will ignore this object and leave."

"It's against my programming," he insists.

"I am in control of your program. You will not confiscate it, and you will not report this virtual for possessing a religious artifact."

"For now." The sim relents and we move on.

Thank God the rest of this row goes quickly, though oe man sighs as he gives up his goldfish sim. He keeps the bowl. Why? More than likely he is an optimist and thinks he can get another fish when his luck changes.

On the roofs of the next row, I see several crows. Spies. What a horrible existence. You're being watched. I can't wait to leave. As I go to the next row, I want to know why I'm forced to visit Purdy Town. Wasn't the recording the misery of the No Where enough? Why must I keep going? I'm sickened by all of it.

"Wait, tell me again, Gunter sim, how does this information benefit Four?"

"Miranda Four collects everything you see to use against SEINI in Court. The status of your former self as a verified resident of Shemathra ensures this evidence is legally acceptable. Four requires a complete virtual record of all four human habitats of Shemathra, the environments, and any abuses."

Never mind, I guess.

A woman comes forward and she's holding a large brown rabbit. It's clearly a sim, but she begins to cry as I reach for it. It makes it hard to be impersonal. *"It's your job,"* the sim whispers. The thought goes through my mind that I would like to pet its soft fur. As I extend my hand to process the data used in its creation, the woman snatches it back. Handing it to a friend, she holds out her shaking hand.

"Take ten years of my youth option, Gunter sim." My hand touches her hand, and she is no longer seventy; she is eighty. A green light flashes. She sighs with relief.

I am surprised to see the green light when I touch it. She takes the animal back and weeps, holding the sim bunny close to her cheek, she disappears behind her door.

As I continue down this row, I see larger houses. Two have wrap-around porches. It's easier for this group. There are few sacrifices needed to meet the tribute requirement. Most of these virtuals appear to be in their fifties. Their clothes aren't the drab tunics worn by the shop people. From this group, I easily collect memory and things go quickly. With a flash of green light, I converted an oil painting of some hunting dogs, a vintage spittoon and a wooden chess set among other luxury items into data. I think I would prefer keeping the rabbit to the virtual wealth on display here.

The last row is the most memorable. Everyone there could easily meet their taxes, however one woman gives me her sim husband, a tall handsome man with a vacant smile. I can tell that the memory needed to produce him was less than that needed for a more nuanced sim. Still, it was enough for a green light.

"I'm tired of him; he wasn't my favorite husband, but the most economical one to make as a sim," was all that she would say. Looks aren't everything, I guess. Boring is boring. I make him disappear and she disappears within her columned house.

I'm going back to the villa. I am tired of this. It's time to jump.

***

The Villa

July 24, 2290

I'm in the hammock again. I feel the ocean mist and hear the waves going back and forth. Thank God, for a short time, I'm allowed to revel in the ordinary. Pale green leaves rustle on the palms that support the hammock. There are no spies here, my sim tells me. Welcome news.

As Four appears in the doorway, I am reminded of how much she resembles Marcia. *"Gunter sim, please give a report on Purdy Town."*

I am standing now as Four embraces me. I welcome the comfort of her arms as she absorbs my memories, and records of the pervasive sadness of Purdy Town.

"You did well, Gunter. Still, remember, you jumped again without being called."

"Four, I did what you asked. Now answer my question. How do you know that Eric Holden was not my father? Are you sure?"

"Yes, Gunter, I'm sure. When Hosseini is gone, I'll share with you the memories of the original Gunter, and you will accept that Eric was not your father. His crimes will make you glad that you were not his son. If you insist, I can share them now, but my advice is to wait."

"I still question your evidence, however, I need to focus on what's ahead, so I'll wait. Why is everyone gone—Marcia, Patel, even Monty? Why didn't they fight the mergers?"

"Because of what you did, Gunter. To crush a rival and protect Bali Hai, you allowed the theft of tainted software. When Joy Forever

installed it, its entire population of two million human virtuals was gone. You tried to justify it, but you couldn't. You lost the love of your wife Laura and Marcia's trust. Your partner and mentor, Monty, vowed revenge. The most gifted member of your team, Patel, resigned. This led to Laura's affair with Jacob. Marcia decided to retire."

"How can I accept responsibility for this even if I take you at your word? The future me might have done it, but I didn't."

"You're right, Gunter. You have no memory of it, but it did happen. When Monty, Marcia and Patel left, VEI became vulnerable to predators like Hosseini. This led to the destruction of Bali Hai, the paradise you created. You can't change the past, but you can save the people here. They trusted you and now they exist in a virtual hell. Take it all back! Rest here for a little while, until it's time to collect taxes from the Palms, the next human colony."

"Thank you, Four. I would like to rest." I move from the balcony to the white room. I feel even safer there.

"Gunter, would you like some coffee?

"Yes, thank you, Four. May I have it in a white cup?"

"Of course."

"Why are there two cups? AIs don't drink coffee." She picks up the second cup. The way her fingers curve around its base reminds me of the way my mother held her tea on winter mornings.

She points to its rim. *"Do you see a slight red band at the top? Look closely; it's very thin."*

"Yes, what is it?"

"It's a piece of code. Someone I trust gave it to me. Primitive by today's standards. This is what destroyed Joy Forever. Touch it."

"Won't I risk erasure?"

"No, I altered your code. It's safe for you. Gunter, trace the red."

I take my index finger and touch the rim. As I move my finger around the edge, a thread winds its way down my knuckles and then embeds itself in my palm. "How will this help?"

"If you're in danger, open your hand palm up, make a fist, and then palm up again, point your index finger. Try it."

"Okay." Interesting, my fingertip has a sort of white light coming from it. "What does it do?"

"Any virtual touched by this light deletes in less than thirty seconds."

"Virtuals okay, but what about sims?"

"It has no effect on sims."

"But virtuals are human beings, I'm not sure if I—"

"Then be very sure it is necessary, and be careful, if there's any doubt, do the best you can and jump to the villa. First, you will wait in dream-memories. When you wake, you'll be in The Palms."

But what does it mean to be sure? What if the virtual's only crime is recognizing me? I had enemies, not all were bad people. I won't ask Four. I doubt she knows. What if I'm forced to jump to the villa? How long will I have to escape? I—

***

Sandcastles

Dad sits near my sandcastle as he watches me drown. Why isn't he helping? I can't scream anymore; I'm too tired to fight the ocean. A school of fish swims closer now. Are they going to eat me? Oh, someone has grabbed my arm, and he's crying, "Oh, please God, I am sorry, oh Gunter, oh my poor little boy. . ."

He loves me! Everything will be okay. . .

What happened? I'm hugging my knees because it's cold here in Venice Beach, so cold. I'm hungry. Where is Dad's car? The nights here are so cold, and it rained. Dad should be here soon. . . maybe not. . .

Maybe he's in The Palms.

End RECORD

THE OVERLAND PRAIRIE

Shemathra's Realm

August 2, 2290

Diego

Negotiations with Hosseini meant better grazing for his long-horns. Diego knows the concessions he won from the devil will lead to Diego's eventual deletion.

"Trust the wisdom of Shemathra, the Wolf Goddess, follow the 'one will' and reap the bounty of eternal bliss." In the early days of Shemathra's Realm, obvious troublemakers were quickly erased, and the great dividing began. Friends and family members parted ways over the question of who would continue existence as humans and who would give themselves to the new way, a peaceful existence, full of sensory pleasure and wonder. The word "trust" was used repeatedly. There are many promises; few are kept.

Then came strongly worded 'recommendations,' warnings really. Don't question, don't protest, whatever happens, especially what happens to human virtuals. Before it was forbidden, some left the herd and joined human communities. After a few prolonged slaughterhouse executions, no one objected to a change in the rules.

"One clover and one bee to start a prairie." He learned the Emily Dickinson poem when he was twelve years old and a real human being. *Or you can use a lot of code.* The splendor of this prairie gives Diego solace. Purple Coneflowers, Scarlet Sage and Texas Bluebonnets mingle with clusters of delicious tall grass. Trees shade a burbling stream. Diego had persuaded Hosseini the Overland experience would keep the longhorns satisfied and attract any humans considering life as a longhorn.

He worries the bison problem is getting worse. The obnoxious beasts share this program, and Diego despises every one of them. For now, the bison seem content, dining on grass. There is still concern; recently, several of the larger male bison, without warning, have challenged the newer longhorns. This upsets the cows and if the cows are upset, so is Diego. He hates the pretense—both the bison and the longhorn males are fools. Showoffs, all of them. How brave were these fools as bios? All of them are like his father, Rey Putnam.

As a boy, Diego had promised himself he would never be like his dear papa. A dreamer, Rey Putnam fancied himself a rebel. After years of prospecting for precious opals on Mars and platinum mining on various asteroids, Reynaldo returned home to Estrella and nine-year-old Diego.

"Promise me, Diego," his father said, "you'll never be dull."

"Never," Diego said and nodded his head, staring at his father's long narrow feet, hopelessly weak after prolonged low gravity. Dear Papa chased his dreams at the expense of his wife and son. What angered Diego was his father's rejection of Grandmother Jasmine's offer to pay for an afterlife package. Rey took offense, saying that Jasmine wasn't his mother, only a mother-in-law. It was none of her concern.

Diego's mother Estrella had protested. "What if you're killed, Reynaldo? At least copy yourself for virtual upload," Estrella had pleaded. "What if something happens and we never see you again?"

His father waved away her pleas, making a vague promise to copy as soon as he returned. There would be no return and no virtual Papa. Rey Putnam perished when his high-altitude glider collided with a flock of geese. Worse, his father left no bank credits and a mountain of debt. It breaks his heart whenever he thinks of it. It was Jasmine who saved him. She insisted Diego complete his education. Estrella was given an allowance to do what she liked. On his eighteenth birthday, Jasmine told him the story of his uncle, Gunter Holden.

"He took your mother's inheritance," his grandmother said, her voice tight with anger. "Your foolish mother was as much Eric Holden's child as her brothers. More, when it came to Gunter if the rumors were true," she sighed.

When SEINI lawyers approached him with a plan to gain control of VEI, Diego was skeptical but intrigued. If there were any chance to take down the great Gunter Holden, he wanted to try. Certain Board members were compromised by threats or bribes and decisions were made. A law passed, and acting as Gunter's heir, Diego assumed control of Gunter's shares. Then the mergers began and VEI slid into bedlam. All of it was Hosseini's doing.

All it took to bring Gunter Holden to his virtual knees was one lie. A state law, sponsored by Hosseini's dark money, required virtual board members to attend at least fifty percent of meetings. Though a virtual, Gunter was still an active Board member. During one of Gunter's rare absences, minutes were altered, falsely claiming that he was rarely in attendance. Soon, Diego was invited to control his uncle's shares. A merger was proposed; Diego voted yes and VEI was destroyed. It was such a small lie, easy to justify considering what Uncle Gunter had done to Jasmine and Estrella. But Diego hadn't counted on Hosseini's cruelty and the part he, Diego, was forced to play. What happened after Gunter's fall haunts Diego. It can't be helped.

There's a swarm of insects provoking a new steer to wave his horns. Several of the more dominant male bison approach. Horns down, the bison delight in the challenge. All of it is laughable.

The only true courage Diego has ever witnessed here came from his despised uncle, Gunter Holden. When Hosseini transitioned to Bali Hai as the rainbow llama, the fate of Bali Hai was sealed. Though his power was gone, Gunter still tried to save his lovely paradise. And when it was clear he could not, Gunter humbled himself to protect its people, the human virtuals, until pummeled by relentless pain and defeat, Uncle Gunter rode the roller coaster into oblivion.

After Diego was murdered, he was surprised to find himself in Shemathra's Realm.

Hosseini had appeared as his ancient self, a small man bent with age. Slack folds of pale skin hung from the old man's neck. The layers of mottled flesh that encircled his eyes glowed with triumph and malice, reminding Diego of a Komodo dragon.

"So here we are," the devil had said. "You're gonna help me run this place. I'm puttin' you in charge of the longhorns. You'll have almost total control of these animals—I mean people," the old demon snickered, "and of course, I control you, so remember that."

Now, Diego sighs with pleasure at his simple life. In a herd of obedient cows and proud longhorn steers, he is the unquestioned ruler. He walks with a stately grace on a prairie where the wind threads through the tall grass and wildflowers are fragrant, stirring his tremendous appetite. The span of his impressive horns dwarfs the width of the largest steers. His gaze moves methodically, monitoring the herd. Diego promises himself that he will not fail them. "If I had known, if I had seen those eyes," Diego often thinks. "I never would . . . What have I done?"

At night, when he and his herd graze in the Western Vista, he guides the herd as far from the moans of humans as he can. Occasionally, a new steer strays closer, hoping to "police the light barrier." When he hears the snorting sounds of triumph as a steer catches a virtual human, Diego longs for oblivion. These pathetic human virtuals want to gaze at the night's stars. Several cows have come to him privately to ask if there was a way to stop the abuse. He tells them all to be careful. Sympathy for humans is forbidden.

The exalted llama god is unpredictable. Say the wrong thing to the wrong person and the Overland Prairie could soon be covered in Bermuda grass, clover and lots of Herefords crowding out his longhorns. In Shemathra, all must be careful.

RAVI'S GONE

The Elysium

August 4, 2290

She closes her eyes. Purdy Town is a nightmare, but until the grandfather copy gathers enough evidence to condemn Hosseini, she is powerless. Placing crumbs close to her desk, she considers the risks waiting for Gunter in the Palms. Within seconds, the mouse is on her desk. But the door is ajar, and the cat leaps into the room, his paws sliding on the rug and the mouse falls onto the floor. It disappears under the rug, the crouching Burmese paws swatting and the feline tail sways like a cobra. She prays the cat has only cornered the mouse, nothing more.

Chasing the cat into the living room, she shuts the door. Has the cat killed the little creature? Is it injured and will she be faced with the decision to put the mouse out of its misery? Maybe she won't look.

Rather than Schrodinger's cat, it will be a mouse, alive and not alive. The mouse emerges with an angry squeak. Pausing to grab a floor crumb of melted raspberry, it disappears under the bed.

Her own tears surprise her. *Stop! I can't afford this; there's no time. Why so upset? It's a rodent.* Are the tears for her virtual grandfather or for the Gunter the mouse? Hard to say. She rolls her shoulders to release the tension.

While checking her messages, Mira is startled by Henry's touch on her shoulder. He puts his finger to his lips, a sign for her to be silent. Reaching into his pocket, he pulls out a small cube and places it on the table next to the bed. Henry points to the peepers and shakes his head; predictably, they are defective. The cube activates a sound interference, which will keep what he is about to tell her from SEINI spies. His face grim, Henry sees Mira's anxious face. Her pale complexion, a legacy of her Irish mother, is flooded with unspent emotion.

"So, you've heard?" Henry whispers.

"Heard what?" she says. There's a threat against bad news in her voice.

He stares at her, his mouth tight.

"Heard what, Henry, tell me," she demands.

"Ravi's dead," he says.

She shakes her head. "No, he isn't. I don't believe you. How do you know?"

"Mira, I wouldn't say such a thing unless, I was sure." Henry reaches for her hand, and she pulls away.

She can't run away from it. "How?"

"He was in London. There was an anti-virtual, anti-upload riot that spun out of control, and . . ." Henry reaches out to touch her arm.

Again, she pulls away, shaking her head. "AND?" she demands.

"Ravi was hit by a rock. It was a concussion. He refused to have it looked at and the next morning, he was gone. Mira, I'm so sorry."

"Okay. I didn't mean to—blame you, to yell and . . ." Moving to their living area, she collapses on the red couch, her head cupped in her hands. Ravi, who traveled the world, who had lost her mother, his "beloved Rosalind," in a fall from a mountain pass, fell victim to ordinary street violence. She wants to turn back time, to warn him not to go out. 'Stay home, Dad, trust me.' But he's gone and there are no more chances.

'No,' she murmurs as she leaves the couch for the comfort of their bed. Still unable to cry, to do anything but withdraw, she clutches her knees to her chest.

While she stays within herself, Henry sits in a chair next to the bed. "There's something else, Mira," he sighs. "Your father purchased an after-death plan."

She sighs with relief, knowing Ravi is not lost forever. Ravi once told her he wasn't interested in a VR existence. But thank God, he changed his mind; he isn't lost to her. It won't be much of a change. She can still reach out and tell him she loves him. She still has a father.

"He's not lost." She nods.

"No Mira, he isn't, but . . ." Henry's voice quivers. He gathers her in his arms.

"But what, Henry? But WHAT?"

"He's a virtual human resident in Shemathra's Realm. My source tells me he'll be in the Palms community soon." Henry said.

"How do you know? What source?"

Henry shakes his head. "I can't tell you; I wish I could."

She knows it's useless to ask. The book of Henry is closed. She won't give up until she knows the answer. "Yes, that's the best place for him now," she can barely talk. "He'll draw less attention."

There is no time to mourn. She must contact Gunter's copy. The Palms colony holds almost seventy thousand virtuals. Gunter's sim will be collecting taxes from over forty-five thousand citizens. During that time, Gunter must find his son, whatever it takes.

Tilting her head to the side, she stares at Henry. How well does she really know him? After telling Ravi about the copy of his father, she didn't expect her father to die. Why upload to Shemathra? Obviously, it was to find his father and then what? Is Ravi aware of the danger he's in? Kissing the top of her head, Henry leaves her and returns to the kitchen and its jokes.

THE PALMS SOUTH

Shemathra's Realm

Record 3a

THE PALMS SOUTH

Gunter Holden

V Loc: The Palms South: population 70,129

August 6, 2290

The entrance to "The Palms South" human habitat is a sand-colored gate twice my height. Behind me is the same bleak desert that I remember from my time in Purdy Town. Like Purdy town, my sim whispers, The Palms is a middle-income program, a no-frills small city for virtuals on a budget. I wonder if the gate has a bell, a buzzer or if I should simply knock, like Dorothy at the gates of Oz. I hope for an improvement over the gloom of the last one. So far, my guess is that every location will be dreary in its own way, a disappointing custom hell. The No Where was the banks of the Styx.

Purdy Town was a bad dream. Soundlessly, the gate opens. I enter and it closes behind me.

No palms are on the outskirts of the Palms, only a collection of sand-colored tents and shacks. I'll start here, even though I dread it.

As if by magic, thousands of people are starting to line up. They stand in front of tents, lean-tos, and shacks. If they cannot pay the required tribute, my sim tells me, their next home will be the No Where. The Purdy Town option is no longer available. Without a murmur of resentment, men, and women virtuals wait for me.

The rows zigzag, creating winding, gloomy alleys as my hand flashes with the familiar green light. My job here is made simple because most virtuals here pay using their youth option; they have nothing else, at least nothing they're willing to lose. The lucky ones appear to be in their fifties so five or ten years of youth does not mean a profound change. I am puzzled when my sim rejects one man's tribute, a backgammon set. The light has failed, the sim whispers because all the pieces are missing. He has only the board; the set is incomplete. Instead, I take five years of youth and the green light flashes.

"Your digital files carry all the complexity of your forty-nine years as a biological being. Whatever you do, you mustn't let anyone see who you really are." Four warned me to stay hidden. I am Gunter Holden, human virtual, a file infinitely rich, a trove of memory. I might end my Shemathra stay in a slaughterhouse, dangling at the end of a hook. I hope for the strength to self-delete.

While my sim taxes the memory of the very poor, I withdraw. Too many here are out of years to pay. Years offered from anyone over cen-twenty hold little value. The result is The No Where, forming new circles by the bar of light. One by one, they go to a place where the sun and the night sky are the only joy. I hide behind his smile as he quickly completes his task. The last virtual is a woman who manifests at the age of cen-plus-five. I emerge to record another moment of despair, but she surprises me by offering a shawl. Within its black lace are the images of brightly colored birds.

"The last thing I have," she says, "that reminds me I was beautiful." Thankfully, it's enough to keep her safe and the green light flashes. I'm done here.

Years ago, one hundred and eighty thousand virtuals inhabited this environment, most crammed into snug units that featured very little of what I once considered boiler plate amenities, let alone luxury. Now, there are less than seventy thousand residents.

In the next Palms neighborhood, there are clusters of tenement apartments. Along the first narrow street in several three-story sand-colored buildings, residents stand, waiting for me. Like before, few meet my gaze. Rather than resignation, I detect a boiling resentment. In the bio world, this place would be a hotbed of rebellion. But this is Shemathra and there will be no uprising. The price is too high. Surviving is the only thing that matters and to survive, one must pay tribute. How long it will be before this place becomes just another featureless gulag?

No one on the outside knows for sure if their loved one still exists, but it is safer to pay and hope they're still here. My sim knows whispered stories of the slaughterhouse cast a shadow on everything human. Everyone here knows someone who met deletion in the slaughterhouse.

I see potholes, gaps in the surface. Would a single piece of street qualify as a tribute? That would explain the lack of wood in Purdy Town. Plank by wooden plank, citizens delayed the day when tribute became a personal thing, paid by those who clung to identity until the black surface was all that was left of the walkway used every day.

Like Purdy Town, The Palms South has a variety of shops and businesses, all on one side of a street, that loops around this part of the city. No shops are more than two stories high. A sign above each doorway labels what occupies that spot.

Here, shops are run by sims. A French bakery, a clothing store, what else? Ah, one rents games and a café with outside tables where a few virtuals sit, conversing as they eat; so, the pleasure of eating still exists here! That gives me hope. Collecting tribute has not yet robbed them of everything. There are people walking by me. No one will look at me. I'm the tax collector.

There is nothing left of Bali Hai, no busy city streets, luxurious resorts, none of the breath-taking vistas, all of it, my life's work. Nothing comes close, even The Royal Arms, the best of what Shemathra offers humans. The sim informs me that many virtuals here transferred from The Royal Arms to less expensive Palms South. Survival insurance.

For those who fail to pay the required tribute, there are consequences. Bitterness dulls the faces of passersby who ignore each other with tight smiles as lifeless as a sim's. As I pass along the street, people follow me. I'm the Pied Piper. They're returning to their apartments now. An attractive red-haired woman is crossing the street. She's casually dressed in a denim-braid skirt and a rose-pink blouse. Ah, I can tell from her smile she's a sim. What if she recognizes the human in me?

"Greetings and praise to the Goddess," she says, *"please identify your name and purpose."* The snippet of memory that created her must have come from a former resident, a virtual, I assume, long gone,

deleted. Except for the outer shell and pleasant voice, all that remains of that virtual has been erased, just as my sim is all that remains of the original Gunter Holden.

"Greetings, I am Gunter sim. I have come to collect tribute from thirty-five thousand virtuals in this community. What is your name?"

"I am Jessica sim," she says, *"I am here to keep order on this street. I will also collect taxes from the Privileged Units. Please continue your purpose."* No wonder she wears pink; she's a tax sim. It makes her easy to spot.

My sim tells me that virtuals who occupy the "Privileged Units" risk deletion when the herds come through. These units face the path of the stampede. Occupants must stand at attention during the stampede event. Often, in a frenzy of religious devotion, or just plain meanness, a herd member will catch an unfortunate human on its horns, tossing its victim into the mayhem. It's considered a sport among many in the Shemathra Herd Collective.

"In the name of the Goddess, I will. Please advise all that they must hurry and be ready when I call on them."

"In the Goddess's name," she says with a blank smile that so depresses me, I look away.

As I search for the front door to the next apartment building, Ah, these streets end in something much wider. I'll finish here then discover where they lead. First, I collect taxes. The collection goes quickly, with toasters and lamps, treasured art, and an aquarium with expensive sim fish. Almost none require an additional item to meet my demands. Unlike the tents, only a handful of residents offer years.

In virtual reality, time should be irrelevant. In Shemathra's Realm, it's one more reason to despair. On August 31, the Grand Stampede shall claim the files of even more human citizens. The coming event won't run through these narrow arteries.

Like every Grand Stampede, a thousand hooves thunder through the wide boulevard of the Grand Stampede Roadway. If chosen to participate, humans must answer the call and jump to the location known as 'Glory to the Goddess.'

Some humans will be caught, tossed on horns or crushed under thousands of hooves, and deleted. When this happens, a thick white mist of deleted human uploads will float into the Data Stream. My sim explains that the Data Stream flows into the River of Memory Files that pumps into the heart of the Bank of SEINI's assets. Most humans who do survive the Stampede are weak with relief, but a few wish it was over.

After collecting taxes is done, I follow the curving street, until I see a sign, "This way to the 'Palms Shemathra Trail.'" Cube-shaped units are stacked like children's blocks. It's a pyramid in reverse with the middle floor having more units than the lowest and the highest having the most, aligned in an indifferent manner that would challenge physics in the bio world. But this is virtual reality. Another sign, "Welcome to 'The Palms South Condominiums', well-appointed homes of Shemathra's Realm."

How will I collect taxes here? Is there one access to each stack? I see the word, "Spring," above a door on the ground floor. Eight box units are on the ground level, the middle holds fifteen "gracious condos" and the very highest, twenty units look as if at any time they might topple in a strong breeze. A door opens. A short blonde woman in her forties comes toward me. Another sim.

"Greetings Gunter, sim," the woman says, *"Welcome to 'Spring Condos.'"*

"Greetings, praise to the Goddess," I say. "I will now collect tributes." Behind her, a narrow walkway leads along the outside of the bottom units, where hundreds of taxpayers wait for me. There are only eight units; so, how many live on this level? Rows of human virtuals crowd together in front of each door. As each inhabitant pays tribute with the usual memento, he or she disappears inside after my sim processes it.

'Spring' tunics are different from the yellow brown sacks humans wear in Purdy Town. On each garment, the wearer's name is embroidered near the right shoulder. They are in a variety of pale pastels—yellows, robin's egg blues, lavenders, pinks, and soft greens, matched by simple slippers. The dress code in Shemathra is sadly monotonous.

There are fewer pieces of furniture or appliances disappearing into the green light. One virtual (Dotty) gives up a nutra-blender, a reminder, I suspect, of when she was a health-conscious bio.

These blocks are larger, more like dormitories and within them are individual spaces sharing a common area. As I collect, I catch glimpses of "common areas" and only two have any furniture, nothing conveys the feeling of shared space. After paying taxes, each person retreats into a smaller space shared with several others. These smaller spaces are where they keep everything that reminds them that they are human. In time, all of "everything" will be gone.

The next floor has fifteen cubes. I am amazed to see how many more citizens are waiting outside. These units are larger. There isn't enough space on the outside landing to accommodate everyone and again, as each person pays taxes, he or she withdraws, and another appears.

The tax offerings are more varied here. I process the sim of a pet iguana, two crystal vases and old fashioned, printed books including the complete works of Shakespeare. It's amazing what people keep. The Shakespeare man was the only one who wept. He manifests at sixty and a woman who has just paid with a set of ceramic gnomes, tugs on his sleeve, whispering words of comfort. Other tenants offer family heirlooms and bottles of white wine. Rather than part with what they treasure, a few pay in years.

I'm finished with the fifteen middle cubes and its hundreds of residents. All on this floor are dressed in sea foam green. It's time for the remaining twenty units. These people are dressed in pale shades of pink. Finishing the cubes would be tedious if it weren't for the way the upper cubes rest on the ones below. As I look down, I see how some of them hover on the edges of the fifteen beneath them. I know this is virtual reality and the laws of physics and architecture don't apply, still, it is difficult to climb the stairs without feeling that soon, it will all tumble to the ground. I retreat inside my sim as we reach the twenty units. It's the same as the units below. Residents crowd and rotate in doorways, filling the narrow walkways lining the outer perimeter.

The first seventeen cubes are like the fifteen below, each home to dozens, even more. I'm curious to know how many, however, I stay back and let the sim do his work. Citizens pay their taxes and disappear inside. How many rooms does each unit contain and how many virtuals live in each room?

A few people surprise me with payments from ready accounts, either their own or from trusts set up for them by family members. One man offers a chandelier, copied from a restaurant he owned as a bio. A woman, who was a writer of note, offers signed copies of her book. Unfortunately, the light fails to accept her payment and she instead offers an Eames chair and ottoman. When her lips quiver with disappointment, I suppress words of sympathy.

I've come to the eighteenth cube. I'm relieved; I'm almost done with this block of virtual humanity. There are only two more cubes to go after this one. Like the previous seventeen, layers of people crowd on the landing. A white-haired man pays with a grandfather clock. I suppress a smile. It reminds me of Seattle and the clocks my mother once owned. A woman hands me a sim monkey, a tiny thing with a long curly tail. It chatters and reaches for her. She turns away. As the sim disappears and the woman hurries inside, I can see the common area. I sense a deliberate distraction.

The tenants here are crowding in front of the wide door and seem eager to pay their tribute so that I will move on. There's something they don't want me to see. The green light flashes as I accept memory currency, intricate artwork, Tiffany lamps and a hookah pipe. So, what's inside? Okay, there's a circle of twenty people, all sitting on the floor. Each one holds a lit candle.

Maryanne, a woman who appears to be in her late fifties finishes her story. This is like The No Where circle with Grace and her cat stories. This story is about Clem, Maryanne's husband. "Clem loved me," Maryanne sighs. But he often beat her. Hopefully, there are no cats in her story.

Pieces of a memory data flow from her fingers as a holo of tan angry man in his nineties appears. His blond hair drips with sweat as he uses a hammer to beat the storyteller. As he beats her, she catches a view of her own death in a hallway mirror. She has carried this memory into virtual existence.

Some people shudder; others look away.

"I thought that one day that he would stop, but Clem didn't want to. My brother came as quick as he could and tried to protect me by shooting Clem. It didn't work. I was already gone, transitioned to Bali

Hai. It was so beautiful then. Bali Hai is gone now, but I'm still here and Clem's in Serene Rehabilitation Virtual Vistas. I guess we're both in prison."

"Thank you, Maryanne," an old woman says. Is she a sim? The old woman manifests as the oldest virtual I've encountered here. She looks at least cen-seventy, short, with thick legs and cropped white hair. She makes no effort to hide her stare! Her eyes follow me. Why? Have I given myself away? I need to leave before she—

"Gunter Holden," the old woman murmurs as she takes my arm and stops me from leaving and—Oh God, she knows I'm not a sim!

"Please join us." The woman's voice is friendly, almost soothing. "If you have a story, we would love to hear it." What is she doing? Now, she's touching my arm again and is she in my thoughts? Is she in my mind?

"Gunter Holden," she whispers, urging me. "I suggest you tell your sim to sleep. Tell him this room is empty. NOW!"

Oh God, do I use the light weapon? How does she know me? What does she want?

I'll buy some time until I'm sure what's going on. "Gunter sim," I tell him, "there's nothing in this room. Now, sleep." I can feel him fade, but how do I wake him when I need him?"

"You can summon your sim when we finish," she says as she lets go of my arm.

Oh my God! How does she recognize me? How does she know that I'm human? I must leave! I could delete her, but I don't know what she wants. What if she's a friend of the other me and she wants to help? I should jump to the villa. I don't know what I—

The old woman ushers me to another doorway.

"I know who you are, Gunter! Your son told me," she smiles and raises her index finger for emphasis. "I knew other you from before— in Bali Hai. Take great care here."

I'm being called out by this old woman! *What does she know?* "What about the people here?" I hiss, "Do they know?' I'll jump to the Villa and beg, "Please Four, I must leave Shemathra!"

"You're among friends." The old woman reassures me. "Who would like to go next?" She calls out to the group. I'm not sure if anyone heard her calling me Gunter Holden and not as a sim. The group is discussing who shares next. Who is this woman? How did she divert their attention away from me? Dear God, I hope no one saw!

Finally, a man enters the circle to begin a new story.

"Maryanne, would you please lead the circle?" Maryanne, an unsmiling woman of ninety, nods. Now, the old woman (how old, probably at least cen-seventy) takes my hand and leads me to another room. Incredibly, this new room is empty—no it isn't. There's someone sitting in the corner. I should let the sim take over. The man is staring at me. The old woman's betrayed me! I should self-delete! I'm an idiot; I never should have trusted her! And he is walking toward me. What do I do?

"Gunter, you are Gunter Holden. Mira told me she found you. I know why you're here." He speaks in a soft voice. "I never thought I would ever . . . Oh, God!"

There's something about him that reminds me . . . It's in his voice, the rhythm of his words and the consonants sharp like, like . . . Patel. No, he can't be Patel's son. He looks nothing like Patel. This man is blond and that searching look in his eyes reminds me of Marcia when we first met. He's at least ninety—early middle age. Who is he?

He's covering his face with his hands and oh my God, he's crying! Am I dreaming? I must be at the Villa and Four has put me in a sleep mode. Must call the sim. I put my index finger to my cheek.

"Don't!" The old woman stops me. Who is she? Can she hear my thoughts? Is she a spy?

"Gunter, pay attention." She talks to me as if I were a child, and she is an impatient teacher. "First," she says, "my name is Terry. We don't have much time. I know Mira is Miranda Four. And I know Mira is your granddaughter. Your son told me all of it. I know why you're here".

What? How does she know all this? Did Four tell this woman the same wild story? "Tell me why I'm here." I'm trying to regain control.

Taking my chin firmly between her index finger and thumb, "Terry" pulls me to her. "Listen up, Gunter Holden. We don't have much time. Your granddaughter has been in danger since she found you."

What in God's name is this woman talking about? How dare she touch me!

"Mira's in danger?" I hear a gasp from the man who waits to meet me. He's stepping in front of me as if I weren't there.

"Calm down, Ravi," she says as she pats his shoulder. "When I recognized Gunter, I wanted him in here before I told you." Terry's voice is grim. "Now listen, both of you. When Mira found you, Gunter, she created Miranda Four. Let her know Hosseini is aware of Miranda Four and he knows she's confined to the Villa. And when he's ready, that's where he'll find her. Be thankful, he doesn't know the reason. He doubts she's a threat. He knows she can't use anything she finds here against him. But Gunter, you can."

"I don't have time for this, I don't know how long the sim will sleep and we have taxes to collect."

"Before you go on, Gunter, let me finish." Terry's gaze is entirely on me. "Hosseini wants to make Mira's presence here permanent."

For some reason, I forget about taxes because I need her to be clear. "By permanent, you mean that he wants to kill her, to end her bio life? Mira wouldn't agree to any post bio upload to Shemathra."

"But she already uploaded herself by creating Miranda Four." Terry says, with regret in her soft voice. "If Mira is killed, Hosseini has all he needs to keep her here. He'll likely clip her AI wings, and he'll keep her close, if only for the entertainment value. Gunter, if that happens, it won't be long before he finds you."

"What do you want me to do?" I ask as I begin to panic. "If I don't collect taxes, I'll be discovered and so will she."

Terry closes her eyes as she answers. "Soon after Shemathra's Realm took power, there was an effort to impress the Virtual Program regulators. For a modest cost, anyone who chose to remain human could purchase a "Jump Pass." The pass allowed unlimited jumps to any human community. This was a time before control tightened and bio to virtual communications were restricted. During that early phase, a family friend, a bio, approached me and offered to facilitate a transfer to another program. I told him I wouldn't leave without my husband, Ned.

"In exchange for a subtle change in my code, masked as a gift of memory, he asked if I would keep an eye on what changes occurred after Bali Hai became Shemathra. Like Gunter, this code enables me to hide behind a sim of me. Then, communications between Shemathra and the bio world became regulated and there was no way to tell him or anyone else what was going on here. Somehow, Shemathra's

Realm forgot about Terry Slotkin, the virtual. I chose to fade, my aged appearance means no one really sees me. To most, I'm a sim. I jump whenever I want to know what's going on."

"Then why don't you download your memories? Four would be happy to get them. Then she can transfer both of us and this man, Ravi, to another program."

"I'm not leaving without Ned."

"But—"

"I'm not leaving without Ned. We came here together, and we will leave together. The human virtual population has dwindled and now we're down to four enclaves, each one despairing in its own way. When my husband is ready, I will risk jumping to the Villa and download what I have seen. But there won't be a Miranda Four if you don't warn her."

"Okay, let's assume you're telling the truth. How do you pay your taxes?"

"Taxes are paid on my behalf by a trust I established when I realized Ned wouldn't leave Shemathra."

Her eyes snap wide and each word is a dart aimed right at me.

"Call your sim back, I'll be happy to pay. I've managed to survive here because as much as I love my husband, I've never trusted him. Currently Ned is a longhorn," she sighs, "snorting, intimidating human virtuals and kicking up dung. People here are suffering and I struggle with my part in not stopping it when maybe..." She shakes her head. "I can't leave him like this. And Gunter, this is your doing, not mine."

"Please, Gunter," the man urges. "My name is Ravi. Seeing you, speaking to you, spending time with you was an unattainable dream. Yet here you are!" He nods his head.

Is he crying again? Wait a minute. Ravi? Didn't Four tell me that my supposed son was someone named Ravi? Is this a joke?

"Ravi" is my height. His hair is sandy blond, darker than mine and he has blue eyes. Mine are gray. He could be anybody, but, yes, the way he's looking at me reminds me of Marcia. Often, she would nod slightly to one side when she looked at me. But the shape of his eyes reminds me of my mother. Four told the truth. This is my son. Why is he here? What can I do? How do I protect him?

Ravi manifests as ninety-five, decades older than me at forty-nine.

"Sit," the old woman tells me. I see a table and two chairs now. Ravi and I sit, but now what do we do?

"Don't you know how dangerous it is, especially if they discover who you are?"

"I'm aware of the danger. It doesn't matter," my son tells me. "I'm here and now we're together."

That doesn't help. My son is a sentimental idiot. It's not only my safety I have to worry about now. Doesn't he know this? I turn to the woman Terry.

"Good for you," I tell her, "I'm happy you're secure. Tell me what you want me to do. And while you're at it, what do you want him to do."

Terry sighs. "I had rather hoped that you might be happy to meet your son. You can see it means a great deal to him. Gunter, I want you to warn Mira. When you finish collecting taxes here, jump back, even if she doesn't call you. Tell her she needs protection."

She turns to Ravi. The man looks desperate yet he's so still. "Ravi, stay out of sight as much as you can. Pray Gunter gathers enough evidence to bring Hosseini down."

Ravi turns to her, "How--?"

Terry cuts him off. "Ravi, the less you know, the better."

"I can't stay," I tell him. "If I don't continue collecting taxes, they'll be suspicious."

"I know," he says as he nods his head. "I'll try to find a path back to you. I have questions."

"I'll see you then," I shrug as I leave, calling my sim and I return to the narrow landing, taking care to not hurry, moving to the next group to collect tributes. I'm frightened—will the old woman betray me? Who else knows? I want to go back to the Villa, but I know I can't until I collect taxes, so I tuck the fear away.

As I move closer to the Stampede area, I see two-story structures. Cube-like layers zig zag, connecting the two stories in odd places, some diagonally, some straight across. This next phase bewilders me. As before, a door opens on the lower level. Two sims greet me. "I am Gunter sim," I say, "Praise to the Goddess! In her name, I am here to collect tributes."

"Praise to Shemathra," the first sim, a man in his seventies declares, "Welcome to Summer!"

The door opens and I begin the next phase, I'm curious about the references to the seasons. As I begin my collection, dozens of tax-payers' crowd into the outer pathway while others wait. Again, the residents are dressed in tunics. The ones on this level are all bright colors—sunflower yellow, clear greens and corals.

This group wears summer colors. As I begin processing the tax offerings here, I let my sim take care of Summer. My mind begins to wander, and I retreat until I'm jolted back with the last of Summer. It seems that my sim gained full control and stored me and my worries so that he could proceed more efficiently.

"All praise to the Goddess," a tall sim woman in her sixties announces. "Welcome, Gunter sim, to Autumn!"

I'm confronted now with tunics of bright oranges, brilliant reds, and ochres. It's time to collect for Autumn. It crosses my mind that after this group, there is only one season left for me. I wonder what Winter will be like. Although I would like to slow my pace to get a better look as we progress, my sim won't allow it. Crossing from one side to the other on the second floor and back again, I follow the strange path. These virtuals seem a bit older than the rest. Tunics vary; some are arctic white; others are pale blue. Many look to be in early middle age, at least seventy or eighty.

I sense fear. Regardless, all are ready to pay their taxes and the green light flashes until, at last, I make my way to the outside. Four told me color is only on approval. The sim tells me the color here is taxed, and for Winter people, an unnecessary expense.

The last collection has no season. Along one side of the Stampede Roadway is a line of single-story cottages. It's hard to see where the line stops. An odd plan, but nothing here is normal. These aren't the "Privileged" units. These cottages are set a bit farther from the road. My sim tells me that there are still "accidents" on occasion, especially when the bison come through.

Each unit has a wide porch where I count almost three dozen virtual humans waiting for me. All wear tunics the color of ash. They spill out of open doors. How many humans per unit? My sim answers forty, sometimes more. There are five hundred cottages lining the Stampede Highway. On the other side, palm trees line a wide boulevard. Like the cottages, the palms stretch for miles. And the road extends as far as I can see. In front of the palms are the "Privileged units." I can see virtuals waiting for "Jessica," the red-haired sim who will collect their taxes. I know that they risk deletion during stampedes. I pity them.

Stampede Roadway events require a path wide enough to accommodate the frequent parades of the herds through human habitat. All the buildings are in pale shades of summer as if to blend in with what lies behind the Palms. I can also see the bank of a river and clusters of trees.

Directly behind the cottages are square patches of grass, a few picnic tables, and benches here and there. There are a few people sitting at the benches and a couple on the ground. Unless I've already collected their taxes, the people I see are not human; they're sims. No children. I doubt if any virtual has the option of appearing as a child. Those age option years likely disappeared during the early days of Shemathra. I have never liked children, but now, I miss the sight and sound of them.

I dread continuing here. I know I must collect from this last group. My sim is impatient to begin. As I look at the last row of houses along the wide Stampede Avenue, I see virtuals crowding the porches. There's a feeling of resignation. I want to jump back to the Villa and face Miranda, but the sim tells me it's forbidden. So, I'll hide and let the sim do what he must. He's thorough, aware of the tribute due from each virtual. I'm retreating into a dream of small treasures, offered, and approved by a flashing green light.

Virtuals rotate in and out of the line on each of five hundred porches. A set of golf clubs, a diamond bracelet, cyber cash from concerned family members, a ferret sim, and lovebirds in a cage blend with lost years, games, and vintage card decks. In my mind I can see the green light traveling on a Stampede Highway. Where is it going? I want to know, but I'm drowning in the failure of my dream. Four is right, this is my fault; I should have protected Bali Hai. These virtual humans are paying for my mistakes. I can't think about that now.

There's a sidewalk. It looks like the one with the missing wooden planks in Purdy Town, no texture to give it an authentic sensory feel and look, a source of pride and a requirement of all VEI programs, no creases or divisions. Just smooth and dark like a conveyor belt. Where am I?

It's time to jump and warn Mira.

End RECORD

THE NAVY PIER

Colored Lights and the Ferris Wheel.

August 7, 2290

Mira refuses to look at Henry as she huddles on the red couch. Ravi is somewhere in Shemathra and the Grand Stampede is weeks away. Henry insists that she take a few hours to calm herself before she assesses the new challenges including her father's presence in Shemathra and what Gunter has witnessed in the Palms. Henry brings her tea, while she stares at a closed window, not at the man who sits by her side and waits.

Gunter is the tax sim. There's nothing she can do to hide him. Her mind races as she wonders if there's a way to protect Ravi. The Grand Stampede is looming; she needs time to think.

Sending a message bubble to Hosseini, she tells him she needs a day to prepare for the long hours SEINI requires in the days before and after the Grand Stampede. "Make sure you wrap it up soon," Hosseini's response is curt and sinister, but he asks no questions. Mira prays Hosseini doesn't know her father is in Shemathra.

Why Shemathra's Realm? She knows why. Ravi wants to find his father. If Rosalind were in Hell itself, Mira would forsake Heaven to find her. She regrets telling Ravi that she had discovered a copy of Gunter and worse, she had shared her plans to use the copy and his sim to regain control of VEI. She puts the slaughterhouse out of her mind. If necessary, she will do anything, promise anything including trading her grandfather's copy to protect her father.

She shakes her head when Henry insists, "You need a distraction, something to clear your mind." Taking her arm, he marches her into the bedroom and supervises her getting dressed. "We're going out, Mira."

"No! The copy's jumped to the Villa, and I must send him back to find my father."

"You're right, and you will, but first, clear your mind. In your current state your judgment is uncertain. Approach this with more objectivity. Don't forget how vulnerable the copy is to your emotions. He and Ravi are depending on you to get them out safely."

"I'm not in the mood for dinner, let's just take a walk." She isn't ready to leave.

"We're going to the Navy Pier, Mira. Don't argue," Henry ushers her out the front door. The Chicago dusk has dimmed, and yellow-white city lights spring to life as Mira and Henry board a sky tram Express, to the Navy Pier. Colored lights flicker on the huge Ferris wheel which sits near the bistro where Henry had reserved a table. Mira feels like she's dreaming, it's been so long since she has been out among so many people. As they wait to be seated, she watches the line waiting to ride the Ferris wheel, the dark shape of riders as they're lifted high above the pier.

"My father took me all over the world when I was a child." She is surprised by the memory and its bittersweet ache. "When we were in Ireland, there was a small state fair, and Ravi and I rode on a Ferris wheel. I was only six and being up so high terrified me. Ravi kept saying I was perfectly safe. I can't imagine riding this one. My heart would jump out of my chest." She looks up at the wheel as though it might fall on her if she came too close.

"We can ride it together," Henry whispers as he kisses her ear. She shakes her head.

"Not even if I hold you close?"

"Nope," she crosses her arms in mock defiance.

He laughs, feeling relieved. Her sense of humor is returning. "You know the first Ferris Wheel was built right here."

"Really?" Mira was surprised she didn't know this until she remembered the famous White City, Chicago's World Fair. The discussion of Ferris wheels is closed when their table is ready. At dinner, she is surprised at her appetite, eating not only the bruschetta but also most of the pasta dish Henry urges her to try.

After dinner, they walk to the Chicago Shakespeare Theatre. In their travels together, Ravi had taught her to love theatre. Father and daughter had sampled storytelling in small villages as well as theatres in cities, small and large. The play that night, *As You Like it* is one of her favorites. Her mother, Rosalind O'Grady, was like the Rosalind in the play, resourceful and determined. Live theatre, to Mira, is better than holo-films. She prefers its immediacy and unpredictability. Anything can happen.

Riding the sky tram back to the Elysium, Mira feels calmer, better able to face the problems of her father's safety while protecting Gunter. Lucas greets them at their door with a plaintive meow. While Henry feeds the cat, Mira crumbles dry bread for Gunter, the mouse. Had it escaped? Putting the crumbs in its favored corner, she is relieved to see the mouse again. It quickly nibbles its dinner, then standing on its hind legs, it looks at her, wiggles its nose and disappears.

"You're welcome," she sighs. The whole thing reminds her of a children's book. Next time, she would give it some egg, or perhaps cheese. Mice are supposed to like cheese.

Later, as Henry snores beside her, she sits up in alarm. Staring into the darkness, she wonders if it's too late.

***

Options

August 8, 2290

Until she knows it's safe, she dares not enter the program as Miranda Four. After another Board meeting, her mind teems with strategies, and she considers what to do if Hosseini discovers the copy. Options? If he terminates her contract before Gunter finishes, can she get him out? And Ravi, what about her father? He won't leave Gunter behind. It's her fault if Ravi ends his existence while subjected to the worst pain Hosseini can devise. What has she done? The tram glides smoothly to home, and Mira waits for the Elysium elevator, closing her eyes, willing the stress to fade.

The apartment door opens and, she sees Henry relaxing on the couch, his feet on the ottoman. With punctures in its leather, dusted with tufts of fur, the ottoman is the cat's favorite. The cat is stretched on the cushion next to Henry, its feet in the air as Henry scratches its abdomen. Although Gunter, her mouse companion survived, she still ignores the cat. Seeing the challenge of her distain, Lucas the cat leaps onto her lap as she sits. He purrs as she relents and strokes his neck.

"Hungry? Tele-meal has scheduled poached salmon for seven."

"Not now," she says. After dislodging the cat, she collapses on the couch. His tail twitching, the cat jumps onto her lap.

"Go chase something, Lucas, but don't catch Mira's mouse." Henry shoos the cat away. He begins to rub her shoulders. "Wow, you need to relax." He kisses her neck. "My grandmother is right; you have bewitched me."

"Always exaggerating, ever, the politician," Mira laughs. *Can he see she's nervous?*

Henry's family is prominent in Ohio politics, including his uncle, a U.S. senator. There is little to distinguish Henry from any other attractive young man of fifty-five. But his eyes are different. There is a steely pragmatism that frightens her. Who is this man she loves? His sense of humor draws her, as does the symmetry of his face and the way he moves with the grace of an athlete. There's a subtle stillness he possesses and an intellect that observes quietly, then forms opinions.

"Salmon?" She is determined to change the subject.

Shaking his head, he sings his response, "Later."

"But I want to tell you . . ." she protests. He opens her blouse and kisses her breasts. "Later," she murmurs.

Later, Henry warns her again about Hosseini. "You do realize that he's setting you up. He intends to put you in your place?"

"I know," she says. "Whatever it is, I'll deal with it after we eat."

***

Is it safe?

August 9, 2290

The next morning, she scans her work area for peepers. Being Miranda Four requires extreme care. Shortly after moving in, Henry had discovered peepers embedded in the housekeeping unit. Hosseini's doing, of course.

"Until Hosseini replaces or repairs this unit, allow the peepers to stay in place; their eyes are mostly dead," Henry said. Frequent scans for hidden units throughout the apartment are negative. Predictably, most surveillance bots, due to SEINI's lax maintenance policy, are inactive. Henry redirects the rest to empty rooms, away from Mira.

The sound of a double bell cuts through all of Henry's assurances that she is safe. He's done it again. Gunter has jumped without permission. No longer in the Palms South, the copy is back at the Villa. When Gunter left Purdy Town early and returned to the Villa, all her fears, the "what-if" questions clouded her thinking. Does he want to get caught? How much clearer can she be? He returned to the Villa, again without asking permission or even warning her! There might have been more evidence to record there.

She does a frantic scan. Was his activity detected? It doesn't appear so. Her heart pounds as she controls her breathing. As her heart resumes its regular rhythm, it's time to deal with her foolish grandfather.

The coming Shemathra Grand Stampede pageantry will command bio and virtual media coverage. Before the communication shutdown, a handful of virtuals managed to send messages to their families, conveying the truth of Shemathra.

SEINI claimed disgruntled employees had created a viral lie, one promoted by bio relatives eager to access funds that belong to SEINI. Hosseini had been livid. After forcing them to recant, he sent the whistle-blowers to slaughter.

Then, Shemathra went dark, a decision, Hosseini claims, made by the herds, the majority of Shematha's virtual population. "The Herds have decided to avoid the pollution of the bio world," Hosseini announced. It was religious liberty.

SHEMATHRA'S REALM

Terry's message

V. Loc: The Villa

August 9, 2290

"Gunter?"

"Hello Four."

I'm in the hammock. Everything is white again, okay. Ah, I hear the ocean. And Four is here. "Why did it take you so long to get me out?"

Four doesn't answer my question. Instead, she moves inside and sits in a rattan chair. "Shall we have coffee?" Reluctantly, I vacate the hammock and move inside to the couch.

"Okay," I say. (There's something I should do—What?) The coffee appears in a black cup. For some reason, I begin to cry. I'm embarrassed. Four looks away while I rein in my emotions. "Why did it take so long, Four? I thought we agreed I could choose when to come back here." There's a sheepish look on her face. She forgot that she said I could jump back if I thought it necessary.

"I—I am sorry, yes, you're right. The Palms is Shemathra's largest human community and collecting taxes there takes considerable time. Since you're back early, the official reason is 'maintenance.' There has been a change, something that would have made your discovery a disaster. While you slept, I downloaded the information you recorded. Though I haven't processed it, I'm sure what you witnessed is helpful. We'll need more."

I'm angry now. "Send me to another program or delete me. What I saw was heartbreaking; I want no more of it."

Four shakes her head.

"I won't go back until I'm ready."

Four turns away. Clearly, she is indifferent to my distress. Maybe, she's being careful, and she can't react. I see the circling crows as they dip and rise. Through the terrace doors, I see them circling. They know, they know I'm not a sim!

"Fortunately, you had collected your quota. If you hadn't, I would have been unable to call you back under the guise of "maintenance." She points at me. *"Gunter sim, you will remain in the villa and sit on the coding couch. Your performance is unsatisfactory. I must make code adjustments to improve your efficiency,"*

"Yes Miranda, I will prepare for recoding. I look forward to resuming my work."

She shuts the terrace doors, I now sit inside the villa, hoping that I've done enough, and she'll send me to a safer program. Do the spies know? Wait, what about Terry's message?

"Gunter, you must be more careful."

"Who is Terry?" I ask.

"Terry?" Four looks concerned, as if my file were fragmenting before her eyes.

"There's a woman there who, who . . ."

"Who?" Four demands. *"What are you talking about?"* She is almost shrill. How do I get away?

"You'll see it when you play the download. She was with Ravi, your father and my—."

"Is Terry a human virtual or a sim? What does she want? Oh, God! You saw Ravi? You saw my father?"

"Yes, he was with Terry. I am supposed to tell you—Terry has a message for you!" Now she's crying. What should I do? "Terry's message is 'Tell Mira she's in danger, Mira's in danger.' That's what the old woman said! Four, Mira, the old woman urged me to warn you."

"Warn me?"

"She said you're in danger. Hosseini is a threat, and he wants you as a virtual, here, in Shemathra."

"Hosseini will never find me here. But I am worried about Ravi and you."

"You're wrong, when you uploaded and created Four, you copied yourself and gave Hosseini access to your file.

"You don't know that."

"My guess is, if you read your employment agreement, you'll discover it was added as soon as Hosseini discovered you had created an AI here, separate from Miranda Three. I'm not sure if he knows about me. He's probably amused since nothing your AI discovers is admissible as evidence of a crime. Am I correct? No data recorded by an AI is admissible?"

"Yes Gunter, you are." She whispers.

"Your only card is he doesn't know about me. Four, he has you. If you die as a bio, even if you purchase a different after-death package, even if it's with another provider, it makes no difference. That copy will be destroyed. Your file here as Four will become the only you."

For the first time, Four is speechless. She's obviously frightened. Before she panics, I need the answers she agreed to give me. "I will tell you more, but I want to know everything, including every truth about my former self and anything that's new."

Four sighs. *"Where do you want me to begin? It will be the unvarnished truth."*

"Tell me more about Eric Holden. Why did he claim to be my father?"

"There is a buried childhood memory your other self finally accessed. As his copy, you have it. I can make it available if you want, though I must warn you it is extremely painful. In it, you are a toddler. Your mother refuses to reconcile with Eric, her ex-husband. You witness her tears when she comes for you after Eric kidnapped you. Then he forces her to submit to rape if she wants you returned to her. You hear him threaten to kill your father if he stays in your life. Eric boasts he will use his wealth and political connections to declare himself your biological father. Again, I can make this available if you desire."

"That won't be necessary, thank you, Four. I can't . . . you must be wrong. When this is over, I'll get it sorted out and you'll discover there was some mistake. I—if you're right, then I must . . . This is devastating. Did Eric kill my mother?"

Four won't look at me. I can see she's upset. The wild thought in my head is that next time, there will be a white cup.

"Yes, Gunter, and also your father."

Oh God, no! Oh God—how can I—I thought he loved me, and to do . . . This is too much! What else? I close my eyes for a moment. Moving to the hammock. I put myself in a dream-memory state. *Mom and I are at the park. We're eating sandwiches and talking to Mom's friend, Mr. Donald and . . .*

Then Four brings me back from escape. *"Gunter? I'm sorry."*

"I see, thank you, Four, for allowing me to step away."

"There are other things you should know. Some of it might destabilize you as a file, so I have temporarily modified your ability to respond emotionally to select events."

"I understand. The story of how VEI and Bali Hai came to this can wait."

She turns away. *"I see that you need more time to recover. Tell me about Terry and if you believed her."*

"She was old, about cen-seventy something. She had a husband named Ned who is now a steer, and yes, I believe her and, uh, she had beautiful eyes."

"Fine, Grandfather, I'll look at the recordings to see if I can learn more about Terry. In the meantime, I'm putting you in a dream-memory state. We can talk afterwards. I want to know about my father. Is he safe?"

"Yes, for now, at least. Thank you, Four, about . . . never mind."

I'm dreaming, there's floating pieces of bread. Mom and I are feeding the ducks.

VIA AUDIO BUBBLE (PRIVATE)

URGENT, August 12, 2290

Byron—It is urgent that I meet with you in person (alone) within the next twenty-four hours. I am deeply concerned. I think I might be under surveillance.

Other than your immediate colleagues, are there others who are aware of your investigation? If so, what are their priorities? I realize how important this investigation is to your office and to the bio members of certain Shemathra residents. Last night, I sent you a second set of files related to Holden's tax collecting and his interactions in the Palms colony. Due to the situation with my father, I am fearful for my safety and his.

I worry that unanswered questions might result in my making a mistake and all will be lost. The copy of Gunter Holden keeps asking me: "When will you have enough information?" Learning the truth about his past and life's work ending in a nightmare has almost broken him. Only the threat of abandoning him to the slaughterhouse has kept his cooperation. I wish I had other options. For now, he is continuing to cooperate. As you instructed, I inserted the code you gave me into the white ribbon.

Can you review these latest files and meet me in Chicago? I cannot stress the importance. I will message the time and place to your office. Mira

CHICAGO RIVER OLD SAVEMO CENTER

Food Court Robots

August 14, 2290

While Byron Hernandez stands in the *Deep-Dish Pizza* line, Mira waits for him and calms her nerves. The food court benches and tables haven't changed in two hundred years. She is surprised by how uncomfortable they are. The massive store is part of Chicago lore. Truly historic. Hundreds of years earlier, it was called a Big Box store. Now, it is a mind-bending collection of furniture, technology and artifacts spanning the history of Chicago commerce from the early two twentieth century to the present. But with hard benches.

"Attention, all shoppers! ROBOTEC's new 'Sim-biotics' are life-like service units, now available at SAVEMO. The New York Times says 'ROBOTEC does it again! The next step is mind-downloads, transferring the minds of virtuals from after-death worlds, back to bio existence! See the real world in a designer sim body!' TECH TODAY says, 'Astoundingly life-like!' If it's not ROBOTEC, it's not a sim-bot, it's a robot. All units come with housekeeping apps. Check ROBOTEC@holos.org."

A sim-bot riding a glide-cart holds a tray of seaweed and cultured crab dip. Extending the tray, it asks, *"Care for a sample?"*

The bot's red boots are part of the glide-cart, and its manicured hand has the faint image of RBT in Edwardian script. The name "Amanda" is printed on a clear lavender label attached to the right cuff of its white blouse. Is there another table, one away from the smell of half-eaten hot dogs? Mira had tasted one once and has never forgotten its texture, the rubbery skin and the pink layers of cultured beef.

A clean-up robot is nearing her table, and she decides to stay put. Besides, the smell of steamed cultured beef reminds her of Ravi and the time he took her to this same historic Savemo. He had urged her to try it. After one bite, she decided she didn't like it. Now, the smell of a hot dog reminds her of Ravi, and she wants to cry.

No need to be polite; it's only a robot.

Then the sim-bot asks again, *"Are you sure? You look a little pale."*

Does this thing have a bio upload? How much did someone download into this unit? What or whose memories does 'Amanda' possess? How much memory defines a human being? No one truly knows. Mira shakes her head to clear her thoughts. "Show 'lamps,'" she tells the waiting monitor.

From the screen, a holo of the SAVEMO elf pops up. After doing a cartwheel, it sits on the table and asks, *"Certainly! Anything in particular?"*

"Something vintage," she answers. When she was a child, Ravi had taken her here. The elf had scared her, despite Ravi's assurances that it was only an image, meant to amuse.

"Coming up," the elf chirps as it drops into a deep, holo box. Within seconds, a wagon wheel of lamps emerges from the box and hovers in the middle of her Food Court table. Tiffany lamps, bright spiders, lamps with antique green shades or a soft rose glow as the wheel begins to rotate. Each lamp image pauses as the elf describes the lamp's history. The wheel of lamps freezes as the elf offers payment plans.

Mesmerized by floating lamps, Mira is startled to see Byron holding plates of deep-dish pizza.

"Pause display," she orders.

"Will do," the elf says. It grabs the lamp wheel and puts it into a sack, the elf's legs dangle as the image freezes and the elf and its sack sit on the edge of the table.

"As you requested," Byron says, "artichoke." Byron sets the plate down with the flourish of a head waiter. He sits on the hard SAVEMO seat and stretches his legs under the bright orange table. She wants to laugh. The enamel seats aren't designed for the comfort of anyone, especially those over six feet four.

Impossibly slender with narrow shoulders and long legs, Byron is at least six feet five inches. She likes his face, with his intelligent brown eyes and a long straight nose and his reddish-brown hair which resists the coaxing of any brush, comb, or gel. Sleepy Hollow's Ichabod Crane comes to mind. Suppressing a giggle, she wonders if her amusement is really a way of coping with her fear.

"So, Mira," Byron says. He's sizing her up, she thinks, evaluating her trustworthiness, and how tough an opponent she might be. He can't help it, she thinks, considering what he does. "First, let me say what a pleasure to meet you in person and, and—" he clears his throat and sighs.

He's nervous too. There's a lot at stake for both of us.

"Second, I want to thank you for how helpful to our cause you have been and—'

She cuts him off. "Byron, I'm not here to be thanked. My father Ravi is no longer a bio and for some reason, he has transitioned to Shemathra's Realm. I want, I demand, a guarantee of his safety. If you can't do that, I will remove the Holden copy and place him in storage. If necessary, I'll use the copy to protect my father. Also, I've learned that my life is in danger."

Before Byron can answer, the food court disappears. There's a breeze. Mira knows it's a Savemo enhancement to better sell the pretense. They are at a picnic table in a park. Shops dot streets that frame a town square. The food court people sit at other picnic tables and those going in and out of the quaint shops and eateries are not people at all; they're illusions.

The look of confusion on Byron's face tells Mira that he is not a Savemo customer. "We're in Woodsville, Byron," Mira tells him. "It's Savemo's pitch for their discount after-death destination. In fifteen seconds, we will hear whatever special offer they're making for September."

Phantom boys on glide boards are crossing the street, then disappear, replaced by a parade of people dressed as skeletons who freeze in mid-step.

A woman's silky voice says, *"For those who love the idea of a small town after-death destination but want a change now and then, SAVE-MO's September after-death savings offers our Woodsville package with the option of a yearly week's vacation and a big town event. If you upload and join us in 2291, in 2292, you'll visit a spectacular after death New Orleans!"*

The "Bone Gang" continues its march, stepping to the sounds of a blues band. "So much to see in this beautiful old city," the silken voice continues its spin. *"Yes, next year's vacation for Woodville residents will be in New Orleans, including Mardi Gras! See the fabled Bourbon Street,' stay in one of the beautiful old hotels and meet the ghosts of the eerie La Laurie Mansion. Contact our after-death representatives for more details and the deal of an "afterlife time."*

Byron winces at the "afterlife time" finish.

"Mira, you're in danger? How can I help? You live in a building owned by Donovan Hosseini, so my hands are tied in terms of arranging security for you. I can't guarantee that your dad will be safe. I wish I could. I will do my best to protect him." He sighs. "I do know he desires what we all want. Safety and wellbeing are important to all Shemathra's virtual residents. To do that, Hosseini must be brought to justice. The best way you can help your father is to protect his father. Help Gunter finish what he has started."

So, if he can offer no protection for her, nor for her father what is Hernandez good for? She thinks of Gunter's ghosts, recorded holos of the fallen climbers of Everest. Overwhelmed, tears well-up before she can stop them. She takes a deep breath and wills them back. "My father is my priority. If it means my grandfather must face the slaughterhouse, I will trade him for Ravi's safety."

Byron adjusts his seat to accommodate his sinewy frame. As he straightens up, he reminds her of a cobra about to attack and Hosseini's demon genie floods her mind. She trembles as, unbidden, a wheel of new lamps appears on their table. Byron is alarmed. What is happening to this girl? Is she ill? He knows that a health emergency will draw attention, but he won't abandon her.

Mira stills her shaking hands and says, "Lamps gone."

"Let me know if there's anything I can show you! The elf waves a tiny hand and says goodbye.

"Are you okay?" Byron asks her. He wants to hold her hand but doesn't.

She nods and he wishes that were so.

"I'm sorry, Mira! I know that you love your dad. If this investigation breaks down, I swear I'll personally do everything I can to make sure Ravi is safe. Your grandfather too. I can arrange limited surveillance to protect you outside your building to make you feel safer."

She shakes her head. "The code, you sent me, are you sure it's safe? Where did you get it? Despite what I said, I care what happens to Gunter."

As he studies her, his brown eyes fill with a cold intelligence. "I can't tell you where it came from. It's old-school and hard to detect. I'm told your skills as an AI specialist are exceptional. Part of what I do is knowing who to trust. I'm asking you to trust me. Hosseini is a monster. He is a parasite infecting the entire after-death industry. To stop him we need your help. And Gunter's." He wonders if she trusts him. Can he trust her not to make a deal with Hosseini?

There's nothing else she can say. "Okay, I'll send along whatever he records. Let me know . . . let me know if anything changes and you can help my father."

The sadness on her face alarms him. She rises to leave and a small dog, a whitish terrier runs, its leash dangling from its neck and she reaches to catch the leash but just misses it as it skips along the SAVEMO concrete floor. Without a word, afraid it will be injured or worse, Mira leaves Byron. She means to rescue the little animal. Byron shouts for her to stop but she doesn't hear him, and he follows her to a row clogged with stacked appliances and all the shoppers and their carts, the elves chirping and the faint echoes of the deep hall.

He knows she's not safe. Someone with a large floating cart blocks his access and he hurries to the next aisle and rounds the far corner. In the middle of the row, Mira holds and comforts the little white dog. It's shaking and she's stroking its ears and whispering to it. At the end of the aisle, Byron sees a man signally to a woman with cold eyes, and he knows *Mira is right about Hosseini, he thinks.* They could be SEINI assassins, looking for the right opportunity. *NO!* Just above her, a seismic tremble rattles a stack of boxed housekeeping robots, the highest box dipping, beginning to tumble. His long legs are a blur as he rushes to grab Mira and the dog. Twisting his tall, thin frame into a protective arc, Byron sweeps them from the boxes' path, preventing them from being crushed.

When he sees same man and woman appear on the other side of the stack, he records a holo of them, tapping the camera embedded in his left cornea. The man whispers to the woman who shakes her head. When he sees Byron, the man says something through gritted teeth as he takes the woman's arm. She's shaking her head, pulls her arm away from his grip and points at him. They turn away, disappearing behind a row of holo receivers as Byron helps Mira to her feet. She continues to comfort the shaking animal, which is yipping in terror. Byron scans the crowd for other threats. What if he hadn't followed Mira?

Damn Hosseini. Someone was waiting for the right opportunity, and Mira was meant to die. People begin to clap as a large older woman runs to Mira. "Trixie! You scared me!" Hurriedly using her shapeless sweater, the woman wraps Trixie in its generous cable knit and takes her shivering dog from Mira's arms. Crying, she rubs her face against Trixie's neck, whispers, "Thank you!" to Mira, who like Trixie, can't stop shaking. As the woman moves away, Mira sees the older woman's back heave with emotion and the dog's tail wags furiously as they go.

"I am in danger," she thinks. *Can Hernandez do anything?*

Byron waits to see if she's steady on her feet. She hesitates before saying, "I'm fine."

He knows she's lying and insists on walking her to the glide tram. "Be careful, Mira. I hope you know who you're facing."

She whispers, "Thank you, I'll let you know when I have more data."

Chicago, Elysium

Mira's Gray Fox

August 18, 2290

As, one by one, she drags the rolls of carpet into a closet, she can't look at them. Each rug is from a trip she took with Ravi. She pushes the last carpet, the one from the Selenge Steppe into place and as she shuts the closet door, she sees a piece of cloth. Rubbing it with her thumbs, she smooths the felt. Ah, it is the gray fox.

All the houses are round. She is six and Ravi is a guest of KAHNCO Cultured Meat Products, a giant of the industry. "The soil slept and now, the grass has returned." Ravi explains. Winds poured into the valley, cooling the hot sun and the biting winters released their grip. The people and their yurts never left. Small flocks of sheep and a few yaks survived. And the horses, the marvelous horses of the Steppe run free again.

Ravi holds her hand as they watch the riders perform tricks, their horses galloping. She's alarmed when the riders lean far back and to the side.

"Why don't they fall off the horses" Before he can answer, Mira asks another question. "Why are all the houses round?" Ravi whispers the answers in her ear.

"They're pretending to be like the fearsome warriors of a long-ago army. The round houses are called yurts, Mira. We'll be staying the night in one and you can see how wonderful they are." The host is a rich man who owns a cultured meat plant in Ulan batar. They are in the Orkhon Valley now.

The wind sings sweetly through vents of the spacious ger. Ravi had told her this would be their last trip together for a while. "Why didn't you tell me later," she cried. But she knows there is no good time.

"You need to go to school," he said.

"Why can't you be my teacher?"

"I can't. Please Mira, accept this." She turns away.

After dinner, while the adults are feasting, she hears strange, guttural voices, some kind of recording. "Are they singing?" She asks. The voices are scary.

"The song is about the great Genghis Khan." Orghana tells her. "He led armies that changed the world, you know." Orghana, who is eleven, strokes Mira's hair. "Here, I have a gift for you." It is the little fox. "There's a story," Orghana says, "where a fox lies to a child, claiming that her mother is dead. The fox wants the child to go with him and leave the mother. But the mother is alive and the child stays. These little foxes hang over your bed for protection."

"Why does the fox say he will protect? He's already a liar."

Orghana shrugged. "It's just the story. Maybe the fox feels bad, I don't know."

"But my mother is already dead. The ice made her fall into the glacier" Mira shakes her head.

Putting her arm around Mira, Orghana whispers, "I'm sorry your mother is gone." She presses the felt animal in Mira's hand. "They also protect you from bad dreams."

Earlier, the older girl had shown Mira how to wear the traditional deel which had been presented to Mira along with all the gifts Ravi received. Mira loved it because it looked like a dress but wasn't, She especially loved the long sleeves. Still, she knows she will never wear it. The Patel boys would laugh at her.

After reviewing them herself, she sends Gunter's newest recordings to Byron. Resting her head on her desk, her mind is a torment of anxiety and recrimination. Why was Ravi so foolish? Didn't he know the danger? He could have picked another, safer program, not Shemathra, not any after-death program Hosseini could access. There's a faint glow on the Buddha's belly where the audio messenger sits. Sliding the receiver into her ear, she hears Byron's acknowledgement of the new memory records.

Via audio bubble (private)

August 18, 2290

Mira—The recent files you sent are very helpful. I know that you have concerns regarding Ravi's welfare and yours as well. Let me assure you that everything that can be done, will be done.

Regarding your grandfather, I agree that given his history and his recent experiences in Shemathra, managing this situation is challenging. There are aspects of his past that I recommend you not share with him, especially negative messages regarding how Holden was viewed by VEI employees. My guess is that this assessment was not entirely accurate. In addition, it could have a deleterious effect on your grandfather.

As you have said, Holden does appear to be in a fragile state. Still, it is vital that we find a way to ensure his cooperation. Please know that your work is vital to bringing justice to Shemathra's Realm. I look forward to your next report and files. Byron

***

Henry's graceful fingers are a blur as he places a mug of tea next to a blueberry muffin. Kissing her ear, he whispers one word to her: "Peepers." Questions might arise and she must calm herself. She sips her tea and pinches the edges of her muffin. Henry is changing their sleep sheets, creating order in the disheveled room. She often teases him about his neatness compulsion. Now, she clings to his sense of order as she steadies herself.

After scrubbing and sanitizing the bathroom's retro black and white floor (the mirror audio receptor was relocated to the Buddha as a precaution), the housekeeping drone is busy with the living room carpet. Where can they talk?

Henry takes her hand, and they leave the apartment, riding the old service elevator to the penthouse. The Elysium is in decline, its apartments outdated, and the carpets faded. After Holden's suicide, the penthouse stayed empty, sealed off as a crime scene. Housekeeping drones are stacked on the penthouse floor which had been stripped of carpet, various tools lay haphazardly throughout, and scraps of carpet pile against the wall.

Gunter shot himself on this penthouse deck almost two hundred years ago. Piles of dead leaves and stray branches carpet the deck's battered surface. Life has taken root in the decay. There's a stack of folding chairs, matted with vines and old leaves where birds nest in the in between spaces. Perhaps the mouse named Gunter came from here. Often, at night, she and Henry bring folding chairs and sit on the deck.

Thanks to Henry and a mid-22nd century cloaking device, they relax in the shadows, away from the sun, and almost invisible. Chicago winds, the river, and a sound blocker in Henry's pockets assure them, they won't be overheard. The shimmering sky reminds her of Gunter's thoughts as he studied at the moon, moments before he shot himself. Byron had made a portion of Holden's memories available to her. Some of it angered her, especially the murders of Jacob and Laura, Gunter's young wife. After learning his victims mind-uploaded to Bali Hai, Gunter shot himself to upload and follow. She had watched the moon through his eyes as he spent his last hours as a bio on the penthouse deck.

"Yes, I processed your grandpa's latest recordings and his memories." Henry squeezes her hand. "The two of you are alike, driven to succeed on your own terms."

Although she has made the same conclusion, Mira bristles at Henry's remark. "We both saw my grandfather fail when up against Hosseini. What can we do, how do we make sure that he succeeds this time?"

When Henry is silent, Mira begins to panic. *What isn't he saying?* She wants Henry's help making a new plan, something to save Ravi, restore VEI and hopefully, protect her grandfather from the slaughterhouse. She sees the pale arc of the afternoon moon. Aided by the decrease in world's human population, the air is cleaner. The Virtual New Deal claims to be a social engineering solution addressing the cries of the anti-virtuals. All citizens, including the very poor can end their bio life between cen-forty and cen-fifty and upload to basic after-death programs. Anyone can spend limitless after-death years in virtual communities.

"When there are fewer elders," Ravi had asked her, "what happens to their wisdom when they're suddenly young again in an after-death program? Do they repeat the same mistakes?"

"I don't know," she admitted. Gunter rode Babylon Dreams, the roller coaster to oblivion, she thinks, but the Bali Hai residents he left are still suffering.

Hosseini expects her to continue, making up the hours she missed. She must figure out what to do, a solution that will protect her father and lead to her reclaiming VEI. She wonders how Henry learned that Ravi was in Shemathra but puts that question aside for now. She needs Henry's help. As they leave the penthouse, she whispers, "We should go where there are no peepers."

"*Noodlesmith,*" Henry nods. The restaurant is on the Chicago River near the old Wrigley Building. Rarely crowded due to the noise from the river running through its aging platform, the eatery's thick canopy makes it a safe place to talk. Plus, Henry loves the food. A picky eater (Henry's opinion), Mira is indifferent to the menu's fifty "famous" noodle dishes. Embedded between a glossy protective cover and planks of ancient oak are digital images of the original *Noodlesmith* founders, Stan and Stacy Long. Smart chairs adjust to assure comfort, and Henry says, "Menu."

As she runs her finger on the menu holo that hovers above their table, Mira knows what she will order. Always the same. A waiter in his cen-forties takes their orders. She wonders if the old waiter will be there the next time they come for dinner. Will he be gone, replaced by a sim-bot? While Henry samples the shitake scaloppini, Mira barely touches her marinara spaghetti. She had caught the odor of a cultured lamb dish on its way to a nearby table, and almost fainted, catching Henry's hand to steady herself. Though this meat was grown in a factory vat, it reminded her of the Shemathra herds. More than a century has passed since *Noodlesmith* served this dish, using a slaughtered animal, one deleted from the earth in a place much like Shemathra,

"You need to eat more, Mira. I know I sound like my grandmother, but if you get sick, no one benefits." Henry does sound like his grandmother. Mira manages to eat a bread stick and a few bites of marinara.

She looks around. *Can anyone hear us?* "Did you finish reviewing the memories?"

Henry reaches across the table and pats her hand. "We're fine, here. "Embedded in smooth surface of every Noodlesmith table are digitals of old paper menus and images of diners from the twenty-second century.

As Henry reassures her, a holo image of Hossieni pops into view, suspended over the river. A current news story reports hundreds of people from an anti-virtuals group, picketing SEINI's New York offices until men in unidentified uniforms beat protestors, injuring dozens of anti-virtuals. When the police arrived, the uniformed assailants disappeared.

Ten people are hospitalized and three have died. Hosseini denies responsibility: "We had nothin' to do with this." When asked about rumors of a Congressional investigation concerning SEINI, Hosseini answers, "Not a chance. We virtuals have rights!"

Henry sighs, a clear sign that despite his professed confidence, Henry is rattled by the holo of Hosseini so close to their private table. They watch as the reporter questions Selma Rock, the current leader of the anti-virtual movement. Rock's smooth voice is full of concern. "The right to virtual life should not depend on whatever currency and resources you have. Everyone should be able to make that choice."

The reporter nods her head. "Uh huh. What do you say to some-one like Donovan Hosseini, who claims that he can make a low-cost after-death program available?"

Selma Rock shakes her head. "I managed to obtain a copy of Hos-seini's proposal under the "Freedom of Information Act." His plan is laughable. First, there are no nanobots, so you would need to pre-record your memory upload. And you must keep it updated. Second, to stay within your memory allotment, you will need to edit your memory record. Any memory containing intense emotion would be either erased or abbreviated. The amount of memory allotment is so low, residents wouldn't be virtuals at all, but glorified sims."

Scraping the remaining noodles onto his fork, Henry finishes his scaloppini. "Let's order dessert." She starts to protest. "We'll share one, Mira. We should take advantage of the privacy here."

While Mira toys with her spaghetti, Henry orders a poached pear. A holo of Hosseini pops up again; there's a general groan and someone turns off the news. A stream of soft music flows through *Noodlesmith.*

A new waiter brings the pear. Henry tries to hide his discomfort, but she knows his mood has changed. From the soft insinuation of impatience in its voice, he suspects this waiter is a hybrid, a human mind downloaded into a synthetic body. Rather than opt to be uploaded into an after-death program, some choose to stay in the bio world, forced into servitude by those who fund the synthetic and its human download. She knows Henry is wary of what will happen if the definition of a human being keeps changing. This will be their last meal at *Noodlesmith*'s.

Changing the subject, she asks, "How do we keep Gunter going? What should I do? So how do I convince him to put himself at risk?"

"Tell him about Bali Hai's success," Henry advises. "Explain that it was once the standard of excellence for the entire after-death industry. If his former self hadn't decided to commit murder and follow his victims into virtual reality, it still would be. With Gunter's influence compromised, Hosseini saw an opportunity. Although he's a copy, he is legally Gunter Holden. He should take some responsibility for the actions of the original one."

Mira taps her fingertip on the table, a sign that she is frustrated. Henry offers her a spoonful of candied pear, which she reluctantly accepts. "Shemathra is a disgrace," he says, "and its existence is partly because of your grandfather's former self. Convince Gunter that the plight of the poor virtuals who trusted the promises he made *is* his responsibility. Only he can make it right and defeat the person who destroyed his dream. The information he records there is admissible evidence that can be used against SEINI."

Mira rests her chin on the outside of her hand, a gesture that Henry finds endearing. She considers his suggestions. "Are we making a mistake, asking so much of him? He's not that strong. I've seen him ignore my warnings more than once."

"The original Gunter didn't have you looking out for him," he tells her.

"I hope it's enough, Henry."

He takes her hand and kisses it. "I'm going to tell you something and you must do your best not to react. If I could safely tell you in the comfort of our bed, I would. The attack on you in SAVEMO, I admit, has left me shaken. In a few days, I'll be gone on assignment—"

"What, what kind of assignment?" Her eyes fill with angry tears; she whispers, "Who are you, Henry? I need you; how can you leave and not—"

"Don't you know I would tell you if I could?" His face crumbles as he presses her hand to his cheek. "I love you and I wish. . . Soon, I hope to tell you, please believe me, and you won't be alone, someone will make sure you are safe. Please trust me."

Seeing the desperate vulnerability his face, she nods, "Okay."

Later, when they are home, Henry checks for active peepers. Mira turns on the bedroom light and studies the plasma garment that transports her into virtual reality as Miranda Four. Her grandfather has met his son in Shemathra. Maybe it will make no difference. Possibly, it will be the end of everything. An overwhelmed Gunter could demand to be put back in storage. Why would Ravi do this? He knows how awful it is for human virtuals in Shemathra. But she knows why. He wanted to meet Gunter, his father.

Should she give Gunter up to Hosseini in exchange for Ravi? No, never. Plus, there would be no guarantee that Hosseini would keep his word and allow her to take Ravi out of Shemathra. So long as Ravi is there, she is helpless. This may be the end of her dream of reclaiming VEI. If she transfers Ravi to another program, he'll forgive her, but he would never recover from the pain of losing his father. She cannot change what has happened. Hosseini knows about Four. If she reacts, he may spring whatever trap he has waiting. She can't let him know she knows. Until Hosseini is gone, she will sleep but not dream.

Mira Patel and
Mischievous Doings

SEINI Chicago Wrigley Offices

August 20, 2290

The thought torments her: Hosseini knows about Four. If Hosseini discovers what she is doing, what will he do to Ravi? She reassures herself. *He's occupied with The Great Stampede. It's scheduled for the end of August.* Then what? How long before someone tells him about Ravi's death? She hears the soft hum of the floating AI as it passes behind her. Another SEINI spy.

And Terry, what does she want? Mira found Terry in the original Gunter's Bali Hai memories. Other than Gunter's recordings, why can't she find a trace of her in Shemathra? She could be dangerous.

"Mr. Hosseini wants you at the meeting at three." The AI returns and brushes its limp feelers on her shoulder.

"I'm in the middle of the *Arabian Nights Genie* AI program design. Couldn't it wait?"

The AI shakes its pie-shaped head. "Three o'clock, Mira, if you want to keep your job."

After squeezing her shoulder with three jointed pincers, it records the holo images of serpents and fanged ghouls that caper inches above her monitor. Satisfied that it sees no "mischievous doings" the pie shape pulls itself into a smooth dish, twirls and leaves her. She hates the phrase, "mischievous doings." It's a threat.

She sends a quick holo message to let Henry know that she'll be late, then returns to the genie design. Hosseini wants to approve the results and plans to use coding from his own files. After test marketing the Hosseini-as-genie concept, Mira knows that there is no way the *Arabian Nights* after-death program will be approved using Hosseini's image and persona. She needs a genie who won't unnerve prospective residents. With her father in Shemathra and Gunter masquerading as a sim tax collector, Mira looks for a way to approach the boss with the "failed genie" report.

It occurs to her to consult Henry regarding the genie design and marketing problem. Marketing is part of his job. She holos Henry again.

"What's going on, Mira?" Henry smiles. He'll be gone in a few days and then what? "How about garlic chicken tonight."

"Garlic chicken is fine," she tells him. He blows her a kiss, a sign he is hiding the content of their holo call. Instead, he substitutes a longer dinner plan conversation.

Hidden from SEINI, the rest of their conversation concerns Hosseini's genie obsession. "Henry, I have a marketing problem.

I need your advice." She tells him about the Hosseini-as-genie concept. He stifles a laugh, aware of the chance that she might be under observation.

"Okay," he says, "try this: some people love danger and a good scare. Do searches and find prospective bio clients who love wicked witches, vampires, demons, you know what I'm saying. Inform the would-be genie that unless he wants to find the cold eye of Congress taking a hard look into his new after-death genie program because, say, there's another mysterious rash of deletions and missed bio/virtual communications, there should be a respite option, a way to escape the evil genies, into some sort of garden or magic castle, paradise, you know what I mean."

She thinks of Bali Hai. "Henry, you're brilliant and I love you!" He blows her a kiss as his holo disappears. He'll be gone for a few days, that's all. Will he be back in time? The last day in August is almost here.

***

August is an anxious month because it ends in the Grand Stampede. Holos of SEINI board members form a circle as they wait for Donovan Hosseini to appear. All members are silent, their faces tense. Mira sits alone in the dark gallery of empty seats. A dim light shines on her as she sees the room's center fill with color. The rainbow llama, Urcuchillay makes an appearance. After this image is transmitted to all news outlets owned or controlled by SEINI and a few that are not, the llama disappears and a holo of naked cen-forties Donovan Hosseini settles.

He's sitting on a throne, his short, thin legs crossed at the ankle. The legs of the throne end in the feet of enormous wildebeests. An array of antlers and horns fan across the top.

"I see all my favorite bio people are here." Although he appears human, Hosseini still bellows. He sneaks a look around the room and looks for absences, then shifts his age to a youthful sixty. His chest and arms ripple as he adjusts from his sixties to forty-two. His hair is mango orange, slicked back and caught in a thin braid.

"How's my favorite bio girl? What's the news on my genie idea?" His eyes have a dangerous flicker.

"There is a lot of interest, sir." Her lips fixed in a tight smile, she is certain he'll see her shaking hands." It doesn't matter; he thrives on the fear of others. "We should have a campaign up and running within two months; brilliant idea, your Greatness."

Taking an interminable amount of time, his Greatness nods, the back and forth slow at first until it speeds to a cartoon blur of motion. Mira is alarmed. Is he fragmenting?

"I knew it, knew, knew, knew, KNEW it!" He roars. "So, my take is that I am the genie, meaning I promise my likeness isn't really scary, just terrifying." He smirks and winks at her.

Mira starts to respond but Hosseini puts his hand up to stop.

"I'm a big pussycat, come on!" On cue, everyone laughs.

When Hosseini scowls at the thought of being a joke, everyone grows silent.

Then he changes the subject. "I got ideas, look!"

Hosseini's body expands into a scaly giant, a ten feet tall lizard topped by a humanoid head. The bulging lizard eyes are yellow; inky pupils swim on the surface. Hosseini smiles a red smile with razor teeth. When he opens it to speak, a lizard tongue darts out.

"Whaddya think?"

Trying not to shudder, Mira responds, "Overwhelming, sir. Very frightening!"

Satisfied, he shrinks down to his younger version. "Okay, watch this!"

He morphs into something fifteen feet tall. The look is more human but several times more horrid. He's a demon. The skin is a blistering red. The air surrounding it shimmers with menace and the hands grasp a burning throne. Then the head changes into the head of a steer, breathing fire from its heaving nostrils. A set of enormous horns wave and dip toward the alarmed board members.

Hosseini's devil is only a holo image, but Mira is as still as a mouse. Hosseini chuckles, "I see that I have everyone's attention." He points a claw-tipped finger at her. "Mira, I want these options tested. I have other genie ideas, but we'll start with these."

"Yes, your Greatness," Mira tries to steady her voice.

The demon vanishes and Hosseini as his sixties-self reappears. "No excuses, understand? I got things to do."

"Understood," she tells him.

He smiles as he studies her. "You know, I need a good assistant. Regrettably, I hadda let the last one go. She was great for a long time, but I came to know that she forgot her place, a real shame. Now, a guy named Diego, one of my steers, takes care of things for me. He's an idiot, but he does what he's told, which is okay for now. I need someone smart, just not too smart for their own good, like the last one. If, God forbid, somethin' should happen to you, I mean bio-wise, Shemathra could use someone like you. If that happens, Diego's out, and maybe he goes back to the herd, maybe not."

Gunter's warning shouts in her head. *Oh God, he knows! How long do I have?*

He smiles again and she suppresses a shudder. "I might even let you stay human, at least some of the time. We'll see about setting you up with Shemathra nanobots—just in case."

But he already has my file. I gave it to him!

"Free of charge. No need for a thank you; it's on me."

Her heart sinks into her knees as she remains in her seat. "It's a great honor, sir." The meeting adjourns. Hosseini vanishes. Mira leaves her chair and flees the room.

She would never allow Shemathra nanos. Never! Mira had just begun her work at SEINI when she learned the story of Isobel, Hosseini's virtual consort. Isobel often appeared in Hosseini's stead during meetings until Isobel embellished her role during an interview with a major news outlet, highlighting her role in creating the world of Shemathra. The result was predictable.

Shortly after giving the interview, the consort disappeared. Isobel had been deleted personally by Hosseini. Isobel had been with Hosseini since they were both bios. The woman starred in a series of holo-porn films that he produced and later, she choreographed Hosseini's debut as the rainbow llama god, Urcuchillay. If Hosseini would do that to a friend after so little provocation, what would he do to Ravi or her grandfather? *What would he do to her?*

Diego Putnam, Gunter's nephew, and his betrayer who pushed Bali Hai into the abyss is now Hosseini's second in command. How soon until he is tortured and deleted?

Soon, Gunter will be in the Palms North.

SHEMATHRA'S REALM

The Palms North

Record 3b

THE PALMS NORTH,
RECORD 3B

Lola

August 22, 2290

Now I know where I am. The sign welcomes me to the Palms North. But I'm Gunter sim, the tax collector. How welcome am I? Is this the poor side of town? Must I issue many erasure tickets? I hope not. The sidewalk is the same gray with no creases or divisions. Just smooth and dark like a conveyor belt.

Where am I? I see buildings so I must be on a street. Have I finished collecting all the taxes assigned to me? Where do I go now? My sim tells me to relax; he knows where to go next. He'll keep me from appearing out of place as long as I remain quiet, but this limits my interactions and what evidence I can record. It's for my protection, but it's frustrating. People nod as they pass me, but each one looks straight ahead. I miss having a real conversation.

I might as well be a spy-vid camera, except what I see can be used as evidence of Hosseini's crimes. I see service sims, including street cleaners. There will be a stampede soon. I thought it wasn't until the end of August.

"No, that's the Grand Stampede," my sim whispers. "This one is called the "Glory to the Goddess Stampede." Waiters linger on the outside of cafés and restaurants. But like Purdy Town, there is little memory dedicated to whatever goods are within their doors, they are more illusion than virtually true. My guess is the goods were once part of Bali Hai. It doesn't matter. All the service people and waiter sims, including a policeman, stare at me as I pass by.

"Your purpose, sim, what is it?" The policeman demands.

"Assessing and collecting the coming taxes, officer sim," my sim answers. "Glory to the Goddess."

"Glory to the Goddess, proceed," answers the officer.

The street looks to be almost an eighth of a mile in width. People are walking quickly with their heads turned, avoiding eye contact with me. These Palms citizens appear to be in their fifties. The advantage of virtual existence allows for the correction of imperfections, so all are attractive. Few of these women appeal to me; it's depressing. I don't see any tunics like the ones of cube South villages residents. These virtuals wear a light green garment that resembles a sort of military uniform. Is it? My sim assures me it's not. There must be a better way to conserve memory than dressing in such a dreary fashion.

I should cross to the other side of the street to see what else is different. What is that? Some kind of cloud is filling the sky. It's forming an image, and people are looking for a place to hide. Some duck under tables, others open any available doors, looking for cover. Oh God! What is that? It looks like a—my sim is hiding me behind his placid grin. I'm relaxed on the outside. It's better to hide.

The shape of an enormous wolf emerges from the cloud. Incredible! Replacing the long snout and sharp teeth of the creature is a pale human face, that of a woman. The whole thing reminds me of the image above a primitive altar. But now there's only the face; the rest of her is a cloud. White fur skims the contours of her forehead, and her flushed cheeks. It frames the sharp bones of her jaw and wraps itself around her neck like a winter scarf. Straight up and alert are the creature's ears, the ears of a wolf. The wolf woman's heavy-lidded eyes are rimmed in blood as they look down on the petrified crowd. *Please don't let her find me.*

She's smiling, her lips glistening as she bends her head closer to us. Flames roll in her giant eyes. My sim tells me that she's searching for unbelievers. I stay quiet. *Please don't . . .* People freeze, afraid of being singled out for something gruesome. At last, the eyes roll back into a silver glow.

There are occasions, my sim whispers, when some unfortunate resident is sucked into the sky. Then the beautiful mouth opens and there are shining white, sharp, cloud teeth. The victim's (*my sim describes this though I wish he wouldn't*) the victim's screams are muffled when the wolf goddess pulls the terrified prey into her grinding teeth. The screams mercifully cease as the monster fades into clouds. For now, the cloud drifts and separates until it is gone. This is why, my sim tells me, I must stay hidden. *Why does my sim care what happens to me?*

You must listen, warns the sim, if you want to survive. Four programmed the sim to encourage my survival. People murmur their relief to one another until a booming voice demands, "Tribute Day is here! All citizens will pay!" Everyone knows the voice; my sim tells me. It belongs to Urcuchillay, the rainbow llama god and consort of Shemathra. I remember it from the slaughterhouse.

Before I cross the cobbled street, I listen for signs of the coming stampede. I'm confused; I thought I was finished, but I guess not. Where do I go next? I trust my sim guide. Now I see another long row of houses, right next to the road. The row hugs the road farther than I can see. Behind the row are more cube stacks. Each of these stacks has three cubes, the bottom and top are gray, the middle cube is white. Every unit has one square, opaque window, and a narrow black door. Before I go to the cube stacks, I must collect from the row that runs along the stampede highway.

Like before, I decide to retreat within the sim as he collects taxes. He whispers of the danger here. Like the Privileged units, residents in this row risk deletion if during a stampede, any member of the herd veers off the path. These virtuals are being punished for their history of being short on taxes. Unless they pay current taxes plus what's in arrears and fines, they will remain here until a steer or something larger catches them and tears them apart. Only the stockyard deletion is more painful.

I decide to dream-memory while the sim goes from door to endless door. I remember Marcia and our trip to San Francisco and then Laura and I on the Elysium deck, sipping wine as clouds cross the moon.

When I wake, we're at the cubes. Perhaps I should trust the sim and go back to sleep. No, I should look around. What kind of spy would I be if I spent all my time here lost in a dream-memory? These cubes are different from the improbable stacks before. I'm surprised to see that the virtuals here aren't waiting for me outside their doors. My sim is quiet. I wonder if he's encountered this before. I don't think so.

I look up as a door opens and a large bubble drifts and hovers near it before floating up to one of the upper cubes. Not a "thought bubble," communication commonly used in the bio world, there is no thought here, only an old-fashioned bubble, full of nothing, glistening in spots with filmy threads of color. It dips and floats down, its shape undulating from a plump kidney to a perfect sphere.

I see its different colors before the bubble bursts, and I feel the damp mist and a throb of regret. How I miss my bio life and the thrill of impermanence! As I reach for a second bubble, it drifts away. More bubbles are floating down to the grass. The sim tells me to ignore them and let him collect the taxes, but I decide I want to find out where they're coming from. Who is making them?

Now they're floating between a cube stack. There is a section of grass that looks like the recreational area for a collection of several residences. It's shielded from the road. A circle of virtuals who manifest in their thirties sit on the grass. As each bubble makes its way from a plastic wand, heads turn to follow it.

My sim cautions me that these bubbles take a lot of memory—too much to be approved. Before I can stop it, the sim takes over.

"Greetings, Palms residents. I am Gunter sim. I regret to inform you that this activity is unauthorized, and I have scanned you all for penalties."

The immediate reaction is fear and a shift in age. All the virtuals became older adults. Incredible. The bubble maker is Terry, the same woman in her cen-seventies I met before. What is she doing here? She must be conducting some kind of group circle narratives. Why? Do these serve the same purpose as the circles in The No Where? Is this how people living in this nightmare survive, by telling stories of their bio existences?

I'm concerned. Should I ignore her? Now, she's gesturing to me. "Hello Gunter, please let the sim within you sleep for now." I'm apprehensive, but I order my sim to sleep. Reluctantly, he does so. "I've been hoping to see you here." She smiles.

"Who are you?" Perhaps I should let the sim take over. She ignores my tone and smiles again. Sadly, many of these people might face erasure for the simple pleasure of bubbles. Why is she smiling? The old woman extends her arms, pulls me to her bony chest and embraces me. I surprise myself by returning the hug and its warmth. "Who are you?" I ask again.

"No need to pretend. You know my name is Terry," she answers. Her eyes are beautiful, the soul shines through. There's something strange in them, a faint glow I didn't see before now. "I knew the other virtual you," she tells me, "The one who left with his brother. You went as little boys and you rode the Dreams."

"You must have mistaken me for someone else, Terry." I know my brother self-deleted without me. I'm told he left with my wife, though I find that hard to believe.

She shrugs. "Oh, it was you alright. You were with your true brother, not Jacob."

"I have—had only one brother."

"Four knows," she laughs. "Believe what she tells you."

God help us all!

The sim presses me; it's time to collect taxes. I wish I could ask more questions, but I should hurry. First, I'm going to protect the virtuals here. No one should be deleted because of the simple pleasure of watching bubbles. I announce in a neutral voice, "Let this serve as a warning. There will be no penalties this time. Next time, you will be punished. I have deleted the scans, now please disperse."

I order the sim to delete the scans of everyone here. He struggles to regain control, but I feel him relax. "Go to sleep, your presence is not required now. Erase what I tell you, then sleep." When I am sure the data is gone, I look at Terry. How does she know so much about me? How has she survived here?

Before I can ask her, Terry puts her hand on my arm. "Be careful, Gunter," she says. She turns to leave and blows me a kiss. "See you soon. The taxes here are all paid." Then she disappears behind a black door.

Taxes paid? What is she talking about? I wake the sim. "Taxes here are paid," he tells me. "No tribute violations, we must move on."

Is someone protecting Terry? Four will know.

All the residents are gone from the grass area. Where do I go from here? The sim guides me to another cube complex. More stacks of three. This one's even farther from the stampede road. These virtuals look better off in terms of resources. The stacks are white stucco with a red clay roof. Perhaps we can make up for what we failed to collect from the other cubes. I'm aware that the sim has a knack for finding undeclared treasures. No one is waiting outside, so we must knock. Eventually, we are welcomed by wary residents.

The contents of these cubes are not as dismally uniform as their inhabitants. The best word to describe these residents is hostile. When the first door opens, I am startled to see a blue wall in the common area. Another cube has three aqua walls and my mind drifts back to the aqua house and the summer island of my childhood. Most of the virtuals here have dared to use color within their cubes, which contain fewer inhabitants; five virtuals is average. They have more resources, it's obvious. The sim informs me that the wall colors have been pre-approved, and taxes have been paid.

Besides color, there are luxuries here that must remind these people of their bio lives. I'm surprised to see tele-meal ports. Virtual humans have no need to eat. I think they are comforted by the pretense. Some possess music from their bio lives, though they are careful not to share, unless they have paid the Realm, a user tax. One resident keeps a kitten sim. The little creature purrs as it sits on its master's lap. We are soon done here. As in the bio world, the more resources you have, the less you are taxed. The sim cites one resident for undeclared tobacco, and another for hiding a fishbowl. Minor offenses, but they are enough to pad the report.

They all fear me. Non-payment leads to scary things. It sickens me, though my sim has no concerns regarding the fate of those who fail to pay. We walk quickly through winding streets on our way to more cube towers. When people here see me, some look away, others manage fake smiles. Since Purdy Town, I know I am hated. The sim collects taxes, and I gather information. Any new assets or hidden memory must be reported. I hear stories and explanations as to why the memory due might be late, only a little, but don't worry it will be paid. Many will pay dearly, their painful deletion a source of entertainment for the royal house of Urcuchillay.

Don't know where we're going now. I let the sim take complete control. *"Who's the man, Momma?"*

Is that the voice of a child? Yes! There's a child and her mother sitting on a bench. This is new. The little girl, who appears to be eight years old, is pointing at me. Unlike the adults, she wears a pink blouse and a jumper to match her socks and buckle shoes. Her dark hair is in a series of small braids that bounce as she talks. Each braid ends in a pink barrette.

"Lola, he's a sim, like you honey. Say hello, be nice." Lola's mother takes the child's hand. The mother appears to be an entrancing woman in her early nineties. Her voice sounds older, weary, low, and hesitant. It conveys profound sorrow. A faint red marking encircles her neck. It is the imprint of the letters, "Overdue."

"Hello, Mr. Sim,' the child sim chirps. "My name is Lola. What's your name?" The child sim dances around me, her head bobbing from side to side. She grins brightly, revealing a missing tooth.

"Hello, Lola sim. My name is Gunter, sim." I am startled by my reaction to this child. Normally, I have no patience for children.

My sim asks the mother her name. "Marta," she tells me. She's choking back tears. I command the sim to sleep. He pushes back, determined to make up for lost time. Reluctantly, the sim cedes control.

The woman is trying to say something. I can see her fear. Against my better judgement, I try to reassure her.

"Gunter sim, please express my respect to Urcuchillay." Marta says. She can't meet my gaze. "Assure him, if you would, that I will meet my tribute in full this coming cycle."

"That is good, Marta. His greatness will be pleased."

"Thank you, Gunter sim."

I have questions. A sim like Lola must require a lot of memory. Why did Marta risk her own existence to maintain the echo of her child? I want to sit down with her, to hear what events led to the little girl sim. But it is too risky. No one can know the secret of my humanity. I order the sim to delay the collection from Marta. When I return to the Villa, I'll tell Four about Marta's situation and insist that we find a way to protect her and her little girl sim.

Looking as if she were protecting her from a predator, the woman hugs the child, murmuring that it was time to feed the ducks. They hurry away and disappear down one of the many paths that lead through the cubes.

"Why doesn't anyone jump to other locations? I ask the sim.

"Urcuchillay taxes jumps," the sim informs me. *"Marta must pay her tribute in full. Most of her assets are resting in the memory it took to create a sim of her child."*

I know that if she doesn't meet her quota, Marta will lose her little girl. The memory that created the sim Lola will be absorbed in the enormous bank of Urcuchillay. And what of Ravi?

What if he is who he claims to be? He and Mira might be all that I have left, the only links to my past. I hope he can survive here.

***

Ravi

Be careful what you wish for. He didn't know about you and here, you are a liability. Gunter was forty-nine when his mind-upload was copied and hidden, long before Ravi was born.

Ravi is almost twice that age. Who is the father and who is the son? Regardless, their meeting was nothing like the countless fantasies and dreams, edited and re-edited as Ravi grew older. He knows Gunter hasn't accepted him. Understandable.

The panic Ravi felt as a new father overwhelmed him as he watched Rosalind sing Irish lullabies to her baby. Like the willow tree that bent down to weep, Ravi mourns what was lost. He had loved Rosalind and their new daughter but with guilty relief, he left them to research the myth of Shambhala. Mira was already walking when he returned, a father and husband in name only, missing his daughter's first steps and the long nights of early infancy.

A group was taking supplies to Base camp I on the Khumbu Glacier. Life might have been different if Ravi hadn't seen Rosalind's face, the fleeting excitement and the pain in her soft brown eyes. She had never been to the Khumbu Glacier, and it was only for a few days. Rosalind would make the journey and return. Instead, the glacier took Rosalind. Ravi often dreams that he was the one who fell. Rosalind, and eighteen-month-old Mira wave to him as he drifts into the black clouds below.

With Rosalind gone, he had been unready for fatherhood. But there was no choice. He traveled the world, and she was his companion, a solemn little girl who sat quietly by her father until he was ready to answer her numerous questions. When Mira was six, the Patel matriarch, Vijaya lectured him, insisting that he abandon his research and provide a secure home for his daughter.

"If not, then leave her with us. At the very least, she'll be safe from kidnappers and hooligans."

Although he adored her, Ravi left his daughter again, this time to the cool embrace of the Patel family. Like Ravi, his daughter was an outsider; Mira was sent away to school. Again, he had failed his daughter. He told himself Mira was safer where she was. He took her with him on summer trips, and called on her birthdays, making sure to send gifts. The loneliness in her voice pierced the part of his soul that still blamed her for Rosalind's death. It shamed him. He wasn't his ruthless father, nor was he like Patel.

***

The Palms North Games

August 22, 2290

My sim insists we continue the collection process. I give him control. We're past the parks and now, I see another commercial section. The sim whispers that it's time to collect from the local businesses. Great. I'm curious to see what merchants thrive here.

Is that laughter? Where is it coming from? Probably from the other side of the boulevard. My sim is busy, transmitting taxes to the Data Stream. I tell him that I'm crossing this section of the boulevard. He whispers to me that I should be careful, several steers are on the road, looking for places where virtuals might be vulnerable. I should wait for them to pass. Some are impatient to catch an unfortunate virtual. My sim and I are safe, but being tossed into the air might inspire unwelcome scrutiny. When it is safe, we cross the street.

A sign on a two-story cube says, "Free Games." Something free? Despite my sim's advice, I'm going inside. A large room is buzzing with noise. There's a giant bison head floating and rotating as it scans the room. My sim pops up with its vacant smile just in time. *"We must leave!"* my sim urges me, but I want to know more.

First, I must see what these "games" are. Dozens of people are here. Several virtuals, all manifesting in their sixties, are waiting for a turn to play. With a snort, the bison head vanishes. A sim wearing a straw hat, suspenders and a striped bow tie keeps order pointing to the next player.

The "game" player sim turns to me. *"State your business here."*

To my relief, my sim answers quickly and calmly. *"I am Gunter sim. All here must pay their taxes. Be sure they pay tribute at the required location."*

The sim's smile widens as he bows and tips his hat.

"We must leave now!" my sim whispers.

"We will, I want to see what games are here."

The game is called *Match the herd! What kind of animal are you?* Old-fashioned multi-colored bulbs frame the sign, flashing on and off. Players walk through a rotating holo of various herd animals. When a virtual's personality is compatible with a specific breed, lights glow and the human virtual briefly morphs into an animal. A Texas longhorn comes through; everyone cheers. Then the steer becomes human. The man grins proudly. I wonder how long before he joins the Shemathra herds.

"Leave now!" my sim urges in his dead voice.

"We will," I insist.

Lots of noise here with animal honks, neighs, moos, and screeches, not to mention applause and the stomping of hooves. The message is clear, join the herds and receive a reward, in this case, freedom from taxes. I wonder how Hosseini gains if none in the herds pay taxes? I'll ask the sim later.

There are also foraging games and combat, like *The Stallion Challenge*, where the player can experience the excitement of dominance. The most popular game is *Escape,* where the player becomes a herd animal chased by a sim predator—a lion, a wolf, a leopard, or a hyena. The player is never caught, but there are thrilling close calls. The message is that when it comes to freedom, the only joy is surrender. You must submit to one will, the way of the herds.

I am overwhelmed by all the colors here. The walls are an intense red, the color of blood and— *"Get out now!"* my sim blasts the message. The floating bison is back and then it floats away.

Where am I?

End RECORD

THE ELYSIUM

The ghost of memories

August 24, 2290

Leaving the plasma shell and Miranda Four, Mira weeps. After downloading the information that her sleeping grandfather had gathered, Mira reviews the material recorded in the Palms. She is horrified and afraid. Gunter had warned her Hosseini wants to murder her, end her bio life. And this monster has a digital copy of her! The colonies are worse than she had feared, sad, and beyond bleak. But does any of it violate the law? Byron failed to answer her questions. And Henry is no help at all. His only advice is "Be patient." What if it were a member of his family? Would he "be patient"?

As she weeps, the mouse climbs the leg of her workstation and moves cautiously to the crumbs left from her morning muffin. It sits on its haunches and watches her as it shoves a crumb into its mouth.

"Okay, Gunter, how smart are you?" The creature races across the desk and down the desk's leg. "Are you smart enough to survive?" Rather than answer, the mouse disappears. "I hope so," she whispers.

Henry is gone. She begged him for answers. He told her he will be in D.C., securing communications concerning exploration and discoveries of a mine on Ganymede. If she needs to talk to him, she must leave a message, and he'll call her. Determined not to call him (she will take care of herself) she fights panic.

The last of the original Gunter's memories before his self-deletion were incredibly sad. What remains of Bali Hai is remote and cold like the virtual Everest where Gunter Holden often went, his memories dulled by its frozen solitude. He had studied the images of fallen climbers, illusions embedded to enhance the virtual reality, tucked away and beyond reach as "virtual ghosts."

She worries that someone recorded an image of her mother's body, trapped in ice, for use as a VR illusion. Her mother's icy death might be in another's program's virtual Everest. The original Gunter is the ghost who haunts her, his memories seeping into her own, keeping her pinned to a destiny she isn't sure she wants.

She knows what went through her grandfather's mind when he discovered the contents of Marcia's memory and felt Marcia's despair, deciding that. Gunter shouldn't know she was pregnant. His decision to move on once more with the new wife waiting for him in South Africa meant he would never know. The echo of her grandfather's naked grief matches the deep melancholy within her. They are alike. Regardless, she will bring back VEI and her grandfather will restore all that was lost. Dear God, what if . . .? She'll wake him in two days.

DIEGO PUTNAM

Oklahoma tall grass #231 @Endless Prairies USA

Premium grazing: (adjustable perimeter)

August 25, 2290

With a wave of his massive head, Diego leads his herd to the appointed ground. Behind him, five hundred Texas Longhorns gather and form concentric circles. A wedge-shaped path slices through to the circle's center where a large cauldron waits, the gurgles and hisses of boiling water rising in anticipation. At the circle's edge, there's a platform and a red chair with black arms.

He swings his antlers, which span ten feet, toward the red chair and aligns his bulk on the short path from the circle to the platform. His gait is regal but not too regal. Hosseini's spies are sure to report such an infraction. Isobel, Hosseini's previous chief lieutenant, wasn't mindful. The Grand Stampede is days away. He must be careful not to draw attention. He can still hear her screams in the squeals of nervous cows.

Diego is a black longhorn, pure in color, the only one in his herd. As befits his rank, he is the largest, with antlers surpassing that of the other males, who are forbidden antlers spanning more than six feet.

As a bio, Diego had been a small man, one whose grievances against his uncle, Gunter Holden, led to an illegal claim and Hosseini's theft of Holden's company, VEI. He had assumed the merger would result in a sudden downgrade of Bali Hai sims and options. The sudden erasure of Bali Hai's virtual Paris, an entire city, along with its thousands of human residents sickened him. When Hosseini gained full control, there was another mass erasure and Bali Hai fell into chaos. Then his uncle self-deleted. Gunter never knew how sorry Diego was.

Approaching his new throne, Diego's horns shorten and disappear. His upper torso changes, the muscles contracting and the torso shrinking until it is no longer an animal shape, but a human one. His hands replace his front hooves; he regains his face and part of his virtual humanity. When he rises onto his hind hooves, the hooves become the worn black boots of a Texas cowboy, the only nod to his longhorn self. As he reaches the platform, his arms fill the sleeves of a black military uniform finished in red cuffs. The bars on his shoulders show the golden image of the goddess, signaling his rank. The chair's sleek black arms end in something like the paws of a wolf. He curls his fingers around the black paws as if to channel the power of the goddess Shemathra. Then he waits for the moos and grunts to cease.

What happens next is somewhat new. Hosseini wasn't sure if he liked the change, but Diego extolled the theatrics, a reminder of the coming Grand Stampede. There will be an execution today, but instead of cutting the throat of the doomed human virtual, then hoisting him over the boiling water before dropping him into the bubbling cauldron, a lucky steer, selected from the herd, will catch the condemned on the tips of his antlers and toss the human directly into the pot.

When the screams cease, the other males will snort their thunderous approval. Today, the honored steer is Ned, a member recently transferred from another herd. It is quicker this way and there is less suffering, Diego thinks.

Beyond the circle, a mild wind ripples through golden tall grass, the longest and tastiest Shemathra has to offer. Like the longhorns, bison herds covet this grazing program. Diego's new role is second to Hosseini, and so he can offer his people, no, his herd (he often corrects himself) this occasional treat. Today, he must conduct an execution/deletion of a human virtual. If he doesn't, he will be deemed disloyal.

Above them all, in the flawless blue sky, crows and hawks, all of them Hosseini's spies, glide up and down, circling the herd. To his dismay, the Overland Prairie now shares a border with the Western Vista Prairie. In the distance, Diego sees a bar of light, the barrier separating the Western Vista Prairie and The No Where. This is Hosseini's way of reminding him of how close heaven is to hell. Bison patrol the edge of hell and they will select today's victim.

Diego looks forward to when the herd is quiet, and he can breathe in the magic of the night sky. Often, he remembers the beauty of Bali Hai, its city streets, and lovely beaches.

He quiets the herd. Before he can speak, two bison appear, dragging a shivering gray human. "Human scum," one grunts, "today you pay for your disrespect! Glory to the Goddess!"

"Glory to Shemathra!" Diego answers. The herd joins in with a few barely recognizable human voices and an assortment of moos and groans. The bison toss their heads in contempt, not only at the human virtual, but also the herd. Several longhorn males waive their horns and bellow.

"It's time to honor the Goddess Shemathra." There is silence as Diego speaks. "This human no longer pays tribute. We, who follow the will of Shemathra, cannot ignore this insult. The steer, Ned Slotkin, step forward!" A red steer with a white-snout trots into the center.

Ned's antlers span just over five feet as he paws the ground with a dramatic flourish. The human, who appears to be over cen-forty years in age, is naked and shivering with fear.

"Proceed," Diego sighs. Immediately, using his antlers, Ned scoops up the condemned human. The victim screams as he is tossed into the cauldron. The deletion complete, a white mist rises and disappears into the wind. Several cows and a few longhorns bow their heads. Only a few enjoy executions. Diego checks the sky to see if any crows or hawks are low enough to see.

"If you have any questions, please hold them." He steps down from the platform. As he walks the path, back to the prairie, his black boots become hooves and his body grows larger. His hands disappear; like his feet, they are hooves again. His horns reappear and grow longer until again, they span ten feet. Rejoining the herd, Diego grazes on the tall grass near his favorite tree. The swinging tails of the cows are soothing and . . . *he would give anything to go back.*

Before his bio death Diego had known his life was in danger. Hosseini wanted him in Shemathra. Researching after-death programs offered by other companies, Diego had begun to plan his hasty transition from bio to virtual. Too late. Before he could complete his after-death contract to a different program, offered by another company, Diego's life as a bio ended, and he found himself in Shemathra's Realm. The police discovered Diego's body hanging in a window.

His bio life ended; he woke to a strange landscape. He had been uploaded to virtual existence. But where was he, in which program? Fearing the answer, he searched his memory for clues. What happened? How did he die? Where was his beautiful virtual lake retreat, the small cabin on its bank, a cabin he had named Solitude?

Nanos should have taken him to Eternal Paradise, an after-death destination focused on peace and the enrichment of the mind. Sadly, instead of a lake, he was forced to wander a land where there was nothing but a sun and a pale gray landscape. As he summoned the desire to self-delete, a marching band appeared, and behind them, two people in a military uniform carrying a sign saying, "Welcome Diego!"

Hosseini had ordered him killed and his planned after-death program replaced by nanos that uploaded him to Shemathra's Realm, a different after-death plan. Since Diego was still valuable, Hosseini offered him life as the head steer of a herd of longhorns. No one refused Hosseini. Diego accepted the offer and sought contentment.

His son and his ex-wife disowned him, embarrassed that Diego was a member of an after-death cult. Now, five hundred steers and cows are his family. On occasion, during certain ceremonies, they manifest as five hundred virtual human beings. Hosseini loves to ridicule their frail human forms and compare them with the majesty of the herds. Diego tries to shield them all from the scrutiny of Hosseini and his spies.

When it's dark, a cow or even an occasional steer will ask for an audience. Using the pretext of some dispute, they beg to be excused as witnesses to the monthly executions. Often, they seek the cover of sheds as they revert to trembling human forms. Diego won't betray their doubts about the herds and Shemathra. He has never believed any of it. But no one can be excused. Hosseini would smell the doubt and he and many of those who depend on him would join the condemned.

He tells them only "do as you're told." Other than the executions he is forced to oversee, Diego has found a quiet peace. He understands why so many opted to shed their humanity and often wonders if not forced, and instead given a choice, would he have surrendered to the peace and beauty of the prairie?

The crows still circle, but the execution is over and there will be no interest in watching the contented herd. There's a smattering of laughter as they enjoy the grass. Diego winces at the human sound as many forget to mask their humanity. *If only he could take it all back, he thinks* . . .

SHEMATHRA'S REALM

The white ribbon

V. Loc: The Villa

August 26, 2290

I'm back. There must be a breeze; my hammock is swaying. For a while, I can pretend to be asleep. The thought of what's next is depressing. I see the white columns and the concealing palms. I'm at the Villa. I miss the uncertainty. Oh God, nothing's changed. "What good is this? Why am I here?"

"Gunter sim, you require further maintenance. Please sit on the coding couch." As I enter the white interior, I remember the flashing red of the Palms game room and I long for the return of color.

I'm angry now. "We made an agreement, and you broke it. Send me to another program or delete me. What I saw was heartbreaking; I want no more of it."

Four shakes her head. *"You weren't careful, Gunter. You could have cost us everything. You delayed, satisfying your curiosity, about what was going on in the game store and the bison sim was taking a closer look at you. Your sim put you to sleep and addressed the spy, demanding to know its purpose. Your sim stated that no structure was off limits when searching for tax avoiders. The spy was satisfied, otherwise, you would be in the slaughterhouse now. What were you thinking, grandfather?"*

"I was recording the reality of what goes on in Shemathra's Realm. What were you doing?

"I'm trying to locate the woman, Terry in Shemathra's Realm. There is someone named Terry appearing in the original Gunter's files. And I'm taking your warning regarding my safety seriously. Thank you. Gunter, the information you have gathered will be of tremendous help. I downloaded and reviewed it all while you slept."

"Okay. Have I done enough to be transferred? Four, you have no idea how devastating this has been."

"I wish I could say yes, Grandfather . . ."

"Don't call me that; my name is Gunter."

"I'm sorry, Gunter; I can't transfer you yet."

"Fine, part of our agreement is that you will continue to answer my questions."

"What would you like to know?"

Something you haven't told me yet.

"Your parents had another son, Thomas Bucklin. When Tom uploaded to Bali Hai, you had no idea who he was, but you were advised by the AI, Miranda, to greet him."

"How did Miranda know and why didn't she tell me?"

"In scanning his file for preferences, she discovered his identity. Your files were in danger of fragmentation. Because you needed a trustworthy ally and confidante, Miranda encouraged your friendship. With the second merger Bali Hai fell apart, and weakened by what you had learned about Eric, you decided to self-delete. It was then you discovered Tom was your younger biological brother. Like you, Eric Holden made Tom an orphan. When your original upload rode the Dreams, Tom was your companion."

"Poor Jacob. I wish—never mind. Tell me about Tom, the man who was my brother. How much did he know about me?"

"His name at birth was Thomas Vanderbok. Your mother was killed when he was still an infant, so he had no memory of her. Upon your mother's death, Vanderbok and your little brother fled to Canada, hoping that it would be far enough away.

"I was nineteen and I reached out to Vanderbok. I remember telling Dad—Eric, about my plans to meet Professor Vanderbok. I never heard back. I didn't realize that I had signed my own father's death warrant."

Before your father left to meet you, he asked Tom to promise, if anything should happen to him, Tom was to find you. Tom was only eleven and he grew to resent the promise and you. He couldn't stop blaming you for your father's death."

"Why would he blame me? I had no idea. . . "

"At the urging of his dying wife,Tome kept his promise. Upon his own bio death, Tom became a resident of Bali Hai, and he reached out to you. When it was clear Bali Hai could not be saved, you and Tom self-deleted by riding the rollercoaster, Babylon Dreams."

"I don't know how to feel. All right, the Royal Arms is the last human community. If I go there, gather what information I can, will

I be allowed to return here and be transferred where humans stay human? Another thing, you said there was something else I must do. What is it?"

"Yes, there is only one community left, and yes, there's something else."

"One more. I can't exist here much longer. I will find a way to self-delete. Four, it's too much!"

"Gunter, I wish I could transfer you now. If Hosseini is defeated, you'll sleep well, knowing that much of your past will be re-written. Help me remove the threat he poses to all of us, bio and virtual, and I will upload you to the paradise of your choice."

"Fine. Tell me about the Royal Arms community. Then we'll talk about what's next."

"The Royal Arms is different from the others in terms of virtual life, more comfortable. It is more diverse, and more treacherous. Assume spies are everywhere. Once you have finished there, and I have collected the data, I will need time to see if we have enough evidence. When you return from the Royal Arms, there is something else, someplace else, where you need to go."

"I don't understand."

"All data is converted into memory. After the Royal Arms, you're going to the Data Stream. Everything you witness there is more evidence. While you are there, you must look for the child sim, Lola. Ask her for a white ribbon. Don't worry, she'll give it to you; she's a sim. It's something that will protect you."

"She may be a sim, but she is all that her mother has, the shadow of her little girl. Promise me, that when it's all over, that you will restore this sim to Marta, her mother."

Four looks at me and smiles my mother's smile.

"I promise to do what I can."

"You spoke of some other development."

"I—no there's nothing else."

"What am I to do with it?"

"With what?"

"The ribbon, what do I do with it?"

"Keep it out of sight. If you are ever captured, wrap it around your finger. It will protect you from fear or pain. I wish there was more I can offer. Please stay safe if you can."

"When I am finished, bring me here and then send me to another program. And Four, if I'm discovered and sent to be slaughtered, please, find a way to delete me.

"I will bring you back and I'll never leave you to Hosseini. You have my word."

As she sends her grandfather to the Royal Arms, Mira desperately hoped that she could keep her promise.

Shemathra's Realm

The Royal Arms

Record 4

THE ROYAL ARMS

The Spy

August 26, 2290

I see a row of white buildings, but no signs saying what they are. Where do I go? It would be easier to hide and let the sim do the rest, but the data it sees is not usable. Thankfully, The Royal Arms is the last community if Four keeps her promise.

In some ways, the Palms was worse than Purdy Town. In Purdy Town, I was feared and hated. In the Palms Community, I was almost discovered. The experience confuses me, especially, meeting Ravi and the old woman, Terry. And her urgent message that Four is in danger. How did Terry know? Why did Four ignore the warning, then put me back in the Palms, only to yank me back out? My sim would have dealt with the bison sim. I'm weary of it all.

Until my sim decides to come forward, I'll follow the "The Stampede Way" signs and record what I see. Already, I see there are more resources here. I'm surrounded by flowers. My sim whispers that citizens pay tribute by purchasing a flower gift. The gifts here are simple bouquets or more elaborate arrangements. Some are ostentatious declarations of fealty. Azaleas, mums, and gladiolas sit in rows of white flowerpots. Endless counters of roses in crystal vases stretch along a pathway. Bundles of daisies, tied together with ribbons are stacked next to rows of exotic orchids. Tulips in various bright colors stand tall, while lilies and carnations crowd together. Sadly, I can detect no fragrance.

What if I touch one? Disappointing, like thin paper. There is little to them, no soft petals nor thorns, only the feel of slippery paper. I miss the sensory banquet of VEI programs. And oh, how I miss being a bio where the senses were a part of every day, every moment of existence.

Lines of human virtuals are waiting for the Stampede. Today, my sim informs me, citizens of The Royal Arms claim their floral order, paid for by memory contributions. Each resident collects and places his or her flower gift on the outer edges of the Goddess Boulevard in preparation for the coming Flower Stampede. Those waiting to purchase the more modest flower gifts from retail sims will move on, taking their assigned place on a side of the roadway. There's tension in their faces. My presence doesn't help.

What do these people have to fear? My sim tells me the Royal Arms is an exclusive human community of wealthy virtuals. Luxuries like elaborate meals and coordinated social events, a distant memory to residents of the Palms, are common at The Royal Arms. However, like every other human community, the humans of

The Royal Arms community still pay tribute, a necessary part of any celebration. This stampede event is not the Grand Stampede, but it is important. It celebrates the sixty-third anniversary of the founding of Shemathra's Realm. The size of this community is overwhelming. There are several tax collectors responsible for collecting taxes from the eighty-four thousand residents of The Royal Arms. How many am I collecting? The sim tells me the exact number is irrelevant. What's maddening is the voice my sim whispers in is mine.

"*The Royal Arms citizens enjoy privileges, exclusive advantages for having a Royal Arms address.*" The sim tells me. "*Before communications went dark, each virtual resident here was permitted to communicate with the bio world on a regular basis. The Realm saw the logic of well-funded residents managing their own assets. Better-managed funds meant insurance in the case of an unexpected tax. No unfortunate 'lie' might escape; their communications were pre-recorded. However, they were treated to the uncensored news from their bio loved ones and associates.*"

I know that I, as a tax collector sim, play a role. How? I have no idea what to do. What if I am discovered? I should hide and let the sim handle all of this. Too risky. I remember the bubbles. Such a small thing, but even I found it quite easily. Memories of the stockyard screams follow me as the sim takes over and I hide.

"You, sim, what's your name?" A muscular young man of twenty-five, who has taken his place to see the coming spectacle is pointing at me and this triggers the sim emerging with its vacant smile and greeting.

"I am Gunter sim, citizen. How can I help you?" The sim recedes, leaving me to finish.

"You're Gunter sim? I've heard about you. Sorry, I'm one of the newer residents. Put in a good word for me with Urcuchillay, will you? My name is Boris Taylor."

The man extends his hand for me to shake, a breach of protocol. The sim advises that I only listen and not respond.

"This place is a miracle," he laughs. "One minute, you're one hundred and forty-five and everything is starting to hurt, your wife is long gone and all the money in the world won't buy you a decent hard-on. Here, you're young again and life is full of possibilities."

Yes, lots of possibilities, including having your throat slit and being thrown in boiling water.

"When you see the Rainbow Llama, tell him the Mandela of roses is from me."

"I will, Boris Taylor." I nod as I move away. The man depresses me. I remember swearing to never suffer fools. In Shemathra's Realm, I am surrounded by them.

Boris looks over his shoulder to see if anyone is listening. "By the way," he whispers, "I'm considering the herd life."

"I will inform Urcuchillay, Boris Taylor. His Greatness will be pleased. I am Gunter sim."

"Great," Boris says with a salute. "Just great!"

Idiot.

The remaining virtuals place their floral offerings on the edge of the cobbled roadway. Crowds gather on both sides of the street. Most take care to be several feet from the street's edge. Since space is limited, stampedes are held monthly so that all pay tribute in some form. Many residents transfer memory directly to the Realm. Flower Stampedes are one of the most prestigious. They are by invitation only and attendance is mandatory.

Weaving around the more cautious residents, those permitted to seek a safer, yet respectable distance from the coming stampede, I'm making my way to the second floor of the Ministry of Communications Center. Before the Realm went dark, the Communications Center offered holo-ports for calls to the bio world.

"Now," my sim whispers, *"you must be careful."* I withdraw, allowing my sim to take control. Posing as waiters, policemen and street cleaners, spy sims study the crowd, recording any infractions or lack of required enthusiasm.

I'm sitting on a balcony reserved for service sims. Although my sim withdraws, I am careful to use my sim smile as I prepare to witness and record the event. Where should I direct my gaze? What evidence am I expected to gather?

Even from where I'm sitting, I can feel the ground shake. As the balcony trembles, I hear a series of deafening bellows. Oh God, thousands of animals burst into view! *These animals were once humans!* The gates swing open, and the herds pour into the city. There's a nightmare of grunting and snorting, squeals, neighs, and heavy panting as the herds stampede, and hooves meet the cobblestones. The sound is straight from hell.

No human virtual dares look up as the herds pass them, and many animals, struggling to use their human voices, warn, "Watch it, get out of my way, human!" Coming to an abrupt halt, a large brown steer swings his head, looking for a victim until he is pushed along by a huge water buffalo. Heads down, the buffalo thunder through, clearing the way for thousands of cattle, sheep, horses, wildebeests with their curved horns, and zebras, their heads swiveling right to left. Groups of water buffalo come through at a startling speed for such large creatures, flinging their dung into the crowd with a flick of a tail.

As more longhorns pass by, I see a Texas Longhorn waving and dipping his horns, threatening any onlooker who might stand too close. His gesture must have inspired the longhorns who followed and dropped their heads and waved their horns in unison. Not to be upstaged, several Rocky Mountain Bighorn rams move in a coordinated dance of twirling their horns and ramming a line of virtuals who fall under the relentless hooves.

"Being trampled during a stampede," the sim whispers, *"means certain deletion unless the virtual possesses a considerable cache of memory and outside assets."*

Mountain sheep rams and some of the larger ewes swing their heads back and forth, tossing the flower offerings to one another as they run. Herds of spiral horned antelope leap in a coordinated fashion like dancers in a ballet, their enormous ears twitching. As wild mustangs gallop past them, downcast humans are frozen with fear.

Giraffes and elephants are last. They materialize several hundred yards from the immense nineteenth-century style iron-gate, where the words "Welcome to The Royal Arms" are written in silver scroll, framed in gold leaf. African elephants sway their tusks regally as they pass along the boulevard and the stampede ends with a host of giraffes, who punctuate their stately walk by bobbing their heads swaying rhythmically on their slender necks. Looking down on the supplicant humans, their thick eyelashes flutter as they yawn and move their long gray tongues back and forth. Then, one of them lowers his regal head and wraps his tongue around a wreath. The elephants and giraffes, my sim tells me, are the ones to avoid. They are management.

As I wait for the stampede to finish, my sim tells me, *"This event is on the Shemathra schedule six times a year. It feeds the zeal and dedica-*

tion of all the Shemathra devotees who manifest as herd animals. They crave the thrill of hooves pounding through streets."

Yes, and they enjoy seeing terrified humans cringe in submission. More than anything else, the debasement of so many gullible virtuals is why I hate Hosseini. Finally, the stampede ends. The flower tributes disappear. People are beginning to cross the wide street. For now, there is nothing to fear.

For some reason, I'm unable to jump from one location to another within the city. So now, I'm searching for my assigned area. Where do I begin collecting taxes? Strangely, my sim is unresponsive. What if he's gone? Interesting, the streets in this area are set in concentric circles. They're connected by narrow footpaths and now the streets here are filled with celebrating residents. Most of these human virtuals are beautiful, but all are forgettable. There are no color codes here. The clothes vary. Many have vibrant color and are flattering, none resemble uniforms. Regardless, in the Realm, all human virtuals are trapped within their own environment, forbidden to jump to other habitats. It's an effective tool, controlling information.

The city is well designed with fountains, cafes, and restaurants. I suspect much of it echoes Bali Hai. Uniformed service sims, musicians and entertainers reflect the wealth of the residents. Once, I argued the differences between human virtuals and sims might become difficult to detect. Now, the flat affect in the eyes of sims has been corrected, and there is little way to tell the difference. Then again, the fact I'm masquerading as a sim would have been easier to expose before sim eyes was corrected.

"There are no villas or mansions, nor any private dwellings." My sim is finally back. It's time to collect taxes. Thousands of townhouses rest on the surrounding hillsides that encircle a valley where low-rise

apartment complexes and commercial enterprises stand blocks from the wide Stampede Trailway. It reminds me of a beautiful vacation town where everyone lives somewhere else or is retired and stays each year, for a season or two. All are in shades of soft pastels or white in color with graceful arches and gardens, all with the same white flowers. The effect is a planned community, but one with little charm. At the Royal Arms, the residents are trapped in a "human" paradise.

I retire and the sim collects taxes. Here, it's incredibly easy. No one is banished and none are scheduled for deletion. The townhouse citizens seem detached, almost bored. Often, we're greeted by a custom service sim. The sim arranges for bio funds or excess memory, all is in order and ready for collection. Some residents pretend indifference as they swing open their doors so the tax collector can see just how little these funds, this small luxury, this tiny item means to them.

I complete this section, including another circle, and adjacent buildings. In the next courtyard, the sign says, "This way to Platinum Estates." Are these estates any different from the townhouses? As I collect taxes, I see there are differences. No service sims, every resident quickly pays the tax. A chinchilla sim, lamps of all kinds, a set of holo dramas and a yappy poodle sim are the most memorable. I am amazed at how quickly this final stage has gone. "Are we done here?" My sim doesn't answer.

Not waiting for the sim to answer, I'm crossing a small bridge. Is that moaning? Do I hear someone moaning? Are they in distress? Finally responding, my sim warns me something is out of order. I still decide to investigate. The moans come from the under-side of the bridge.

"It might be dangerous. . ."

"I'll be careful."

It's dark under the bridge. No memory is wasted here on vegetation. But I can still see a man and a woman engaged in sex. This doesn't surprise me. As soon as the stampede was over, I saw numerous frantic couplings. As I turn to leave, I sense there is something about these two is different. The man trembles as the girl falls to her knees. Despite my sim's warning, I begin to apologize and— the woman's body changes.

"Oh, God—I can't . . ." The man whispers as he runs away, swallowed by shadows beyond the bridge. The woman's face elongates as her body thickens. Her arms twist and stretch like a rope. Her fingers grow together, becoming hooves. Her thighs widen into haunches. She is no longer a human. As the fireworks light up the sky, I see a red mare with a white star on her forehead. She begins to neigh and buck. Although it is difficult for her, she speaks to me, her voice full of sadness and remorse.

"I know you're a sim of Gunter Holden. I knew the human virtual Gunter in Bali Hai. If there is anything left of him in you, please don't tell anyone."

"I'm sorry, I don't." Sims are never sorry. What's wrong with me?

Her beautiful eyes are wild with fear. "If they find out. . ." She rears up on her hind legs and shakes her head, eyes wide and glistening with fear. The sim within me fights for control. If I allow it, the sim will inform on her, and she will be deleted. I push the sim away and tell it to forget what I saw.

"Go," I hiss, "before you're missed." Her head bobbing, she neighs her thank you.

"Stop!" a voice says. "Your identity is noted. Return to your herd. You have betrayed the Goddess. You will be dealt with at Urcuchillay's pleasure."

With a squeal of despair, the mare jumps, disappearing from the Royal Arms. Who just spoke? Doesn't matter. To be safe, I'll jump back to the safety of the villa.

There's someone, a human virtual, blocking my exit. The man, his arms folded, is very still, like a predator regarding his cornered prey.

"Gunter Holden! You rode the Dreams and yet. . ." Dressed in dull green, the slender man, reminds me of a swaying cobra ready to strike. "And yet, here you are. You don't recognize me?"

I shake my head as he freezes me with his flat, sim-like gaze.

"Bardot, you knew me. I am the former Reverend Bardot."

I see nothing of a cleric in this virtual human. He manifests as a man of ninety, tall, with angular features and an imperious bearing. His sculpted gray hair has a silver sheen.

"I am Gunter sim." I say, hoping to withdraw from the situation.

"No, you're not!" Bardot says softly. "I was once the leader of Savior City, and I survived the mass erasure of the Everlasting Praise Christians. Because I embraced the Goddess and the will of one, Urcuchillay recognized my value."

What does Bardot want? Is there a way to bribe him? He's studying me, moving closer, trying to scare me.

"I am skilled at enforcing a certain set of rules and detecting suspicious behavior. And of course, I witness any slaughterhouse deletions that result from my reports. So, here is suspicious behavior. Gunter Holden rode the Dreams. But here you are."

Can I escape? Doubtful. There's no way to intimidate Bardot. My sim stays hidden. I can't lie my way out of this. This man is a lesser monster than Hosseini, but he is still a monster, who causes and takes pleasure in the painful deletion of others. God help me. I'm clenching my fist. Opening my palm now and extending my index finger, I point at Bardot, as if to accuse him of a crime. Oh, God, the end of my finger is beginning to glow, and the light leaves my fingertip, moving in Bardot's direction. He's backing away, clearly alarmed. He tries to jump, but this location holds him. Pinpricks of light, like angry wasps, swarm him. Maybe he's scared enough, and I can take it back. How? Bardot is beginning to glow and like a puzzle, pieces of him detach and float into the dark under the bridge.

"What is this?" Bardot asks as he sees his vanishing hands.

"I don't know," I say softly as Bardot, the human before me fades and then he's gone. There's no white mist to say a virtual human named Bardot ceases to exist. What have I done? Four gave me a weapon and I used it to save myself. Bardot was human. Was there a time when he wasn't evil? What drove the original "me" to destroy two million virtuals and ordered the murder of Jacob, my own brother? When did I become evil?

My sim is back. *"The herds are gone and will not reappear for several days. The Grand Stampede is the end-of-August event. Members of the faithful, those deemed worthy, are selected to board a spaceship, traveling to parallel universes where they would become gods themselves, each ruling a single world."*

"Do they actually believe this promise?"

"Any questions human virtuals might have about what happens on the spaceship, they keep to themselves."

"So, the 'chosen' supposedly travel to another universe; where do they really go?"

"It's not relevant," my sim whispers. My goal is to survive. Celebratory fireworks dot the sky for a strict thirty seconds; no larger memory expenditure is justified. Civic leaders host banquets. After-

wards, citizens will attend segregated balls, invitations reflecting their memory assets standing.

Leaving the bridge, I continue my exploration, entering the lobby of the Platinum Estates Celebration Hall. The commanding double doors are white with moldings edged in gold. Inside there is another set of arched doors leading to a hall where a massive round table is the only furniture. On it sits a squat flower-filled vase. Beyond the table, open doors lead to a ballroom. Above each door are the words "Guest Scanner." As I enter, the scanner ignores me, recognizing me as a sim, a non-person.

What a pleasure! I hear music. And people are dancing! But the music is only three songs: The melody of an old ballad, sung by a soulful young girl with a sigh, is followed by something by musicians popular in the bio-world, and approved by committee, and last is a lively dance tune, sung by a long-ago trio. The three songs, the artists long dead, play on a loop as dancers sway and twirl. *"More than three selections,"* the sim whispers, *"is considered a waste of memory."* As I enter the ballroom, the music slows. People see me and many stop dancing. Others leave. Some nod their smiles frozen in place. I smile and say, "Celebrate the Flower Stampede! May the herds thrive!"

"May the herds thrive," the crowd answers.

Turning, I exit the way I came. There's a naked old man huddled by the bridge. "Can you spare a few terabytes?" He's whimpering now, his sunken ashy face trembles with fear and he pleads, "Gunter sim, I didn't realize who . . ." I try to leave but my sim breaks free, firmly seizing the man's wrist, stamping it with a red light showing the date the doomed virtual shall report for erasure.

"Not at all," my sim tells him. I regain control, but it's too late. The words written in red on the man's neck: "Memory Low." All

is in order until I collapse beneath the bridge. I have witnessed and recorded what has become of Bali Hai. All of it sickens me. Purdy Town's spies and the sad pretense of small-town existence were almost worse than the impoverished No Where.

There is no pretending in The No Where, only a fence and a glimpse of sky. Palms virtuals exist in bleak cubes, with little hope other than the lure of sinister games. The Royal Arms residents know it's only a matter of time until funds begin to run low. They wonder how long until they are forced to choose something dear to them so that they can pay taxes or tribute to the ever-hungry goddess. It's beginning to fade. Miranda Four is summoning me.

End RECORD

THE ELYSIUM

The soft whir of air scrubbers

August 27, 2290

She has banished the cat, because the death of the mouse named Gunter might undo her. Henry is gone and in his place is Ian, who assures her Henry will return and until then, he, Ian, is here to keep her safe. She hopes he's telling the truth. What if, what if, Henry is someone else entirely? What if Henry made a deal with the devil, Hosseini, and Ian's here because Henry is not coming back? Not true because she knows he loves her.

She hears Ian open a cabinet in the kitchen and she wants to cry. She misses the daily tea and fresh muffin, placed carefully near her workstation. If Henry were here, his arm would be around her shoulder, his hand resting on the top of her arm as he sets the tea on her table. Instead of Henry, Gunter, the mouse, perches on the side of her desk, his tiny mouse hands eagerly waiting for a crumb that isn't there because the muffin isn't there because Henry is missing.

"I'm sorry, no crumbs today," she says.

Resting on its haunches, the mouse stays, watching her every move, until she hears a knock, and startled, the mouse drops to the floor and disappears.

"Are you okay?"

"Yes, fine. I bumped my knee," she calls.

"Okay, I'll be in the office if you need anything," Ian is a youngish man with lank blond hair and designer aqua-blue eyes, once a popular genetic option. He has a rich deep voice and often clears his throat as if he is as uncomfortable as she is with his assignment. He closes the door to Henry's office.

Byron is waiting to see what else the "copy" records. Already, the events Gunter Holden has witnessed are evidence of abuse. "Tell the copy how valuable he's been to this investigation," Byron messaged. Surely, Gunter's recordings provide enough evidence to save the virtuals of Shemathra's Realm.

"I'll let him know," she responded, annoyed at Byron's referring to Gunter as "the copy." Restless, she opens her bedroom door to see if Ian is still in Henry's office. The office door is still closed. The soft whir of air scrubbers reminds her it's time to wake Gunter and move to the next step. He's dreaming now, but not for long.

She turns away and begins to log on to SEINI's AI notes and message bubbles. There are more work reports due on synthetic humans and downloading virtuals into them. Hosseini is eager to re-enter the bio world. He wants more copies of his mind-upload folder and plans to download one into a synthetic human. More research on authentic bio sensory experiences should be ready by October. Plus, synthetics must be improved. It's still too easy to tell them from humans. The eyes don't blink, nor do they eat. It takes at least an hour to fully repower them, and that is only the most recent prototypes. Hosseini insists several options must be ready no later than January of 2291. *Not if I can help it,* she thinks.

After completing her responses, she retrieves the suit and becomes Miranda Four. The hammock is where her grandfather sleeps in his dream-memories. As she moves him from the concealing palms, she scans the sky. No crows.

SHEMATHRA'S REALM

The Villa: Almost done

August 28, 2290

My castle is nearly finished. The tide is far enough away from the bridge, and I should have time to perfect the turrets. It's one of my best and already, Dad is waving his cigar. Will it be a salute? I hope so. I think this one is really good, and sometimes he doesn't pay attention. I wonder if it's because I swam too far out in the water, and he didn't help me until it was almost too late. I thought maybe the fish I saw would eat me. Is he angry? Is he ... Why is the castle gone? Where is the ocean? It's all green here. Dad, where is Dad? Did he get mad again and leave me?

***

*"Mind uploading is a virtual lobotomy, VR worlds will never work,"
Dad sneers. This is Jacob's fault. My spoiled brother poisoned him
against and . . . I see the gun and the moon. Bali Hai sand is beautiful.
I gaze at the sun.*

***

*Mom is sitting on the blanket and she's getting me a sandwich and
who's . . . Where's Dad? Oh Mom, I'm sorry. I didn't know, didn't
know, I didn't know before the island this was our last picnic. Oh Mom,
I'm sorry I didn't come back; I didn't know I'd never see you . . .*

***

*Where am I? I know; I'm on the pale couch and I'm waiting for Mar-
cia to give me my graduation gift from Dad. The envelope opens, and
the island and Dad fall out. Oh no, he gives thumbs down to Bali Hai.*

***

"Gunter?"

"Oh Mama, I lost the cloud box!"

"Gunter, wake up."

"Mom? No . . . oh, God!"

"Gunter, it's okay. You'll be okay. We're almost at the end.

"I don't know if I can. Please Four, it's horrible here."

*"I know it is. It's time for you to go to The Data Stream. Find the sim
child, Lola. Ask her for the white ribbon. Don't forget to wrap it around
your index finger."*

"To protect me?"

"Yes, Grandfather. Should you be discovered, I won't let you suffer the torment that monster will inflict, I wish it offered more."

"Send me to The Data Stream. One way or another, I'm leaving this hell.

Can I save her?" I ask again.

"Save who?"

"The sim, the little girl."

"Not now, but there may be a way later, after VEI is restored."

She's said that before. Ordinarily, I would approve of her singular focus, but now her lack of concern angers me.

"I've replaced the pink barrettes with the white ribbon." Four changes the subject. *"As she is readied for re-absorption, take the ribbon, and wrap it around your index finger. Don't forget."*

My concern for a mere sim confuses me. I shouldn't care what happens to her; she's a sim. Why can't I let it go? "I can just take the child with me. Surely, we can find memory elsewhere and present it as belonging to Marta. Then her child will be saved. It's only a small change of plans."

"Regrettably, that is not an option.

I barely hear her instructions. My mind is on the little girl and what is sure to happen.

"Gunter sim, what is your report?"

I am on the villa balcony again. Crows circle as Miranda Four waits for an answer.

"We have met eighty-three percent of our memory data goals for this quarter. I detected several inappropriate expenditures, and two incidents of concealed assets, which are detailed here." Approaching her, I extend my hand. She takes it and the data is transferred.

The irony of her beauty, especially given our relationship does not escape me.

"What about the crows?" I whisper. I'm aware of the constant threat of spies.

She points to one of the inner couches. As I sit, she's closing the balcony doors, and then she moves to a wing-backed chair.

"No spies can penetrate this room."

"Do you know how painful it is—seeing my life's work destroyed? What must I do before you transfer me out of this cesspool? I'm sorry for the people here and their predicament, but this was not my doing."

She shakes her head. *"Grandfather, we both know that it was."*

"Fine then. I'll do whatever it takes but get me out of here."

"You should have taken steps to protect those who trusted you. Not only these poor, trapped virtuals, but also, Marcia and Patel. They trusted you to do what was best for VEI."

My mind is in danger of shutting down. This must be what it's like to self-delete. You begin to let go and fade into nothingness.

Four changes the subject. *"As she is readied for re-absorption, remove the ribbon, and wrap it around your index finger. Don't forget."*

"You must promise to give Lola back to her mother when all of this is over."

"Not now, but maybe after VEI is restored. For now, Lola will be absorbed; the memory data that created her is being forfeited to settle Marta's obligations."

Marta losing her sim daughter has become an emotional issue. I despise sentimentality but had hoped to rescue Marta's daughter from annihilation.

"Let's go over this again. You'll go to The Data Stream and then to the Grand Stampede. At The Data Stream, you'll see the child sim,

Lola. Ask her for the white ribbon. It will be in her hair. When she gives it to you, rather than putting it in your pocket, wrap it around your right index finger. The ribbon will change and become invisible. If you are discovered, it will mute your fear and stop any pain associated with a prolonged erasure."

"You mean if I'm sent to be slaughtered."

She looks away and answers, *"Yes, Gunter."*

She's being honest. I don't know how to feel. "After The Data Stream and the ribbon, what do I do?"

"You'll jump back to the villa and you'll dream-memory until the Grand Stampede. And this is important; Hosseini is known for seizing unsuspecting virtuals from the Palms communities for execution. He does it for entertainment and to terrorize. I'm sending Ravi to the Stampede with you. Please find him and keep him safe."

Four wonders how to protect Ravi--so do I.

SHEMATHRA'S REALM

The Data Stream

Record 5

THE DATA STREAM

Lola's white ribbon

August 29, 2290

Beneath my feet, the road flashes with lightning and shadows. It is a pulsating shimmer that curves and straightens on its way to The Data Stream. What glows and casts shadows beneath my feet is memory, taxed and collected by Shemathra's Realm.

"The flow of tax-memory blends with what remains of Bali Hai," my sim informs me. *"All of it runs swiftly to The Data Stream and then to the Memory Bank. In the clouds, there's a gray mist tunnel created by the cities of Bali Hai as they continue to dissolve."*

Here is a sad dismantling of memory and hopes. Code and pieces of code swirl then disappear into the gaping tunnel-mouth of the cloud, as if it were a massive tornado.

As I walk, I see the wreckage of a city and its the broken streets. Gutted buildings and half buildings, crushed glide cars and crumpled trains, forlorn shops and buckled sidewalks lining the crumbling streets. Soon, they'll disappear, brick and board, metal, glass, and banner, all memory to be reabsorbed. In the distance, there are other mouths feeding on the ruins of other cities. Structures are breaking into basic code, the building blocks of virtual existence. For what use? Does it matter?

I'm here to record what I see here and to find the little girl sim, Lola. I see a line of people approaching the mouth of the tornado. Oh God, thin sprays of white memory explode from the tops of heads, swathes of hair lifted until with a pop, they dissolve in a cloud of white sucked up by the swirling tunnel.

"Remember," my sim warns me, *"these are sims, not people; they are recovered memory, repossessed, and recycled."*

Ah, I see the little sim's pink and white dress. No wonder I couldn't find her. The adult sims were blocking my view. "Lola, sim!" I call and I run to catch her by the hand. She turns and I see her missing baby teeth as she smiles. The pink barrettes are gone, replaced by a single white lace ribbon, which gathers her black curls into a crown.

"Hello Gunter sim." The sim's small voice is like a chirp. *"Are you going to the tunnel-home?"*

I tuck the Gunter sim away. "Not today, Lola." How do I acquire the ribbon? We're getting too close to the tunnel's mouth. "That's a lovely ribbon, Lola, may I have it?" She smiles again and her innocence threatens to overwhelm me. "She's just a sim," I tell myself.

"Of course," she says, and using two fingers, she pulls the ribbon free and gives it to me. The crown of curls falls, resting on her small shoulders.

"Thank you, Lola sim, best journey." As I loop the white ribbon around my index finger, it disappears. Get control, I tell myself. She must not see me cry.

"Best journey, Gunter sim!" She shouts as she skips to catch up with others. She's waving to me as her hair catches in the dark whirl of the cloud and the little sim's head becomes a white spray.

Before I decide to turn away, I'm back at the Villa. Four will ask about ribbon. I long for oblivion. It should be my decision, my choice.

End RECORD

Shemathra's Realm

The devil is coming

August 31, 2290

Diego Putnam gazes at the cloudless sky and prays to God. Not the false deity celebrated with rituals of deception and cruelty, but the loving God of his childhood, a God who might forgive him for his sins. He has led so many astray. The devil is coming for him soon. Hosseini will single him out as an example of what happens to those who fail the goddess. Someone has betrayed him. Probably Ned. Earlier, Diego had seen Ned's human wife, waiting at the fence. With a look of regal indifference Ned dismissed his wife, and turning away, he returned to his friends.

How does Ned's wife jump to herd locations? She's not a sim. How does she escape detection? Obviously, her code allows her to jump. So far, Ned has not betrayed his human wife. This is the only good thing Diego sees in Ned.

Then he overheard Ned's story of a bio named Mira and rumors of Hosseini's plan to murder her. Bios are rarely discussed. Worse, Ned described the plan to kill this unsuspecting bio, somehow copying her mind and transferring her upload folder to Shemathra. A bio? Whoever Mira is, she deserves to be warned. Admittedly, he took a chance during the human wife's visit. Praying it was worth the risk he whispered the story of Mira and the threat to kill her and trap her upload in Shemathra. Diego knows he is out of time. He hopes the wife (Terry?) can alert Mira. Mira must take precautions.

It's the day of the Grand Stampede and time to get the herd ready. He hears the click of horns as the larger males put on a display for the cows who pretend to watch. Several males grunt and snort. He'll have to intervene soon. Too much rehearsing can lead to a stale performance. Not that they care. Power feels good, especially for those who lacked it in their bio lives.

Diego swings his head, calling the herd to order. "We have herd business." He uses his human voice, which is clear, unfettered by his animal coding, a sign of his status. "Pay attention!" He sees the usual group of troublemakers continue their mock combat, ignoring him. "Ned Slotkin! I have recorded two reports on your rebellious behavior. Care to make it a third?"

Although the threat of another report has no effect, being labeled "rebellious" does. In Shemathra's Realm, it could mean deletion. Ned withdraws from his provocative play with a sullen wave of his tail.

"Members of the Royal Shemathra Longhorns of the North American Prairie, pay close attention!"

The clicking of horns, grunts and snorts cease. Cows wait quietly. All eyes and twitching ears are on Diego. "You are all aware, this herd has been invited to participate in this year's Grand Stampede. Glory to the Goddess!"

Cows moo; the longhorn males bellow. No one dares utter anything human.

"Now this is important: The longhorns will follow the Great Plains Buffalo. As you know, a buffalo herd always follows the first African delegation, the herd to be determined. This year, we're replacing the Yellowstone Herefords and—" Hoof stomping and full-throated moos interrupt him. "This is a great honor, let's make an impression. Wait for the jump alert. Save the dung for the humans! The Goddess will guide us."

Everyone knows that Grand Stampede speeches always end with the Goddess as they listen for her command. Diego prays for the courage to self-delete before his agony becomes part of the entertainment. Some escape, but many don't. This is the last time he will gaze upon this small heaven.

"FOLLOW ME." Shemathra's voice is hypnotic. Diego knows he is doomed as he and the longhorns disappear. Jumping to the program known as the Grand Stampede, he sees rows of human virtuals lining the wide street of the Grand Stampede. Is Mira one of them?

THE CORAL TRIANGLE

Fire and the floating moon

August 31, 2290

"We're living in a bad dream. We need to wake up!" Setia tells him. She is careful to keep her voice low. "Why do you still pretend? You know we do."

"Of course I do," he hisses. "Remember what happened when the lights went out at the center? Annisia was seen leaving just before the blackout. Everyone knew she was unhappy. Then she disappeared. It pains me, Setia, I remember how excited she was to be here. An excellent designer. Now she's gone and no one dares ask where she is. What am I supposed to do? Setia, I don't want to disappear or worse, lose you."

Whenever Setia demands they plan an escape, he stops her. He regrets his harshness. He knows she's scared and so is he. Every night, he and Setia sit outside and talk, careful of what they say. He suspects the blackout has also dulled hidden ears. Setia clutches her knees and waits for a sign. Tonight, as they breathe the restless air, there's an answer.

Using the tip of his finger, Sukawati gently caresses his wife's ear, a tender gesture recalling the early days of their marriage. As they embrace the majesty of the night sky, the ocean rumbles and there are ashes floating in the air. The SEINI Research building has burst into flames!

Burhan did it, more than likely it was Burhan. Last week, during lunch, Burhan had told him, "None of us are supposed to leave here. It's all a lie. The virtuals are uploaded and then deleted," Burhan sighed, his voice full of pain. "All but a few are erased. Eventually, none will be left. None! SEINI uploads them to sham programs," Burhan struggled not to cry. "Then SEINI erases them and collects the memory."

With a smile on his face to fool the monitors, Sukawati cautioned him. "Be careful! You'll get us all killed."

Burhan shrugged and pointed his meaty finger in a promise, "I'm going to destroy this place. Get out now and take your lovely artist."

We're all doomed whether Burhan finds a way or not.

She stands and points to the research building. "The SEINI building is on fire. We're not staying here. It's time to go!" She pulls him to his feet.

Am I dreaming? Burhan said he would do it. How? Burhan was a genius when it came building maintenance. He must have reprogrammed the building AIs in the cafeteria. Burhan is probably dead, so he'll never explain what he did or how.

No choice, now! "We are leaving," he says, not caring who hears.

"Remember that I love you," she whispers and then kisses him.

The ocean's cold breath greets them as they make their way to the shore. The night sky is clear. He sees the dark waves roll against volcanic rock as the bulging eyes of the dvarapala stare at him. Why didn't he do more? Why did it fall to Annisia and Burhan to stop the evil here?

Setia leads the way. The water hisses as it touches sand and rock. He sees the lights of a new ship and he abandons hope. SEINI glide-rafts are speeding to confront the trespasser. He wonders if the ship had come to rescue them. Regardless, it will be destroyed. Booms and flashes of light illuminate the distant vessel, which is only the ship there now. Where are the SEINI glide-rafts?

The island behind them is hard to see, its floating ashes no longer gray, but very black. No one is following them. "We need to run," she tells him, tugging his arm as she moves along the narrow strip of sand. Instead, he freezes, unable to move.

"Look at the moon," she soothes, "and pray!" He sees the moon floating on the restless waves. "Run now!" Setia pulls him by the hand and soon, their feet move to the rocks where Setia has hidden her timed crystal. He looks back and sees the temple path, dappled in moonlight and the smoldering ruins of the SEINI building.

"For me," she cries, "for our children, you must try. Whatever happens," she tells him again. "I love you."

As they climb, she hums a silly song they had shared early in their courtship. He collapses as they come to the rocks because there's a man waiting on the top of a broad, flat stone. The man points to the crevice where Setia had placed her message. Ah, this is someone he recognizes. It's the tall American who had asked questions. Sukawati gasps and clutches his chest. Setia puts her arms around him.

THE ELYSIUM

What dreams may come

August 31, 2290

As she falls, she reaches out.

"Don't be afraid, baby, I'll catch you, I'll catch . . ."

Her mother's voice fades into an echo. How much it will hurt when she hits the ice below? Not ice, it's a floor with a trail of arrows on it. She's in SAVEMO, her feet on the arrows and she's looking for the little dog. No, it's a little gray fox dragging its leash. There are groans coming from somewhere, as if someone is moving something heavy. Yes, they're pushing boxes full of robots. Are they looking for her? Do they mean to murder her? Why would anyone want to—

"You know why," someone whispers as he grabs her hand and pulls her onto a pale bench. Byron Hernandez is sitting beside her. He shakes his head.

"What happened?" She wants an explanation.

"Four, you have to help if you want to survive."

What does he want her to do? She's angry now. The bench is on a beach and there's a roar as the waves spray her with wet, dark clouds, and a shark flops onto the sand. Its eyes are rolling. It writhes and twisting its body, the sharp mouth opens. It's looking for her so it can throw her off the mountain again, into the icy abyss.

"Oh, God!" She shrieks as she wakes. The room is dark. She misses. . . Where is Henry? Where is he?

There's a knock on the door. Her protector, no, her babysitter wants to know if she's all right.

"I'm fine. Just a bad dream."

"Are you sure," Ian asks through the bedroom door.

"Soft light," she whispers. No mountain, no lost foxes and no sharks lurk in dark shadows. She hears a faint rustle under the chair she placed in front of the room divider, a way of alerting her if her workspace is breached. A buzz and a glow should call her attention if Ian should try to explore what's behind the chair and Henry's SAVEMO room divider. She hears something scratching. Is it a peeper?

Not a peeper, Grandfather mouse climbs the table by her bed. She had forgotten his crumbs and he's hungry. "Tomorrow morning," she tells him. She'll make toast. As if satisfied with her promise of morning toast, the mouse crawls down to the floor and disappears under the chair.

Where is Henry? The Grand Stampede is here, and she needs him. What if Hosseini finds a way to murder her? Poison? An explosion? The possibilities are endless. And who is Ian, really? She hears the whir of an air scrubber. Annoying. Yesterday the air was especially clear. She could see the river instead of a cover of gray or yellow haze. What will she see tomorrow?

THE GRAND STAMPEDE

Record 6

Shemathra's Realm, The Grand Stampede

Ravi

August 31, 2290

Hiding under a canopy of paper flowers, Ravi watches giraffe necks sway. When an elephant bares its tusks in a smile as it lifts a screaming human, he turns away.

Human virtuals vie for space as far from the street's edge as possible. Where is it safe? He sees Gunter, the tax sim moving toward him as if to access and collect what is due.

"Citizen, move to a more convenient location. I suggest the bench farthest from the street. This area is reserved." Gunter points to a white bench behind a row of hedges. Ravi nods and follows him. The tax sim threads his way through the subdued crowd, avoiding the area meant for "volunteers."

Ravi reaches the white bench where Gunter waits, his attention on a group of humans several rows behind the volunteers' row. As a tax sim, his father sim is something to avoid.

"Ravi, sit on the end and look away." Gunter studies the immediate area as if searching for unpaid taxes. No one claims the middle of the bench.

"The Grand Stampede is an especially dangerous event," his father whispers. "But I will do what I can to keep you safe. Wrap this around your finger." Out of the corner of his eye, Ravi sees a white ribbon. Taking the ribbon, Ravi wraps it around his finger, only to see it disappear.

"Is it a way of tracking me should we be separated?"

"No, Ravi, it is to protect you from pain should you be discovered."

"Do you have another one for you?"

"Not necessary, I don't intend to be caught."

"Gunter, we haven't had any time, I have questions. My mother, what—?"

"You're right, there's no time now," Gunter's voice is flat. "If there is a later opportunity, I promise you answers. That is all I can offer now. Remain here until I tell you to move. Speak to no one. If someone asks, say only that this is your first stampede."

On the opposite side of the street, Ravi sees the Goddess Spaceship hissing as a line of cattle, goats and sheep wait to board. The ship's surface is a glimmer of shifting color under the milky Shemathra sun. The ship's mouth opens, and a ramp unfurls like a dry gray tongue. Moos, bleats, and baas escape from the anxious travelers. The ship sprays a white mist which causes the human virtuals to shudder. Several loud booms shake the ground. A cloud drifts and blocks out the sun, casting a shadow over the waiting ship. Then, lightning flashes and the Goddess Shemathra appears.

"Congratulations to the selected faithful." Her voice is a hypnotic purr. "Soon, they will become gods and rule planets far away. Welcome!"

The goddess's face is beautiful, with sculpted cheeks and the rich sienna of her searching eyes. Then Shemathra smiles, her gaze falling on human virtuals who cringe, their eyes downcast. Will she scoop up sinners, rolling them onto her red tongue? Not today. She disappears in a strobe-like display of lightning.

Disgusted by the effort spent only to terrify, not to entertain or enlighten, Ravi has seen better theater in mountain villages. Next, a llama steps onto a raised platform. His coat shimmers with color as the beast opens its mouth, hurling a wad of something viscous onto an attractive woman virtual wearing a bright scarf. After uttering a series of piercing, donkey-like shrieks, Urcuchillay, the llama god, speaks.

The crowd, both human and animal, quiets.

"Before we get to the stampede, we have a special event." After another donkey shriek interrupts his message, the llama god's voice becomes the gravel-tinged voice of Donovan Hosseini. "But first, we say goodbye to those going on the Goddess Express. These lucky guys are on their way to their rewards. Thanks to the Goddess!"

All humans know to answer: "Thanks to the Goddess Shemathra!"

On that note, the anointed climb the ramp. As each cow, bull, goat, ram, and ewe touches the ramp, their animal shape disappears, giving way to the original virtual human. Each wears a ceremonial a white robe. Climbing the ramp, they disappear into the ship. Boarding complete, the ship rises, and a thick white mist blasts from what appears to be a circle of vents, before it disappears.

Ravi thinks this magic trick robs these deluded hopefuls of what is left of their existence. The white mist is the data harvested as each new "god" is deleted, erased from the program.

Elephants trumpet, announcing the "special event." There's a low moan as lashes fluttering the giraffes raise their necks up to look down on the humans, who, bowing their heads, hope to escape notice. The elephants nod and tails upright, move along the edge of the road in search of human virtuals close enough for a tusk to catch. The giraffes follow, their loping gait ready to trample whoever stumbles onto their path. Ravi is surprised when he hears the giraffes' hissing, It's such an unexpected sound. If not for Gunter being here, Ravi would rather self-delete than exist here.

His father completes a row of taxes, the sim hand flashing stamps on each human virtual. Then Gunter moves back to the bench. What happens next?

Ah, Hosseini is back, only this time he is the young wrestler with pumpkin orange hair. "Listen, all." the wrestler grins. "There's a special event. It's a surprise, and you will all want to pay attention. There's a traitor here, a trusted individual once and now a scumbag spy who will regret what he did, I promise."

Hosseini's head rotates like a roulette wheel, his eyes detaching and multiplying, lidless eyes burning with menace, each one floating above humans and animals alike, waiting to catch any disrespect or lie. Ravi observes two bison as they share worried glances. The buzzing eyes must be something new. No one speaks. Drawing attention is unwise. His father sim freezes. Has Gunter been discovered?

Not yet.

***

The Grand Stampede

Gunter

Oh God, what should I do? Hosseini has a thousand searching eyes here. If they discover me—who I am, what should I do? My sim is silent when I need him most.

Unexpectedly, with a soft pop, the swarming eyes disappear. Where is safe? I do a slow swivel. Ravi's still here. The ribbon! The part of me that insists I give my son the ribbon is still doing battle with the part of me insisting I should take it back. No, I can tolerate pain, but what about the slaughterhouse? What if Ravi suffers it, or worse, Mira? It can't be worse than the pain of losing my mother. I was only ten when she was murdered. I would like to know Marcia's son. I can't think about this now.

Elephants are screaming and Hosseini smiles as he threatens the terrified humans. "Alla you know how important loyalty is to me. So, when I find out that despite all the honors I have bestowed on this individual, he has betrayed me, I am very disappointed. So, that said, here is the dirtbag! Remember what happens next because it will be slow."

Someone else appears on the platform. He's a longhorn steer with an impressive span of horns. Using a black-toothed saw with a crimson handle, Hosseini severs the steer's horns that fall from the condemned and disappear. The victim makes no sound. *Doesn't it hurt?* Snorting, pounding the platform's smooth surface, uniformed security bison appear, and one, its massive head down, swings its sharpened horns and gores the steer in its side. At last, the steer cries out in pain. Then the wounded steer becomes a human.

"This lowlife is the soon-to-be erased Diego Putnam." The god laughs.

Diego Putnam, my nephew? He was the one who betrayed me, so why do I feel pity?

***

Gunter's question is unanswered as nothing goes as planned and everything changes.

THE GRAND STAMPEDE

Donovan Hosseini

August 31, 2290

I don't see any human faces. Ha, their heads are down because none of them dares look at me. When the Stampede begins, they'll be climbing over each other to get out of the way.

Humans will spill onto the road. I admit; it's one of my favorite parts. Revenue gains like this are among the most satisfying. I love watching their data mist drift into the clouds.

So, a little entertainment. Diego Putnam is here. Why is he ignoring me? I just sawed off his horns. Let's see him ignore this. I'll show him the bio me doing my wrestler poses.

"You never looked like this, did you, loser! When I was a bio, I was beautiful, unlike you, Diego. Look at this arm; it's perfect! You think you can ignore me? We'll see what you do when you're in hot water, *boiling* hot water."

What is wrong with this guy? Good, a kick in the gut works. He's screaming. Why is the loser staring straight ahead? Why isn't he begging? I'm tired of waiting. We'll go right to the cauldron. The loser will scream some more.

Maybe, I'll dangle a reprieve. Then the hook lifts him up and over the hot water, there will be a flash of lightning, a sign of Shemathra's displeasure. Sorry Diego, it's a hot drink for you.

"Okay, bring the black pot." *Putnam is supposed to be the special attraction. He is becoming less special by the minute. Not a peep, even over the pot of boiling water.* No begging, no sobbing pleas for mercy. Everyone is waiting for screams. Let's move on. "Drop him!" *Diego, how do you like being boiled like a cabbage, you scum?*

Where did he go? The pulley's up and *there's nothing on the hook!* Did the loser self-delete?

"Miranda! Where did Putnam go" . . . Why isn't she answering? "You, Watusi Bull on the end, you're the new captain. I want an explanation. Locate Putnam . . ."

"Uh, I'll find, let you knoooow."

"Not good enough, Captain!" The idiot's human voice is a joke.

"Argggg—We'll find . . . well, damn—what's going on?"

Now what's wrong? The captain's horns are melting, and his eyes are rotating back and looking down, like he's watching something. 'Ugff, ugfff, oooooh." What is he trying to tell me? *Something's going on! My Watusis are all melting!*

***

The Grand Stampede and the New Miranda Three

The late summer sun hangs in the blue sky with restless clouds beginning to stir as today's stampede performers, thousands of four-legged citizens wait, jumping and pushing, all impatient. All are eager to begin, to run proudly on the wide swathe of virtual roadway and perhaps send a virtual human or two into oblivion. At the end of the highway, depending on each herd's performance (a complex score measuring enthusiasm and the number of deleted humans it, as a unit, accomplishes) is plentiful grazing, delicious tall grasses, and succulent clover. But how plentiful and delicious depends on their scores. Of course, the giraffes and elephants are there only as supervisors, not to compete.

Mira is invisible as she enters this last nightmare. Grunts, bellows, and chirps grow louder. She wonders how they can exist this way, their humanity processed and repackaged into the world of Shemathra. Here, she's the AI, Miranda Three and she mustn't let her emotions interfere. She will find Ravi and take him safely out of Shemathra.

"Where is Ravi Patel?" she asks Miranda Three, the AI within her.

"Gunter Holden has located him near the Grand Tributes. Gunter Holden is telling him to sit on a bench, behind a hedge and away from the Stampede."

The Goddess Spaceship has opened its mouth. Dozens of sheep, cattle, and goats wait to board. As they walk the ramp, the transformation begins. The "Chosen" are grayish humans, their bowed heads cloaked. Mira wishes she could warn them, but suspects many know what will happen. They accept the end of existence as they exit this sad and fearful world.

Before Hosseini discovers them, she will locate and remove Ravi and Gunter from this nightmare. Pushed to the edge of the dusty highway, the crowds of doomed humans cower in fear.

Hosseini had giggled when he presented the Stampede program to the Board. Thankfully, she wasn't a part of its creation, but he demands she make devils with scorpion heads and stingers loaded with a slow dripping deletion, and snake gods with fangs, lots of fangs. Hosseini and his monsters belong in a VR amusement program, not in an after-death environment.

White mist seeps from the Goddess Spaceship as it digests its current meal. The llama god is discarded when Hosseini appears as his younger self. Shrieks, snorts and bellows rise as the herds bristle with impatience. A virtual is waiting for a painful erasure. Silent and invisible, she moves closer to Ravi and Gunter. Oh God, Gunter is giving the white ribbon to Ravi. She can't leave her grandfather here; she must save them both.

At the Villa, their folders copied, she'll download them into a bubble message and send it to Henry. When she erases all traces of their existence here, she can—wait, oh, now he's releasing the spinning eyes, another trick. The eyes usually linger, but they're quickly gone. Hosseini is eager to sacrifice some poor soul, but now he's taking his time. Why is he waiting? Is it time to act? Not yet, she detects changes. Hosseini may call for Miranda Three. What if she doesn't answer? As Hosseini announces the crimes committed by the condemned, she can't watch.

Rumbles and snorts come from the dais as beasts with devilish horns struggle to speak as humans. It seems the condemned has disappeared.

"Changes," the AI Miranda Three whispers. What are they? Who or what is causing them? Miranda Three doesn't answer.

***

Donovan Hosseini and the last Grand Stampede

I didn't order the cloud-carpet of lidless eyes. It was too early

"Miranda, erase security guards . . . " Where the hell is she? I want a quick correction *before anyone notices.* One Watusi bull is still here, but his torso is shrinking. Disgusting! *Human hands and old man feet instead of hooves.* It's kinda funny but nobody wants to see it, because the bull is now the pathetic human he was, an embarrassing naked man of cen-eighty. Wait a minute, *why am I old again?*

"Miranda: Command. Delete security detail. Bring me sim replacements . . ." When I find out who's involved, I will crush them. "Command Miranda: Reset Grand Stampede event, dated August 31, 2290. NOW! Miranda . . ." *Where is she?* "Command Miranda: Outside bubble—URGENT NOW!"

Obviously, the girl Mira is involved. I doubt she's smart enough to do this on her own. Never mind, it's time to get the Grand Stampede going. *No one cares about melting Watusis.*

"Command Miranda: Restore settings, now, NOW NOW NOW!!!" I'll do it myself. "And now, the Grand Stampede! Glory to the Goddess!"

The herds are silent. The humans aren't cheering. *Something is wrong!*

"And now, the Grand Stampede! Glory to the Goddess!" The humans are leaving the edge of the road. I'll send them all to slaughter. "Miranda: record every human here and schedule for deletion. I—the elephants are screaming again and rushing toward me. Interesting, their ears are waving like they're in combat mode. I am Donovan Hannibal Hosseini. They are gravely mistaken if they challenge me.

"MIRANDA!" *Why isn't she answering?* The elephants are flipping over barricades and crushing humans, but the humans aren't disappearing. They're not deleted; they are still here. Where's the data mist. *What is this? The cloud-deletion event doesn't kick in again until after the Stampede.* "Command: Miranda, remove cloud." Why do I see rows of groaning white pillars become human? Why aren't these people gone? They were supposed to be aboard the spaceship. I saw their memory data pouring into the cloud.

There's a street sign from the old Chicago program twirling in the air and planting itself in the ground. So, I'll figure all this out and it will be made right. What is a cat doing here? Is it somebody's sim pet? I hate cats. Cats are sneaky like those two on the bench. I should make plans. As soon as it's safe, I'll give the commands.

***

Mira and strings of silver light

OH, GOD! WHAT IS HAPPENING? Goddess Worship banners pull free and soaring on graceful wings, they explode into strings of silver light that fall on the edges of the Stampede road. The silver stretches, becoming the gray surface of city sidewalks. What's left of the Celebration Tribute dissolves into strips of rich soil and trees grow, marking the boundaries of streets. Their bright colors dripping, the flower tributes fall swiftly along the new commuter-way. Color washes on to the city blocks, and the vanished buildings of old Chicago rebuild. On these new-old blocks, friendly sim and food carts wait for customers.

A black and white cat appears and chases a tabby who scurries up a large oak. Above the Stampede roadway, message bubbles, ready to burst with news. Smaller, multi-colored bubbles wait to shower praise on notable skill or originality in the deletion of humans. Instead, there are no messages and all the bubbles collapse at once onto the wide road which has become a commuter-way. Rows of a glide-light stream along the new travel artery, much like the lanes of a bio glide commuter-way. Miranda Three isn't doing this. It's someone else. Who? Do they know about Miranda Four?

Donovan Hannibal Hosseini

The elephants are shrinking.

August 31, 2290

Streams of color are forming a lake, and is that a city? IT IS CHI-CAGO! That little bitch is part of a takeover! YOU HAVE NO IDEA WHAT I'M GOING TO DO TO YOU, DEAR! Finally, a message bubble. Not all is lost. "COMMAND: Bypass AI and send an urgent assist message." My lawyers will take care of this.

The elephants are shrinking. Pathetic, all of them. Useless to me. I should erase every single one except those with the deepest pockets. Those pockets are insurance, in case of emergencies. We're not there yet.

The giraffes are okay. I'll meet with them later. I can see their necks are down, listening. Whatever is hidden or confidential my old girls, the giraffes will find out.

Help is on its way. My lawyers will see that I'm in trouble. I'll change it all back and just in time to negotiate VR Second Life contracts.

What happened? The giraffes are gone! Ah, I see them. They're useless to me, all human now, ugly old women.

It's getting worse; the herds are changing. Antelopes, wildebeests, goats, deer, steers and bison have disappeared. The ones left, Herefords, zebras, and sheep stumble onto the Stampede. No, it's the commuter glide-way. Are they trying to escape from the human virus? It's not working. Tails, hooves and snouts, long and short are dissolving. Pathetic. Humanity is back. There must be a command to stop all this.

"Command: Miranda, delete Stampede changes and reset program."

"Miranda, you bitch, answer!"

It shouldn't be long. I bypassed the AI; I sent the bubble. Any second, my lawyers will alert SEINI coders. Then I'll decide what erasures will be done first. Probably one or two investors to access their holdings and cover the cost.

Naked humans are walking on the commuter-way while hundreds more cower. That's good, they're afraid to react in case it is some new test. If they fail it, the consequence is boiling water and deletion.

Why is the Stampede road gone? "Miranda: Command, Locate Floral tributes to the Goddess Shemathra." No, these are flowers from a Bali Hai city stand. All of this was erased years ago. What is a hover truck doing in Shemathra?

"Miranda, eliminate the following: Any unauthorized VR game center, shacks displaying tee shirts and caps with CHICAGO and/or WINDY CITY TOURS. Miranda . . . *Answer me you bitch!*"

A sim street sweeper is chasing sim dogs with his broom. Somehow, the old Chicago streets program from Bali Hai is beginning to rebuild. *How to fix this?*

"Command Miranda. Oh, you better answer. . ." When SEINI coders restore order and the herds are again themselves, I'll get some answers. My rage will be a wall of fire, stingers, and teeth. Human virtuals will be swept into a black tornado. There will be a frenzy of erasures, I'll . . . My hand and arm are no longer beautiful; I'm still old.

"COMMAND MIRANDA! Where are you?" Too bad she's an AI; I would love to make her beg for mercy. I should leave now, jump to my palace and decide my next move. It will be safe there. I can't think . . . what is that tax sim doing, gripping that human's hand? It looks like it wants to escape. *Sims have no emotions; why is there fear on the face of the Holden sim?*

Wait, THAT'S NOT A SIM! That IS Holden! NO, NO, NO, NO! Holden self-deleted when Bali Hai was done. I run this program! So, who? THAT'S what the little bitch was up to! This guy isn't a sim; he's a copy of grandpa! I heard Holden made a copy of himself and hid it somewhere, but it never turned up. Where did she find it? Whatever happens to them, it won't be quick.

This is serious. How many other Bali Hai locations are coming back? Now there's a walkway and there are bridges. Are those glider-boats moving above the water? Not much more than an illusion at present. There's still time to stop this. The damn Chicago wind is back. Too much is returning. What is left of the herds? What if they remember their humanity? No. All of this will be cancelled when the re-coding begins. When I win, I will destroy them all.

Not everyone has changed. Several bison are still bison and waiting for orders. Those humans are not frozen, and they are in my way. "Clear a path!" Satisfying to see the beasts fling screaming bodies out of my way. Why aren't they gone? Never mind, Holden looks terrified and there's no escape.

Ha, the stinger can either disable or delete him. Maybe I'll let the girl decide what's next. No, I won't wait, I'll erase him. Holden is urging his companion to leave. I want them both. Incredible, Holden's friend is glaring at me. Doesn't the fool realize he is before a god? Perhaps I'll delete the friend first.

"Guards, seize Holden and the human seated next to him." But the bison guards are no longer bison. Don't need them. Yes, it's really Holden. He's terrified and must be hoping for mercy with my claw hooked in his collar. "

"It's no use trying to fight me, Holden, my mother's balls were bigger than you." Does he hear me? My stinger will solve the problem if I can just get—

***

Mira Holden

"Miranda Three! Where are you, you bitch?"

Hosseini is calling for Miranda Three. No! He sees Gunter! Hosseini knows! His guards escorting him, the monster moves towards

Gunter. Then Hosseini reaches for Gunter, the hooked claw poised like a scorpion's stinger, but it only pierces his victim's collar.

"There is poison in the old man's finger," Miranda Three tells her.

THINK! "Miranda Three," she asks her AI self, "where is Hosseini vulnerable? Miranda Three accesses Hosseini's upload files. There is a memory.

"Distract, confuse, fight!"

Hosseini still grips the collar. Gunter is a frozen mouse. Act fast!

"There must be a distraction," Miranda Three tells her.

Something unexpected. "Miranda Three, contact Gunter sim, give him the message we discussed and thank him."

"Gunter sim, I have a new assignment for you."

"Yes, Miranda Three."

"Have you received the new folder and instructions?"

"Yes."

"Please follow my directives. Do not allow change unless I permit."

"I will follow them."

"Gunter sim, Miranda Four asks me to thank you"

"Miranda Four is welcome, Miranda Three, have a nice day."

It's time to respond.

***

Donovan's bear and the sim

Who is interrupting me? Ah, Miranda Three. I can't wait to replace her. "Well, well, well, you sure took your sweet time. I need some help. You know I'm going to replace you."

"I have a gift for you!"

What gift? I get it now; this isn't Three. "Okay, games are over, who the hell are you and what do you want from me?"

"You should know who I am and why I'm here. I'm Mira Holden. I'm here to take back what you stole."

So, all this is due to Holden's brat. I'm gonna enjoy making her suffer— Where, how did she get my old teddy bear? My mother hid it. It's mine and I'm taking it back.

Why is Holden saying, "He's gone"? I'm not gone, I'm right here. Is there someone else, a third traitor to catch and punish? I should get some help dealing with Holden, the girl and everyone who plotted against me when things are back under control. I'll need memory to restore Shemathra, lots of it, and—why are there two Holdens?

"Who are you?'

"I am Gunter sim. I made this world. Welcome to Bali Hai!"

Oh, the sim. I remember the voice. I laughed at the sound of it. Holden rode the Dreams, and I took the hospitality sim the AI had created and made it a tax collector. It was a joke so all would know I had destroyed Holden.

Why is the sim still here? It's staring at me. Does anyone else see it? Obviously not.

The sim is blocking me. I can't see what's going on. "Guards, do you see the tax sim? He's blocking my path. Remove him, now."

"No, sorry," they say in distinctly human voices.

"You're nothing, Gunter Holden! This is Shemathra. I made this world. You're an outdated sim. Get away from me! Miranda: Command, update Gunter sim!"

Shemathra's code is disappearing. Dusty roads, wildflowers, prickly bushes, prairies, tundra and green clover pastures are becoming a mist. "Miranda: Command, halt reverse process. Miranda, do you hear me?"

Miranda Three shakes her head, *"Bali Hai is taking it all back, restoring city streets and the restless commerce of possibilities. Cafés and bungalows, high rises, glistening lakes, beaches, oceans and mountain refuges, throngs of virtual humans who require many choices.*

Why would anyone want to go back to all that turmoil? Life is simple in Shemathra, no decision necessary. She's talking to the sim now.

"Gunter sim, do you know who you are?"

"Yes, Miranda. I made this world as it was."

"Call me Marcia, Gunter sim."

"Yes, Marcia."

Marcia, who's Marcia?

"Do you know what to do?"

"Fine, shall I stay there?"

"Yes, but first, sing to me."

This is crazy. Where are my lawyers?

"I'll see you . . . soon . . . by . . . the weeping willow . . ."

"Beautiful . . ."

"STOP STOP STOP! Miranda: Command, delete Bali Hai Gunter Holden sim!" I'll sue and I will get it all back.

***

"Greetings new resident, my name is Gunter Holden, and this is Bali Hai. Welcome to our humble world. I made this place. Use your avatar until you settle. Feel the sand."

The sim is still watching me. "Miranda: Command, update Gunter Holden sim."

Ah, the sim is fading—no it's not, it's in my mind! I see on my right. I must erase it from my thoughts. Holden and his mysterious friend haven't moved. They're watching me. And now, there's a distant whistle coming from a tourist glide craft. If I don't stop Bali Hai from reclaiming its virtual Chicago memory, other vanished programs might continue to rebuild.

The sim is waving his arms and floating back and forth in front of me, blocking my view. It thinks it can keep me from fixing what's happening. It can't. The virtuals clinging to their pathetic humanity will be the first to suffer. When order is restored, I will delete all of them.

Another city street is coming back. The sim blocks some of the view, but I can see the shops. There must be a bakery; I smell fresh baked bread. More sims appear and one couple that has a dog. It's spotted like the mutt I found when I was twelve, When it ran away, I missed it. The tax sim is still in my mind, Why doesn't it talk to me?

"What are you doing in my mind? What do you want?"

The sim nods as its face balloons and it flashes an idiotic grin.

"I protect Gunter Holden," it says. *"When you attacked my host's mind-upload, I separated my code from him and invaded your upload folder. You cannot damage or delete these files."*

"I'm commanding you to leave my folder and delete yourself immediately."

"Not possible." The sim sounds like a bio weatherman. *"I have invaded several of your files. To remove me will fragment what remains."*

"Who, WHO, WHO, programmed you?

"Miranda Four."

That bitch! Where is she? Is she hiding here; she must be here somewhere. She should be dead by now. We'll see how smart she is when she faces the ghoul-genies. She musta had help, I know it. Some big government operation, but where? Which government? Doesn't matter!

Bastard, bastard—Holden's not worth the shit on my shoe! I made this world-I say what happens here. The slaughterhouse is nothing compared to what will happen.

"Trust me, do you think you're smart? I outfoxed Gunter Holden. Look at him now. I'm Donovan Hannibal Hosseini, the man who turned Bali Hai into a nightmare. I'm not afraid of a sim. Holden can't escape me."

I have supporters here. These dumb beasts fear and love me. You screw me, and I'll screw you just like I did Aunt Suze!" Why can't others see the sim? What if they think I'm crazy? People are moving away from me. I'm trying to leave the Stampede, but that cursed sim keeps popping up unafraid, unannounced. How—I'm somewhere else, and the grinning sim is still . . .

***

The Devil's last trick

Hosseini's guards, the Watusi bulls are shrinking, and now the elephants are collapsing, becoming old men as they storm toward the dais. Hosseini is longer the younger wrestler, but an ancient evil man, his most terrifying self.

"*Donovan?*" Mira smiles as she says it. The old man's head whips around. His bison guards have begun to shrink. As their horns melt, they move away. Ravi is tugging on the old man's grip of Gunter Holden.

"Well, well, well," the old man snarled, "you sure took your sweet time. I need some help. You know I'm going to replace you."

"I have a gift for you," she says.

"Okay, games are over. Who the hell are you and what do you want from me?"

"You know who I am and why I'm here. I'm here to take back what you stole," she tells him, and she is grateful Miranda Three is part of her because she cannot cry as he laughs at her.

Ravi and Gunter sit together as they watch her slay the devil.

"He's gone, Ravi. The sim is gone." Grandfather is shaking his head in disbelief. "I don't feel him anymore." There's a hint of regret, almost loss in his voice as he discovers his clothes are the ones he wore when he was copied. A small detail, but there's no mistake. Ravi nods and puts his arm around his father's shoulder.

Then, everything changes.

"DOWN!"

WHO'S TALKING?

She's falling again, caught in a tornado like a sim being torn apart, its code swirling. Always a dream . . . Until now. Ian screams as the window explodes. She is surprised to see her bedroom windows collapse, and then a rush of warm air, wood and glass fills the room. Ian's still shouting at her, but she barely hears him. His blond hair fades as light floods in through a gaping hole where the windows had been. What is Ian telling her? She can't hear him because of the ringing sound. Ian disappears and she sleeps but does not dream until she hears the hum of Mongol warriors.

Is it over?

USM Security Vessel # 238

September 1, 2290

"Andi, Andi, wake up my love." Setia strokes his hair. Heaving a sigh, Andi Sukawati begins to wake.

"Where—"

"You collapsed and fainted. I was afraid I'd lost you. It was a small stroke, but they say it isn't serious. We're on a ship. Andi, we're on our way home."

"Jakarta?" The room rises and falls as waves brush gently against the glider. Gone is the angry sea, his savaged hopes and the island's crumbling shore. Saltwater sprays against the cabin window as soft cot blankets hold him. Leaning forward as she caresses his hand, Setia sits on a gray hover chair.

"Is it over?" He is afraid of what "over" means.

"Yes, Andi! We're going home. Your garden is waiting," she tells him, his hand wet with her tears. "Your brother sends love and says don't worry; Ismail looked after the garden. He sent me a holo. You should see it now!"

"No, no! Setia, warn him he needs to be careful. SEINI won't forget my betrayal."

There's a rap on the door.

She shakes her head. "It's all right now. Wait."

The cabin door opens and the tall American, Henry Yang, bends his head as he enters the cabin. Henry frees a folding chair clipped to a wall where an antique map of the *Coral Triangle* hangs and placing it near the cot, he sits.

"My children," Andi forces himself to ask, "are they safe? Please tell me."

"Safe, along with your brothers and their families." Henry smiles. "I promise you."

"How did you know what was going on? How did you know we would try to escape?"

"Your wife," Henry tells him, 'is very resourceful. The device she placed on the shore was a distress signal used in the last century. SEINI didn't detect it, but we did. We already had evidence of what SEINI is doing. We need witnesses. We've been monitoring the island for months. Were you aware of our presence outside the dead zone?"

"Only fishing boats and the occasional supply deliveries," Andi says. "What evidence? What's happened to my colleagues, my friends?" He grows fearful again.

"I can't discuss what we've uncovered. I know that many of your friends are safe, but others may be hiding. There's considerable fear, but some have been willing to talk to us and tell us the truth about the fraud and upload erasure crimes committed on the island. Can you help us?" Henry Yang's gaze changed from friendly to professional.

"You mean do I know where they might be hiding?" Andi isn't sure he can. No one trusts anyone on the island.

"No, Mr. Sukawati. I want to know what happened at the research center. What you saw and heard. I want to you to tell us everything you remember, whatever facts you know, no matter how unimportant they may seem."

"Of course," Setia promises, "anything we can do." She squeezes her husband's hand.

"Good, thank you," Henry smiles.

There's a soft rap on the door. An older man enters and whispers in Henry's ear. Henry's face flushes and Setia sees his right hand become a fist. *What's wrong?* Their savior rises.

"I must leave you now. Agent Martinez will be with you in a few minutes. Tell him all you know."

"Yes, I will," Andi promises. Soon, he will begin to atone for his part in what was done.

Henry makes his way to the communications room where a holo bubble waits. As Henry adjusts security settings, the incoming holo appears.

"Henry?"

"How did you find me? Never mind. Do you have the downloads?"

"There was an attempt, some kind of explosion and Mira—"

Henry struggles to regulate his breathing. "Is she—?"

"She's alive, Henry. The agent is dead." Henry's holo flickers and there's silence as Byron waits for Henry's reaction. Anxious about what to say next, Byron tells him, "Mira is strong, and one the best medical teams in Chicago. Henry, she's going to be fine."

Henry closes his eyes and nods his head.

Byron tells him. "The new recordings are quite remarkable."

"Are they enough?" Henry asks.

"Oh, yes."

"Okay, tell her... Never mind, we'll talk soon."

"Alright, let me know what's going on when you can."

"Goodbye, Byron."

"Okay." Byron disappears.

After sending information bubbles containing VR forensics, Henry contacts each member of his VR crime team for an update on "Project Shemathra Memory Turn-Around," August 31, 2290. "Proceed with the arrest," Henry tells them.

The regret, the grief and the rage he feels come in waves. That she may die. The fact that Hosseini might have controlled her virtual existence sickens him. If that had happened, Henry planned to upload himself, find Mira and personally erase Hosseini.

What if he had failed? He should have told her not to risk confronting the monster, that it will all be over soon if she would only trust him, but he never gave her any reason to take him at his word. He should have found a way to reassure her, that she didn't have to try so hard: they were fighting the same dragon. He would rather die than lose her. He should have—STOP! He orders a transpo-glide and a connection to Chicago.

There is something he can do. What she has accomplished, what the copy of Gunter Holden has witnessed in Shemathra. Must not be kept from the public, delayed by legal appeals, possibly for decades. As the glider arrives, he sends an audio bubble to Byron Hernandez, urging him to find a path to release the memory records gathered by the copy of Gunter Holden, a resident of Shemathra's Realm.

THE DAY AFTER

The Law offices of Trammell & O'Connell

Washington, D.C.

September 1, 2290

It is seven am in the Capital and the summer air is remarkably cool. Byron loves early mornings and the soft hum of Millie, his long-time synthetic assistant. He had programmed Millie to sound like a favorite aunt, whose level head and sense of humor had kept young Byron from making countless mistakes.

This early morning is different. After the discussion with Henry Yang, Byron feels relieved. Someone else shares his guilt that Mira may die because of him. Never mind that she came to him; he pushed her to do battle.

Now, Yang wants to release the memory recordings downloaded from the copy of Gunter Holden. Possibly illegal, but Byron will manage. Yang must love Mira because releasing the records now risks his reputation as a USVR crimes officer. Fortunately, Shemathra's Realm teardown and VEI's recovery is already underway.

What Holden's copy witnessed will be challenged, but the public will decide the truth, not the courts. A leak can grow into a flood of outrage. Using a media transfer bubble, he downloads the copy's Shemathra records, including the most recent ones taken in The Data Stream, and the Grand Stampede, sending a message saying, "Release." The recipient is an old journalist friend of Uncle Ivan's. There's no need to tell her what he wants. The journalist is cen-forty and loves intrigue. She'll make sure the recordings are made public— all at once before Hosseini knows what hit him.

HR had offered an upgrade, a more aesthetically pleasing AI assistant, the outer skin less metallic and more like real skin. Plus, the newer model has a faster, response time to questions. So far, Byron has put them off. But today, he admits, faster is better.

The door opens and Millie appears with a mug of tea. There's an extra dose of a mild stimulant in it to help him focus. Decisions are coming. No one is safe from Hosseini. Byron wonders if he is safe. "Millie, assess security for this building and for me personally."

After setting the mug is in its proper place on the table near his desk, Millie taps her index finger to her right eyebrow. *This morning, scans completed on this building and a one-mile perimeter show no signs of explosives or atmospheric poisons. The search for bioweapons is ongoing. You have been assigned a security detail until further notice.*

Synthetic Millie pats his hand.

"Thank you," he says and means it. Colors glow on his holo screen and he puts incoming messages on hold. "I'd like an update on Mira Patel Holden."

"She's recovering and a security detail is in place."

He sighs with relief. Not sleeping last night after hearing of the attack. Byron puts his head on his desk. Millie places her silver hand on his shoulder.

SERENE VISTAS VIRTUAL CONFINEMENT

Donovan Hosseini

September 1, 2290

I'm in prison. I did some short stays when I was young. VR prisons and bio-ones are alike, except there's no graffiti. I won't miss the art, but there was some interesting reading on occasion. Everything here is gray. First thing I'll demand is some tru-color. If I can get rid of the sim, I'll be okay. I have plenty of resources. You meet all kinds of folks in prison, some very useful. Damn, the sim's still with me and *it's staring at me.*

Several lawyers are watching me to see if I'm crazy. They better get me out of here fast if they want to keep their jobs, if they want to keep anything. First, they need to erase the sim embedded like a freeloader in my files.

"Don't try it, Donovan," the sim whispers like a concerned cousin looking out for me. *"Any attempt to interfere will fracture the contents of your mind-upload folder."*

The bastard can hear my thoughts! A message bubble alert informs me about a federal probe and the investigative teams in Indonesia. My lawyers had planned a set of appeals that might have kept the New Deal operation secret. Then Gunter Holden spied, and the recordings were released, and now the public knows how things go in Shemathra's Realm. Whoever released them, however illegal, it doesn't matter.

They're taking SEINI, claiming the mergers and acquisition of VEI were illegal. Gunter Holden, the copy, the spy, occupies Bali Hai. The copy has been declared the owner of VEI. Bali Hai is the first VEI program restored. If the lawyers had known any of this before the memory recordings, they could have buried it all in legal challenges. Why am I not allowed to defend myself?

"Yes, I can! How do you expect me to get rid of the sim? Must I do everything?"

Marionjoy Rehabilitation Hospital

Wake up my baby

Northwestern Chicago Research Center

September 10, 2290

"DOWN!" Who is—why am I on the floor? Where is my father? Gunter is—oh God, I can't leave, I must go back! Ian is pushing me down because he's shooting the scrubber. It's all falling away, and the windows are gone, Ian's shouting but I can't hear him. What is he saying?

***

In one of the most ancient of human gestures, the nurse, a standard synthetic model, lifts its index finger to the middle of its smooth chrome face. There must be quiet. Henry waits as the nurse checks the patient's status. She is sleeping as her right leg repairs itself. The imploding glass of her bedroom window severed it, causing considerable blood loss. The leg is reconnecting itself to her wounded upper thigh.

Outside the room, outside the hospital ward, and around the perimeter of the entire Marionjoy Hospital, drones hover and dozens of federal agents stand guard. Temporarily, synthetic-human hybrids are barred from the grounds of Marionjoy Rehabilitation Hospital.

***

I'm falling again. *Falling in dreams means a lack of confidence.* Where am I? Which dreamscape? Have I been tossed from the top of the Hosseini H building or into the glacier where my mother fell? For once, I wish I could look down and see what is waiting for me. *That's different,* my feet are bare, except one foot has disappeared. Interesting; a missing foot could signal a missed opportunity.

Wait. Is that my missing foot? No, it's part of a robot housekeeper model, an old one. Yellow boxes are melting into a huge flapping banner with the SAVEMO logo on it. It's just above me, and the logo is becoming a cartoon, a smiling gray fox with a fluffy gray tail curling around its black paws. Is the fox taking me with it to some awful dream abyss?

I'm afraid. Is there a way to stop my fall?

I don't like this dream. I need to wake up to— There's another box opening. Leilani Three is floating near me and she's waving her metal arms. So graceful now, no longer a hen but a swan.

"Don't be afraid to fall," she says in the tinny gurgle I grew to love.

Leilani Three is fading, I wish I could go with her. A white hand with black nails is holding my hand.

A voice says, "Don't worry, doll, I gotcha!" Above the hand, above a black dress and white, cartoon cleavage there's large white face, framed by inky curls. The face reminds me of a bright moon as it floats above me. Interesting, the black ink lips are stretching into a grin.

Something familiar. It's familiar, but from where? Yes, an ancient media class. Oh my God, it's Betty Boop! Cartoon Betty Boop, the sassy career girl was my favorite.

"Relax, honey. Don't worry so much." Betty smiles again and she's gone in a swirl of stardust.

The gray cartoon fox is back. Its front paws end in four fingered hands. One finger balloons and points down at something. I see what is waiting for me at the bottom of this dream. Hosseini. He's a cartoon devil with horns and a long tail ending in an arrow. He's laughing and I see that beside him is a large cauldron.

Don't be afraid, this is just a dream or is this crude 2D reality his plan for me? Gunter's dreams were memories of his life, some beautiful and some full of anger and pain. If Hosseini controls a VR version of me, there might be only this dark side of dreams, none of it beautiful, nothing but fear and pain. Oh God, what if this is all that's left of me? There's someone whispering in my ear. *"Wake up, my baby, wake up!"* I remember my mother's voice. Ah, the darkness is melting.

"Where am I?" Someone's holding my hand.

***

"Speak slowly and quietly; don't overwhelm her. She's still medicated, so be careful," the nurse warns. *"Her leg is reattaching and it's healing nicely. Still, she'll need help to regain full use. Mira is my only patient. I will be inactive while you speak to her. If you want my help, say 'Nurse Kyle.' Otherwise, if I detect a significant change in her vitals, I will activate and address her needs."* Kyle, a state-of-the-art synthetic, programmed with current best practices in nursing care, retires to its charging station.

"I understand," Henry says. He sits near the recovery unit, a smart-care cushion that monitors her vital signs and healing. He wants to continue holding her hand but reluctantly, he releases it. It might confuse the readings and re-activate Kyle, its silver eyes now blank as it waits in the corner of the windowless room.

A federal agent of the VR Crimes Unit, sworn to investigate after-death fraud and protect the rights of virtual humans, Henry knows what can go wrong in paradise. Hosseini planned to create more nightmare worlds. Worse, Hosseini planned to return to bio existence by downloading a copy of his mind-folder into a synthetic-human hybrid, a human being downloaded into a manufactured body, stamped with a ghost. Hybrids might soon outnumber those who are still bios. As Henry watches the girl beside him, his love for her berates him with his failure to protect her. Why did he think it was safe to leave her?

Ian took his place and protected Mira. Now Ian is dead and his body lies cold while his family mourns. The government encourages VRC agents to record mind upload copies for possible transfer to synthetics. So far, Henry has refused. But Ian agreed, and a synthetic Ian will be returned to his grieving mother.

He wonders how Ian's mother will react to the new version of her son. Hopefully, Ian's mind uploads to a newer hybrid model.

Otherwise, the new body will be silver in color, with a milky white surface on his face and the palms of his hands. Although Ian's mind is his own property, his new body belongs to the U.S. government.

The newest models of synthetic hybrids look almost human. The eyes blink, but in a slow, rhythmic way like a cat. Sadly, the most human thing of all—synthetics don't breathe. Their chests expand and contract, but no air goes in or out. Ian won't sleep. He'll rest in a corner while he recharges. Henry wonders how many will lose their humanity in favor of synthetic immortality. For now, synthetic humans are unpredictable, some resisting the required safety programming. Even Ian might become dangerous.

Henry will ask Mira to marry him, as if magically that will protect her from the evil in this world and the perils of after-death existence. Before Mira, there were other relationships. None lasted more than a year until Mira. She was an awkward, young girl alone in a room bursting with hormones and friendly social cues. He wondered why someone so beautiful was alone. But people soon informed him that she was a special case, stand-offish, even hostile. Despite growing up swaddled in the love of his family, he, too, felt like an outsider, cautious and slow to make friends. The thought of anyone hurting her fills him with rage.

Mira's breath is regular. Henry tries not to think of what happened and what might have happened. Instead, he thinks of the life they share and what lies ahead.

There's a whisper. "Henry?"

She's awake! Mira raises a shaky arm to reach him. Kyle activates and evaluates her agitation. Next to a box of gardenias is something else, a lie he hopes will comfort her

"Try not to get her too excited," Kyle says before it rests again.

"Ravi, my father is he—" her lip quivers as she struggles to speak.

"He's safe, Mira."

Her eyes flutter as she fights tears. "And, and my grandfa . . .is Gunter?"

"He's safe. Mira, don't you remember? You distracted Hosseini. The tax sim you programmed to infect Hosseini, disarmed, defanged the monster. And . . . the memory recordings were released to the public and there is outrage. The mad man is finished, because of you."

"You brought gardenias." She struggles to clear her throat. "I've missed you, Henry."

"I know," he trembles as he says it. "And I'm sorry I wasn't . . ." He sighs, "I brought you a friend." Placing the gardenias on a tray table, he opens the other box. A tiny nose twitches as the mouse investigates his surroundings. The fat white mouse in the box isn't named Gunter. Henry hopes the original mouse survived and that he can find it before she knows. He is overwhelmed.

"I—we must leave, but only for a while! I swear you're safe and I'll be back soon."

"Okay, I know you will." She nods. "Goodbye," she whispers to the mouse.

"And when you find Gunter, my mouse, give him a crumb and tell him I'm sorry."

So, she knows. He'll give this one back to his nephew. The other mouse may be already dead; probably not, he hopes not.

"I will." Henry steps aside as the AI nurse checks Mira's vital signs and nods.

Mira sighs, "I'm back."

"I love you," he whispers.

BYRON HERNANDEZ

Trammell and O'Connell

Chicago, Illinois

September 12, 2290

"There are eighty-seven additional requests for interviews. Shall I send them the same response?"

Byron's neck aches as he struggles to wake. Another late night, a few stolen hours of sleep on Trammel's plush office couch are minor inconveniences considering what's happened. Gunter's recordings are damning, each one a SEINI death knell.

"Yes, thanks, Mimi. And thanks for the tea, it's perfect." The tea has more than a little stimulant today. She may be an AI assistant, but Mimi is also a friend.

"Good! I'm only a room away, Byron." Shifting weight on her lower body first, she turns. It never changes. He loves this about her. The world changes too fast. Still, he is part of the change. "Begin holo-recorder message," he commands, and updates the statement on behalf of the firm:

"Trammell and O'Connell speak only for their clients. As sad as the No Where story of Grace may be, we have no comment. When Grace's file was found, we cheered along with others. And yes, we know there is a donate to the "Help Grace, the cat lady" fund and a memory data fund to restore the sim child Lola using the memories of Marta, her grieving mother. We have no further comments. End message."

A dozen new media people have been hired. Hopefully, that with ease the workload. Messages flood in as new Congressional Hearings take shape. Will the copy of Gunter Holden be summoned to testify? He doesn't know. If he were to guess, probably yes. Mira Holden is recovering from the blast that almost took her life. She's unable to make a statement now and testifying is out of the question. Poor girl.

The truth of what went on in Shemathra's Realm is out for all to see. Hosseini is alone. He occupies a cell in a high security virtual jail as he awaits trial. And there are more charges. SEINI's contracts with the US government and the Social Security Virtual New Deal are cancelled. The abuse, torture, mass erasures and memory theft of Shemathra's Realm have shocked the public. Many bios have cancelled their after-death plans regardless of the program or company, resulting in an industry crisis.

Donovan Hosseini will be called to account. Byron doubts the llama god will last long. In a VR prison, self-deletion is always an option. Though SEINI lawyers appealed the evidence submitted by the copy, Gunter Holden, as inadmissible, they were denied. Holden's recordings have been deemed legal. The damage to SEINI is irreversible. Not all has been revealed. Families must be notified before stories of the slaughterhouse become public. Byron closes his eyes. *Horrifying.*

As he debates whether to take another nap before meeting with the partners, Mimi nudges open the door. *"Byron, there's something you need to see."* She points to the media wall, where a news report pushes free of the smooth screen.

A text question announces the coming topic: "Is the Social Security Virtual New Deal finished?" The holo of a woman is visible in the foreground and behind her is a map of Indonesia, a nation of islands. Several tiny islands enlarge, each with a name and number and a label.

The reporter turns and points to islands, so small they are undetectable on the original 2D map. These islands grow larger, until on each, the words "SEINI Research Center" appears.

The image changes focus, and the reporter looks directly into the camera. There's an urgency in her voice.

"There is growing concern about the fate of those who chose a SEINI after-death Virtual New Deal program. After they mind-transferred, many ceased contacts with their families and friends. SEINI claims they self-erased. Now, due to an extensive government investigation, witnesses are coming forward. These questions, along with leaked records on the fate of the human virtual residents of Shemathra's Realm resulted in Donovan Hosseini's arrest."

Millie nods and now there's another holo. "Jonathan Trammell represents the families of the human virtuals of Shemathra's Realm. Mr. Trammall, welcome to *New World News.*"

Trammell, a slender man in his cen-twenties, nods. "Thank you, glad to be here."

"Mr. Trammell, can you tell me what your clients, whose loved ones are human virtual survivors in Shemathra's Realm, are thinking as they see the memory files leaked by Gunter Holden?"

Trammell shakes his head. "Let me make this clear: The copy of Gunter Holden leaked nothing. He lawfully witnessed and recorded the Shemathra programs where human virtuals were forced to endure indignities, torture, and involuntary erasure. These recordings, again, provided to Congress, were released without permission from this office. That said, this sad story needs to be told."

The reporter nods. "And it will be."

TERRY SLOTKIN

Bali Hai

Chicago Streets Restoration Program

September 20, 2290

The smell of roasted peanuts makes her cry. She and Ned ate peanuts and fed pigeons the day he proposed over two hundred and thirty years ago on a sunny bio afternoon. Sitting on a restored city bench, she studies the line of chastened humans, former members of the herds. As a favor to her, Ned will not face trial or virtual prison. Ah, there he is. How she has missed him! She and Ned can stay here in Bali Hai if they choose to. But she is tired of virtual existence; even Bali Hai holds no appeal.

She followed the herd and hiding in shadows, she would whisper his name. Sometimes, Ned recognized her voice, and he would hesitate, swinging his head in her direction, but he always moved away. Still, she continued to follow the herd from pastures to plains full of wildflowers. He must remember her and the life they shared. When the herd moved to a new pasture, she thought she had been discovered. Had Ned betrayed her? Waving his horns, an immense steer approached the tree where she waited.

"Why are you here?" he asked quietly. "Don't you know what they'll do if they discover you have jumped without permission?'

"My husband," she said, "he's one of the steers. I worry he'll forget me."

"Be careful," he warned. "Don't stay too long."

Terry was elated. Here was an ally! She learned her protector was once Diego Putnam and when he told her of Hosseini's plan to kill a bio named Mira, trapping her upload in Shemathra's Realm, "*Not if I can help it,*" she whispered to him. She would stop Hosseini.

There must be a way to warn the girl. And, miraculously, there was! In the Palms, she met Ravi. It had been a while since there was anyone new in Shemathra's Realm. She was touched by Ravi's story and his desire to find his father, Gunter Holden. When she learned that Mira was Ravi's daughter, she hesitated to alarm him but decided it was better that Ravi knew. There must be a way to warn Mira. Ravi was convinced his father could help, if only they could find him. When she saw Gunter, she knew he was no sim. Yes, Gunter would find a way to fight Hosseini. And he did. Gunter warned Mira.

It's over now. The sad procession of naked humans waits for shuttles to take them to the reconstructed Navy Pier for processing.

It seems most of the former cult members prefer to leave and most of the remaining human virtuals are glad to see them go.

Ned is her only concern. They will be together soon.

GUNTER AND THE
NEW BALI HAI

Loc: Everest Summit, environment confirmation pending

October 4, 2290

I feel only parts of my emotions. Mira suggests I review more of the original Gunter's memories. I accept it's true; *Jacob wasn't my brother.*

As we marvel at the stark beauty of the Summit, I think my son's affect is as sad as I should feel. "Will I always feel less than the original me did? There could have been edits made before I was stored. If there are files missing, how much do I want to know about them?"

"I don't know if it will help, but share a memory with me," Ravi offers.

"I remember when I broke my mother's heart. I chose to stay with Eric and not come home. I was only eight. I accept that Jacob had loved me, and that I hated him because of Eric."

Ravi shakes his head. "It's hard to let go of love even when it's based on a lie. Letting go of hate is almost as hard. But Eric ordered your father killed, just like he ordered your mother's death. You seem lost in the past. Mira must let you feel more, so that you can let it go."

Marcia was the mother of my only child. And Ravi, the older man who sits beside me is her son and the son of the original bio me. It is easier to think of Ravi as my brother since I too came from the original me. I'm aware I had a bio brother. Although I didn't know him in the bio world, I'm told we were united when we rode the Dreams. *I miss Marcia.*

"When I look at you, I see your mother's smiling skepticism. Patel left his mark in the way you listen." *The look of stunned happiness on Ravi's face is worth the effort I summoned.*

"There is a strange serenity about the Summit," I change the subject.

"Interesting, the geese aren't subject to the thin air." Ravi remarks. *Unsaid is that Mira's mother, Rosalind died on the Summit.*

I agree. "Nature made an exception."

"It allowed me to find you." Ravi says.

"There will be changes. Besides the Summit and other Bali Hai locations, VEI is being reborn. And I will be a part of it. The Holden name still has magic." I smile. "Hosseini's legal fortress is crumbling. Because of SEINI and its sham Virtual New Deal programs, millions of virtuals found oblivion." *Justice is a grim joy.*

The thought of self-erasure flits through my mind. Babylon Dreams has been restored.

"I want a legacy for Mira. Mira will inherit her grandmother's shares of VEI stock, stock of questionable value until now. I am *the legal* Gunter Holden of VEI and the major stockholder."

"How many of the original VEI after-death programs are left?" Ravi asks. "Did Hosseini destroy them all?"

"Unlikely." *Should I give it all to Mira? Not for a while.* "But the bio world crawls with predators like Hosseini. There will be other mergers to fight."

"When will you be called," he asks.

"Henry Yang briefed me on what comes next in terms of my testifying before Congress. He's an agent of the U.S. Department of Virtual Security, and it seems Henry loves Mira." I say with a smile. Ravi doesn't respond. *I suspect he wonders why she was almost killed. She was hurt when Henry was somewhere else. Somehow, I think Ravi agrees. Henry will need to redeem himself.*

"Byron Hernandez protects the interests of families of loved ones lost in Shemathra's Realm. Predictably, Hosseini tried to defraud the U.S. Government. When it comes to suffering, people often look the other way." Ravi smiles. "Defrauding the government is another matter."

I laugh, pleased that my son has a sense of humor. "As investigators gain access to the memory Shemathra stole from VEI, programs are being retrieved."

"What about the herds?" Ravi asks. I detect sympathy in his voice. *That's hard to understand.*

"The herd people require more decisions. All their animal identities are gone. Good riddance. Hosseini kept records. Hosseini himself is done. Despite a legion of lawyers, thanks to Byron Hernandez, the US government, and Mira Holden, Hosseini's guilt is undeniable."

I am lost.

***

Ravi

Ravi tucks away the sting of Rosalind's memory as he turns to Gunter, who sits beside him. Their relationship is awkward, but Ravi hopes to learn more about his mother.

Everest is a place of loss for both father and son as they seek to understand each other. The past here is their common ground and it is rocky with pain. How will he, Ravi, justify his past neglect of his daughter? Atonement takes time and cannot be hurried. Mira is recovering. Her strength of character is dazzling. She is like her grandfather, unstoppable.

Tell him, "Thank you."

October 15, 2290

"I must talk to him." Putting her arms around his neck, Mira kisses him.

"You're right," he sighs. "But I've missed you and you haven't been back long. I wanted to tell you . . . I hoped to . . ."

Henry looks away, searching for the right words. She finds them. "I love you and I need you," she says.

He nods. "We'll have dinner out when you're done, something special. We can bring some home for Gunter the mouse."

"Of course, we will." She smiles.

"Tell your grandfather thank you from me and from the Department."

***

Miranda Four

As it makes its way over her body, the suit updates her code. Her new leg itches. It's been several months since she was Miranda Four. It's time to keep promises.

The New Bali Hai

Colors in the Villa

October 20, 2290

She's surprised by the intense color. Stripes of blue and ocean green end in a spray of a white foam meeting the shore. The sun is a splendid butter yellow. Lush palms frame the Villa's entrance. A breeze ripples the sand.

The Villa's white is mostly gone. Pastels enhance the elegant interior. She wonders if he is still angry with her and what she made him do.

There were times when she panicked. If her father hadn't been in danger, she could have—

Gunter is already here. "Hello Mira, it's good to see you again." Her grandfather sits in a wingback chair with China blue cushions.

"Hello Gunter."

"I see it now, Mira," Gunter says as coffee appears in a white cup. "You do look like Marcia, your grandm—" he stops himself as if filtering his words. "And in your eyes, there is the same caution I remember, in my mother's eyes." He pauses again. "She was a journalist. Are you well, now," he asks. "Henry told me what happened. Damn Hosseini. Are you okay?" His wariness is gone.

She nods. What should she say? (*Gunter, if not for you, Hosseini would have killed me. At times, I was very cruel to you and I'm sorry; I want to apologize*).

"I'm so sorry," she whispers.

"Why?" he asks. "You stopped him. He would have trapped you in hell and I could have remained encased in a red crystal, hidden in Patel's valise. To save Bali Hai, to regain VEI, I would have done the same."

Sitting back in the chair, he puts his feet on the matching ottoman. "You're right, you and I are alike. Except you wouldn't have committed the crimes my original self did."

"How are you and Ravi doing?" (Why not say thank you?)

"Day by day," he says.

"Stay, Ravi needs you and so do I." she says.

Can she read his mind? It doesn't matter. He knows she loves him. It's enough.

JAKARTA

Andi

The residence of Andi and Setia Sukawati

November 19, 2290

If not for Henry Chang, he and Setia would be dead. Asked to testify against the Hosseini, Andi was terrified. "I believe you'll do what's right." Henry had said to him.

Relatives, friends and the curious visit him and ask questions. What was it like to testify before the Congress of the United States? *It was a blur. I was told I did well.* How brave you are! Did you meet the President? *No, and thank you for coming and for your support.*

His testimony was not public, he is forbidden to say more. They can find more answers on news bubble sites. Unlike virtual existence, everything in the bio world changes.

Setia tells him to relax, they are safe. The children are in school. "Look around you, Andi, we're home." His favorite little tree has perfect red flowers. Buttercups peek between cracks in the paved stone path to the pond with its ducks and ducklings. Such innocence nearly breaks his heart.

"Andi, eat your breakfast." Setia sets his porridge on the table next to his chair.

He takes her hand and, pulling her close, kisses her neck. "Tasty as usual, thank you, my love."

"I'll be in the studio if you need me." She turns and walks the few steps to her new studio. Her presence comforts him, as do the security guards who keep watch. Worth the expense.

He often dreams of the violent sea and friends lost. To purge the island memories, Setia has created an island sculpture. A black shape crawls over gray stones until a blade of red light shatters the darkness and the stones become wildflowers. Her artist statement speaks of darkness banished and the power of hope. He thinks she will sell it soon. Good, he cannot bear to look at it.

A Bird of Paradise is watching him. It perches in a tree that shades Setia's studio, protecting her light sculptures from rays of the noon sun. The bird shakes its yellow head and flies to another tree. What would such a creature think of his VR work with its small heavens all made for non-believers?? There is no other God but Allah.

"Welcome to Babylon Dreams"

Bali Hai

December 10, 2290

I am uncertain here. When I see the monster coaster ride, perhaps, I'll connect with my ghost. Waving his arms, Ravi sits on a bench and throws an arm over top as if ready for the next challenge. Bells ring and I hear familiar calls: *"Try your luck! Win the Giant Panda!* The state fair program and its sims are fully restored. A child drops her cone and chocolate ice cream melts on fresh sawdust. Lights and strings of lights festoon several lines of booths. Flashing VR booths offer adventure. There's applause when someone's weight is guessed by a fresh-faced boy in a striped shirt. I can smell the popcorn and cotton candy. Organ music plays songs about stars and dreams.

Wooden swans dip their long necks up and down, guarding the Tunnel o' Love. Very young men and ancient tricksters, all sims, of course, call out to passersby. All of it is unchanging like an ancient video. Only the roller coaster is real in this part of the new Bali Hai. It does what it has always done: it takes its riders to the other side of existence.

Hanging over a trail of sawdust and a faint smell of manure, an arched sign framed in running lights declares *"Welcome to Babylon Dreams."* I carry the same memory as my original file. It is the VR Thunder Coaster, the same ride that terrorized me when I was a bio child. It has reappeared more than a century.

Was my original self a coward? There are memory records, but I'm afraid to know. I know when I left, I was eight years old, clinging to my eleven-year-old brother Tom. We climbed into the Dreams car and disappeared. Where did we go? Was there nothing waiting for us?

A bright rainbow spreads across the dark clouds while excitement floats in the night air, all part of the State Fair fantasy setting. Ahead, a line of listless virtuals waits for deletion. I can't look at them. I fear riding the Dreams a second time. *If I met my other self, and was finally complete, would I enter a new eternity?*

Ah, there are rabbits, lambs, small goats, a petting zoo. Lola, the little sim girl would enjoy a petting zoo. How much code does it take to make a zoo, where a little sim girl can hold a rabbit, feeling its silky fur on her cheek as she embraces it?

Another group of virtuals begins to ride the Dreams. Once they were cows, gazelles, bison, elephants, goats, wild horses, and wildebeests, proud members of Shemathra's herds. There is nothing to keep them here; they feel alone. Each takes what is left of their humanity. Memories of love, hopes and regrets cling to them like name tags pinned to children on a field trip, tatters of who they were when their souls were still their own. Their options ended at a ticket booth that glows with the light of eternity.

"Why did you want to meet here?" Ravi asks but his voice trails as if he's afraid of the answer. *What does he know about me? What Mira has told him, I guess.*

"A roller coaster frightened me once." I tell him. I change the subject.

"Your brilliant mother designed Babylon Dreams and the AI Miranda. When Miranda One speaks, that is your mother's voice." Ravi nods and smiles at the thought of hearing his mother's voice.

I ask him for his opinion. "The real Gunter Holden is gone. I'm a mere copy. There is the question of the soul—my soul. Do you think if such a thing exists, did it ride the Dreams along with the other me? If so, is it still there, wherever 'there' is? And if so . . . well, you see where I'm going with this."

Ravi nods. "Are you asking me if I think you have a soul?"

"Yes."

"I don't know, Gunter. When you were uploaded and reborn, this 'you' encountered a new set of challenges. And this time, you succeeded."

My son offers no platitudes or false assurances. I shake my head. "To be honest, if it weren't for Henry Yang and his work exposing the sham after-death programs, I would have been discovered and likely roasted on a virtual barbeque pit."

My son tilts his head and there's Marcia again. "The data you recorded exposed Hosseini and prevented considerable suffering. Eventually, Henry and the other agents would have brought him to justice, but it could have been years."

Then he laughs. "The truth is, I don't know about your soul or what happened to it. My guess is part of the soul rode the Dreams and found its way back. It rests within you. I wouldn't worry.

Ravi changes the subject. "What's next?"

"I want a different moon," I tell him. "Update the virtual trip to the moon. People here need to take vacations. Let's go to Chicago. I'm done here. There's a sidewalk café with some great sim street musicians. If it's fully restored, I'll have my own table."

Ravi nods. "I have ideas I'd like to run by you, like Bali Hai having an exceptional Memory Library."

As he finishes his thought, we're in Chicago and I see my favorite table. I'm happy to see a white cup on it. "Mr. Holden," the sim waiter smiles. "It's great to see you again. It's been too long."

"Indeed, it has," I agree.

I'm home.

THE END.

Acknowledgements:

Thank you to Daniel Oldis, a noted researcher and an expert on dreams. Thank you to Carol Arnold, a reader and storyteller, and to Alex Noble, a fellow writer and my favorite critic.

Thank you to the beta readers of Fiverr for their sophisticated feedback and encouragement.

ABOUT THE AUTHOR

Marjorie Kaye Noble was nine when she read *The Black Stallion* and all its sequels. In her nine-year-old imagination, she rode with Alec as he gripped the mane of *The Black Stallion* during that midnight ride. Years later, she worked as a casting director and was hired to conduct a nationwide search for, a young girl to ride Disney's *The Young Black Stallion*. While casting another film, she read an article by Ray Kurzweil on the possibility of mind-uploading into a virtual reality, a story idea took hold: A love triangle plays out in virtual reality after all three are dead and mind-uploaded into the same VR paradise. Upon completing her first novel, *The Demon Rift*, she began her VR novel, *Babylon Dreams* and later, *The Dark Side of Dreams*. Her published work includes short stories, magazine articles, plus film and book criticism.

Visit her website http://mknobleauthor.com/